"I suspect," Picard said, "that the Trexatians find the Repoki backward and naïve."

T'Lana gave an affirming nod. "This is the greatest challenge to a lasting peace. Apparently, our efforts seven years ago were unsuccessful in terms of assisting the Trexatians in becoming more open to other cultures' perspectives. . . ."

As Picard listened, a comment formed in his mind about the need for a swift resolution. But as T'Lana continued, her voice slowly faded and became unintelligible, like the far-off buzz of an insect.

Pressure mounted in his skull; soon even the buzzing was silenced by the pulse of his own heart.

This is not happening, Picard told himself with infinite force, infinite fury. He would not permit a nightmare spawned by events long past to become reality. Whatever this was, it had nothing to do with the Borg.

STAR TREK

THE NEXT GENERATION®

RESISTANCE

J. M. DILLARD

Based on
Star Trek: The Next Generation
created by Gene Roddenberry

POCKET BOOKS
New York London Toronto Sydney

Pocket Books
A Division of Simon & Schuster, Inc.
1230 Avenue of the Americas
New York, NY 10020

This book is a work of fiction. Names, characters, places, and incidents either are products of the author's imagination or are used fictitiously. Any resemblance to actual events or locales or persons, living or dead, is entirely coincidental.

This book is published by Pocket Books, a division of Simon & Schuster, Inc., under exclusive license from CBS Studios Inc.

First Pocket Books paperback edition September 2007

POCKET and colophon are registered trademarks of Simon & Schuster, Inc.

For information about special discounts for bulk purchases, please contact Simon & Schuster Special Sales at 1-800-456-6798 or business@simonandschuster.com.

Cover art by Tom Hallman

Manufactured in the United States of America

10 9 8 7 6 5 4 3 2 1

ISBN-13: 978-0-7434-9955-2
ISBN-10:   0-7434-9955-7

For Sara
Heer's* to hope

---

* Misspelling intentional.

Prologue

———•———

IT BEGAN AS IT HAD BEFORE: CLAUSTROPHOBIC dreams, a sense of impending evil, the shattering of sleep with a desperate, rasping gulp of air.

In darkness, Jean-Luc Picard threw back tangled sheets and rose. It seemed he had done so countless times, had risen in the grip of a vague terror and made his way, blind but knowing, through his unlit bedchamber. He entered the lavatory and paused in front of the mirror.

"Light," he uttered hoarsely, and there was light.

In the glare he winced at his reflection. He looked the same: clean shaven, with lean, sharply sculpted features, a gleaming bald crown. Yet something was subtly different, something was subtly *wrong*. He studied his face intently, seeking explanations for his sense that he, that his entire world, had gone awry.

Beneath his left cheekbone, the skin twitched. The movement was barely perceptible. Picard leaned closer, grasping the edges of the cool counter. Had it been his imagination, the product of paranoia triggered by the elusive, disremembered dream?

No. The muscle in his cheek spasmed again, briefly, then rippled. Alarmed, Picard placed a hand to it and felt a hard object beneath the flesh, an object that was neither tooth nor bone, but inhuman.

He withdrew fingers that trembled despite his efforts to steady them. The object pushed hard, now, against the inside of his cheek, like a child-sized fist trying to force its way through his skin.

The sense of pressure mounted until it became nigh unbearable. In horror, Picard watched as his cheek stretched beyond all possible limits, until the hard, steadily lengthening cylinder emerged from within his body and erupted through the flesh.

Astoundingly, there was no blood, only a single bright flash of pain. A slender, gleaming silver arm emerged and extended itself a hand's breadth, then paused an inch before the mirror. A whir: the servo's end bloomed and opened, revealing skeletal fingers, razor-keen, deadly fingers meant for grasping, killing, transforming . . .

"The Borg," Picard whispered. Flashes of the dream returned: infinite rows of metallic honeycomb cubicles, filled with the assimilated, mindlessly awaiting a directive; the surgical chamber, efficiently modern yet medievally grotesque, its walls lined with prosthetic limbs, eyes, sharp saws, burning lasers; worst of all, the queen herself, no more than a disembodied head with shoulders, her dark lips curved upward in the most wickedly smug of half smiles, her liquid black-bronze eyes full of promise and threat . . .

We were very close, you and I. You can still hear our song.

Not again. Not again, not again.

Shining metal fingers clicked and flexed inches away from his eyes, blotting out his reflection, his individuality. Picard sank to his knees, still gripping the counter. This time, his shriek was not silent . . .

The sound—which emerged as no more than a loud groan—jarred him to full consciousness. In the instant of disorientation that followed, he pressed his palm to his cheek and discovered, to his profound relief, only human flesh. His breathing was shallow, rapid; he forced it to deepen and slow, and let reality reclaim its hold on him.

This was his bed, and *Enterprise*'s night. He was now, truly, awake.

"Jean-Luc?" A voice, soft and drowsy, beside him; the sound of long, slender limbs sliding against sheets. "Jean-Luc, you're all right. You were dreaming."

"Beverly." His voice was hoarse with sleep; he cleared his throat. "Yes, of course, I'm fine. Just a dream."

She rolled onto her side. He could see her silhouette though not her expression; she had propped her elbow against the pillow, then rested her head upon her palm. Her hair spilled down to brush his shoulder. "What was it about?"

He tensed slightly. He knew the nuances of her tone well; she was the doctor now, not lover or friend. And she was asking a question whose answer she already knew.

"I was talking in my sleep, then," he said flatly, wryly.

She nodded. He sighed as she persisted: "Feel like talking about it?"

"What's there to say? I don't know why I'm dreaming about the Borg. It was all resolved long ago."

Even before she spoke, he read her skepticism in the way she slightly drew back her head. "A wound as deep as yours won't ever heal completely, Jean-Luc."

"Then help me forget." He took hold of the arm supporting her head and gently pulled; she didn't resist but laughed and let herself roll toward him, almost on top of him. He gave her a swift kiss, and they smiled at each other in the darkness.

"I'm sorry it still troubles you," she said gently.

He shrugged. "It's not troubling me. It was just a . . . subconscious hiccup, that's all." He stroked her hair. "Sorry I woke you. Go back to sleep."

She yawned, then settled against him, her cheek nestled beneath his collarbone. In an instant, she was out again—a doctor's talent, learned long ago in medical school. He teased her about it, but it was a talent he envied, especially now that he lay staring up at the night ceiling fully awake, feeling the regular rise and fall of her breath against his ribs.

The dream left him troubled. He had not thought of the Borg in a very long time. He could not remember the last time he had consciously relived the horror of his existence as the human/machine hybrid named Locutus. He did not understand why such memories should surface now. More important, he did not know why they should prove especially disturbing.

In his ear, the faintest of whispers.

"What?" He tilted his chin down to glance at Beverly. She was soundly sleeping; he decided she had murmured while dreaming. He gazed back up at the overhead, then closed his eyes, determined to dismiss all foolish anxiety and return to sleep himself. He drew in a breath, then released it as a sigh and let his body rely completely upon the bed for support.

Another whisper, too soft to be intelligible.

Picard opened his eyes. This time, he did not look down at Beverly; this time, he knew that she was not the source. For the solitary voice was soon joined by another, then another . . . until it became a faint, distant chorus of thousands.

You can still hear our song.

It was, Picard knew with a certainty he wanted urgently not to possess, the whisper of the Collective.

It was the voice of the Borg.

1

———◆———

BY SHIP'S MORNING, PICARD WOKE TO FIND Beverly gone and his mind clear, free of its nocturnal terror. He dressed, and by the time he mentally reviewed the tasks of the day, he had convinced himself that the Borg chatter had been no more than a vestige of the dream.

The first stop was engineering. Picard entered to find the android B-4 sitting, legs sprawled with unselfconscious gracelessness, clad in the mustard jumpsuit he routinely wore. His expression bland and benign, B-4 let his ingenuous gaze wander, without curiosity, over his surroundings. Picard could not determine whether the android had actually registered the captain's entry, or the presence of Geordi La Forge or Beverly Crusher.

"Captain Jean-Luc Picard," B-4 said at last, without inflection. From experience, Picard knew this was not a greeting; B-4 was merely parroting the name of an object he recognized. But for the sake of the others, the captain took it as such.

"Good morning, B-4," he said briskly, with false cheerfulness. Silently, he nodded a greeting to La Forge and Beverly.

Geordi stood next to the android. Beverly stood across from the two of them, her arms folded, her expression carefully professional, that of chief medical officer and nothing more. Technically, since B-4 was not human, what was about to occur could not be called a medical procedure. Nonetheless, Beverly had insisted on coming.

Geordi's features were composed as well, but there was a poignant undercurrent in his prosthetic crystalline eyes. Data had been his closest friend, and spending time with B-4—Data's double in physical form only, certainly not in personality, intelligence, or attitude—had only served to underscore the loss of that friend. Geordi had worked the past few months with B-4 in hopes of summoning Data's memories—to re-create, if possible, all that Data had been.

The effort had proved cruelly futile. B-4 had regurgitated names, snippets of events from Data's past, but had never put them into context, had never shown the slightest interest in their meaning.

But as he had wandered the *Enterprise*'s corridors, Geordi so often in tow, B-4 had kept Data's ghost alive for them all. Picard still struggled with a sense of guilt: in the most human and loving of gestures, Data had sacrificed himself so that his captain and crewmates might live. Even months later, Picard was visited too often by the horrible instant of materializing on the bridge, of seeing the dazzling flash of the *Scimitar*'s destruction, of knowing that Data was dead, incinerated into non-existence . . .

There had not even been time enough to say good-bye. He missed Deanna Troi dreadfully; she was serving with her husband Will Riker aboard the *Titan* now, and only in her absence had Picard come to realize how much he had relied on her as a counselor not only in professional matters but in personal ones as well. He was limited now to re-membering what she had told him shortly before she left the *Enterprise* with Will:

Data's final act was one that brought him the most happiness; it gave his entire existence the greatest meaning. Yes, he could have lived cen-turies longer . . . but what's the use of immortality if there's no meaning to it?

Case in point, Picard thought, looking at the an-droid in front of him. As the captain took his place beside Beverly, B-4 sat staring vacuously, oblivious to the feelings of the humans surrounding him. Data, of course, would have been keenly aware. Pi-card tried, and was entirely unsuccessful, to sup-press a memory: Data, standing in the scalded dust of the desert world Kolarus, lifting B-4's head from the sand and holding it before his eyes in unwitting imitation of Hamlet contemplating Yorick's skull. *Brother,* Data had called him. So like Data, to have yearned for the closest of human relationships.

"B-4," Geordi said, with the same gentle tone he had used so often with his old friend, "do you realize what we're about to do?" La Forge unconsciously fingered the laser wrench in his hand. Nearby sat open storage compartments: one the size of a torso, another that of a human cranium. A third was designed to house limbs. B-4 would soon return to the state in which they had first discovered him: disassembled.

The android looked in turn at each of them: Beverly, Picard, then back at Geordi.

"You are sending me away," B-4 said.

"Yes," Geordi answered, his tone infinitely patient. "You're going to the Daystrom Institute. They're going to study you and learn about your design, how you were made."

"How I was made," B-4 echoed tonelessly. He glanced at the storage compartments, then at the deck.

"We're going to deactivate you now," Geordi persisted. "Most likely permanently. We talked about all this, remember?"

"I remember," B-4 replied, distracted by the movement of another engineer passing by en route to her station.

Apparently more for himself than the android, Geordi added, "It's a good thing you're doing, B-4. You're helping science."

After a brief silence, B-4 looked up at La Forge and asked abruptly, "What is it like to be deactivated?"

Geordi was caught off guard; Beverly stepped in.

"It's like . . . nothing," she said. "Like being nowhere at all. It's not uncomfortable. Humans might compare it to a dreamless sleep."

"Nothing?" B-4 tilted his head in painful imitation of Data.

Geordi recovered and nodded. "You won't see or hear anything. You'll no longer receive any input."

B-4 blinked, considering this. "That sounds very boring. I do not think I want to be deactivated now."

Geordi shot an openly helpless glance at Picard. Beside him, Beverly shifted her weight, clearly uncomfortable.

"B-4," Picard said sternly, "it's too late to change your mind. You already agreed to be deactivated. That was a good decision, one you must abide by." Now was not the time for dialogue. True, the situation might trigger memories of a lost friend, but swift action was required lest it turn maudlin. B-4 was not Data, and that was that.

There followed a slight pause. "All right," B-4 answered mildly.

Picard directed a curt nod at Geordi. "Please deactivate B-4, Mister La Forge."

Geordi hesitated no more than a heartbeat, then with his free hand, reached for a panel at the back of B-4's neck, opened it, and pressed a control.

B-4 froze: his eyes no longer blinked, his head no longer moved, his limbs no longer fidgeted in realistic representation of human motion. Even the blandly pleasant expression had resolved into one of soulless vacancy. In less than a millisecond, he was transformed from sentient being to inanimate object.

Picard had expected the moment after to be the easiest. To his surprise, it was the hardest—for there, in front of them, sat Data, just as he had appeared all the times they had been forced to shut him down. There was no longer B-4's vacant expression and witless repetition to remind them that this was someone, something else. Picard's throat tightened; he recalled a time, many years ago, when Command had wanted to deactivate Data for study. He remembered how hard and eloquently he and Data had argued against it, and won.

Now it felt as though he had ultimately lost.

Standing beside Picard, Beverly gave a few rapid blinks, then regained her composure. Geordi, his tone soft, his words forced, said, "I'll finish up here, Captain. He'll be ready for shipment within the hour." He lifted the laser wrench in his hand and fingered a toggle.

"Very good," Picard said. He turned on his heel and tried to leave Data's memory behind, in engineering—just as he had earlier dismissed the dream about the Borg.

It had been a strange night, followed by a strange morning; Picard could not entirely rid himself of the odd feeling the world had somehow gone awry. Nothing more than mental phantoms, he exhorted himself. Nothing real: just ghosts. Ghosts and whispers . . .

As he rode the turbolift up toward the bridge, Picard's mood gradually began to lighten. His next task would be a far happier one: he had been planning an announcement with great care. The previous night, after he had received some anticipated news from Starfleet Command, he and Beverly had each enjoyed a glass of wine and laughed over his nefarious plan for delivering said news. They had planned, too, a small celebration of the senior crew after hours.

Picard was nearly smiling when the turbolift slowed and arrived at the bridge, but by the time the doors opened, he had already forced a frown in order to produce a properly grim expression.

The *Enterprise* bridge was a study in silent efficiency: a recent transfer from Security, Lieutenant Sara Nave, straw-colored hair loosely coiled at her neck, sat at the conn, studying the stars on the main viewscreen. Nave's serious expression and consummate professionalism belied her off-duty behavior. At the academy, she'd had a reputation as a fun-loving hellion—the captain recalled that several senior officers had used the same label for him. Unlike her captain, Nave had graduated at the top of her class and was one of the best in her field.

Born on Rigel to human parents—both of them high-ranking officers in Starfleet—Nave had been a prodigy, convinced from early childhood that she wanted to follow in her family's footsteps. Her academic record was stellar enough to convince Starfleet Academy to grant her early admission; after an accelerated program, she graduated at the age of eighteen. She was now twenty-five, with seven years of outstanding service under her belt—though it was hard sometimes for Picard to believe it, given the fact that Nave looked even younger than she was. Her pixielike features would always give her the appearance of youth, even into old age.

She was not a tall woman, though her limbs were lithe and long—yet her strength was formidable, in part because she had started in Security. She regularly practiced mock combat with Worf using the *bat'leth*—the quarter-moon–shaped Klingon scimitar—albeit with a slight handicap. Picard was glad to see the two had formed a friendship. Worf did not take easily to new people.

A faint crease appeared on Nave's brow as she manipulated a control, keeping the ship on course for the planet Repok. The Repoki had agreed to permit the Federation to help negotiate a truce with their neighbor, Trexat. Commander Worf had command of the bridge, his bony brow knitted in a perpetual slight scowl, his hair falling down his broad back in a long russet braid. Picard was still not quite used to the sight of Worf in the big chair.

Over the past months, the Klingon had behaved with uncharacteristic restraint, a degree of somberness that Picard attributed to grief over Data and the reassignment of so many crew members. The number of changes had required all of them to adapt. It had been hard enough, in the past, when the crew had lost the *Enterprise* herself; it was harder still to lose each other.

At the sound of the doors opening, Worf swiveled in the captain's chair to glimpse Picard; not quite simultaneously, the Klingon rose and moved for the first officer's position. Picard passed by him, turning his face just enough to order sternly, "In my ready room, Mister Worf." He glanced back at navigation. "Lieutenant Nave, you have the bridge."

The captain did not await an answer but headed directly for the ready room and his desk; he settled behind it, aware that the Klingon was following closely. The instant Worf entered, the doors snapped shut, and Picard gestured for him to take the hot seat.

The Klingon never looked comfortable sitting; Worf would far prefer to be standing at attention. Instead, he rested his great bronze hands awkwardly on his knees, looking like the essence of regretfully coiled power.

Picard forced away the smile that threatened, and with a calculatedly reluctant expression, launched into his performance. "Mister Worf," he began, his voice low, "for the past few months you

have, in my opinion, fulfilled your role as temporary second-in-command most admirably."

"Thank you, Captain." Worf shifted uncomfortably beneath the words of praise, poised on the
edge of his chair, eager to vacate it as swiftly as
possible.

"However," Picard said, "I'm sure you can understand that the time has come to find a permanent replacement." He paused a full two seconds to
increase the sense of drama, relishing his role. "I
want you to know that I made the case quite forcefully for keeping you as first officer. But Starfleet
Command had already made its decision long before my recommendation." The captain lifted his
hand in a rehearsed I-did-all-that-I-could gesture,
then sighed.

Worf was as motionless as stone.

"I'm afraid, Mister Worf, that I received the
name of the new permanent first officer last night.
He will be filling the position immediately."

If Worf felt disappointment, he did not show it;
Picard would not have expected him to. "I understand, Captain. Shall I return to my old post?"

The question caught Picard off guard. He had
been counting on the Klingon to ask the name of
his so-called replacement—especially since the officer was to take over immediately, which implied
he was a member of the current crew. Wasn't Worf
the least bit curious that someone of lesser rank
had been promoted over him? This was not how Picard's little joke was supposed to play out.

Perhaps he had inadvertently offended.

"Mister Worf," he said finally, his tone lightening; at last, he permitted himself to smile. "Forgive me for teasing you. I am proud to report that Command has approved my recommendation and appointed you permanent first officer of the *Enterprise.*"

A pause followed. Picard absolutely expected to hear the words, *Thank you, Captain,* but they never came.

"I am sorry, Captain," Worf responded. "I must refuse the commission."

At first Picard was certain he had misheard, but the longer the words hung in the air, the less he could deny them. His first instinct was to ask, *Are you mad?* His next was to consider that the Klingon had turned the joke on him. But there was no hint of merriment in Worf's eyes; he fidgeted a bit in his chair, obviously eager to be done with the encounter.

At last Picard said, "Worf . . . I'm afraid I don't understand."

"I must refuse the commission," the Klingon repeated.

"I understood *what* you said," Picard countered gently. "But I don't understand *why* you said it."

Worf lowered his gaze. An emotion flickered in his eyes, one that the captain could not precisely identify: reluctance? pain? "It is . . . a personal matter, sir. I would prefer not to discuss it."

For a moment, Picard was rendered speechless.

Finally, he said, "Commander . . . I respect your decision and your right to privacy. But of all candidates, you are the most qualified—and I would prefer you, above all others, as my Number One. Could I ask you to take some time to reconsider?"

Worf met the captain's gaze directly once more, and Picard detected a glimmer of misery. "I have made my decision, sir," the Klingon said.

There was nothing more to be said, the captain realized, with a sense of profound disappointment and disbelief. He straightened, his manner formal. "Very well, Mister Worf. You may return to your duties . . . as temporary first officer. I hope you are willing to continue in that role; it will take some time for me to find another qualified officer."

The Klingon gave a nod and left with obvious relief.

Picard did not follow immediately. He remained behind his desk, contemplating whether or not to inform Starfleet of Worf's decision. Worf seemed determined—but Picard's instinct said to wait, to give him time.

The captain sighed. For the second time that morning, he found himself desperately missing Deanna Troi's counsel.

Worf returned to the bridge and carefully settled into the command chair, ignoring Sara Nave as she half turned her face away from the conn to give him a curious, sidewise glance. He had never felt comfortable taking the captain's seat; of all places on the *Enterprise* bridge, he deserved to be there least.

When Captain Picard had first asked him to take over Commander Riker's position, Worf had considered refusing. But at that moment, the captain had had no other senior officers to choose from, no one from the original crew who had served him so long, who knew the ship and the captain so well. Refusing then would have put the captain in an unacceptable position, since Starfleet had to conduct a search for a replacement. Given the captain's exceptional standards and the reality that most highly qualified officers were already content with their current assignments, time was needed.

Worf's loyalty would not permit him to leave his captain without a seasoned second-in-command. But he thought it understood that his assistance was only temporary; he thought it had been clear that he could never accept a permanent position as Picard's Number One.

Indeed, he had been perplexed by the fact that the captain had even considered him. Worf's sense of shame was still so great he regarded it as tangible, as visible to others as the Klingon sash he wore over his uniform each day.

He had sat in the ready room looking at Captain Picard after the announcement, but the face he had seen had been the dark visage of the commander of Deep Space 9, Benjamin Sisko. The words he had heard were Sisko's as well.

As your captain, it's my duty to tell you that you made the wrong decision . . . they'll probably never give you a command of your own after this.

Sisko's assessment had been humanly soft, even weak. Had Worf been serving aboard a Klingon vessel, he would have gladly accepted death as his rightful due.

Sitting now on the bridge, the Klingon stared out at the streaming stars and saw a different face—this one pale and beautiful, framed by long hair the color of fertile soil. The features were young and delicate, but the spirit behind them was ancient and fierce.

Jadzia. The memory of his wife provoked no less pain than it had the day she had died.

For love of her, Worf had deserted his duty to Starfleet. For love of her, he had forsaken honor.

Only a few years ago, he had gone with Jadzia into the steaming jungles of an alien planet; their assignment was to meet with a Cardassian spy, Lasaran, who had critical information. Information, Worf reminded himself unhappily, that would have changed the course of the Dominion War . . . and could have spared millions of lives.

But Jadzia had been injured in a surprise attack and began to slowly bleed to death. Warrior that she was, she had struggled to fulfill her duty for as long as she had been able, hiking alongside her husband through treacherous terrain. At last, the loss of blood left her unable to take another step. If

Worf continued on to the rendezvous point, there was no doubt that Jadzia would be dead before he could return to her.

Worf's choice had been clear: save his wife's life, or obey his duty and keep his meeting with Lasaran.

He had chosen duty at first, at Jadzia's urging. But each step that took him farther away from her caused his determination to falter; with each step, his love for Jadzia tugged at him until he could resist it no longer and went back to save her.

Afterward, when Jadzia was safe, Captain Sisko had confronted him with the news that, because Worf and Jadzia had not helped Lasaran escape, the Cardassian had been murdered—and his information, which might have helped end the bloody war with the Dominion, was lost with him.

In the end, fate had its way: Jadzia and Worf had only a few more months together before she died—a victim, in a misfortunate place at a misfortunate hour, murdered by a wraith-possessed Gul Dukat.

It was not a death befitting such a proud warrior.

Worf could have given her such a death—performing her duty, in an alien jungle. He could have given her honor, then, and saved his own.

But Captain Sisko had been right: he, Worf, had made the wrong choice. And although Starfleet might be willing to forgive one of their officers such a terrible lapse in judgment, Worf could not.

Being first officer of the *Enterprise* meant that he would at times be in command of the finest vessel in the fleet, a responsibility of which he was unworthy.

Picard remained in his ready room for several moments afterward. Worf assumed that he was already contacting Starfleet Command, informing them of the need for a new first officer.

When Picard at last emerged, Worf leaped to attention, ready to turn the bridge over. But the captain passed by without meeting anyone's gaze. "As you were," he said tersely, then moved swiftly for the turbolift.

Once he was gone, Worf resettled into the command chair and sighed. On the viewscreen before him were stars, but all he saw was Jadzia's face.

Picard hadn't contacted Starfleet at all; instead, he made up his mind to wait. There was no logic to his decision—none at all—only the nagging intuition that the way to convince Worf to accept the promotion would soon come to him. Perhaps it was foolish; the *Enterprise* needed a permanent first officer, and the sooner Starfleet was notified of Worf's refusal, the sooner someone could be found.

Locating an officer of Will Riker's caliber (or, for that matter, of Worf's) who happened to be available for reassignment would not be easy.

Just as it had not been easy finding a replacement for Deanna Troi.

Picard thought of Deanna and smiled. What would she say, knowing that he had just chosen to ignore Worf in hopes of changing the Klingon's mind?

In his mind, he heard her voice—full of both consideration and candor—tinged with that strange throaty Betazoid accent:

Captain, you know very well how stubborn Worf can be. There's about as much chance of him changing his mind as . . .

Silently, Picard finished the imaginary statement for her.

. . . as me changing mine?

He pictured her giving a stern, emphatic nod, with a glimmer of humor in her black eyes. *Precisely.*

Picard's smile faded; he sighed. It would never be possible to find another Deanna, or a friendship like the one he'd had with her. Certainly, the new counselor was nothing like her. In fact, it had taken Command some time to convince him, despite her impeccable qualifications, that she was a good match for the *Enterprise* and its captain.

Picard was focused on the position of ship's counselor for good reason. On his way to the bridge earlier, he had received notification that the shuttle bearing Deanna's successor would soon be in transporter range.

In the midst of his reverie, his communicator chirped. He pressed the badge. "Picard here."

"Ensign Luptowski, transporter room two, sir.

The new counselor should be arriving in approximately two minutes."

"On my way."

Picard stood next to the transporter operator—a recruit from the academy, twenty years old if he was a day—and watched as the shimmering miasma on the pad slowly coalesced into humanoid shape.

The body formed first. It was short, very slender, decidedly feminine. The hair that appeared was blue-black, with a fringe of carefully trimmed bangs that partially covered a high forehead and upward-slanting eyebrows. The eyes were heavy lidded, large, and almost as dark as Deanna's; the nose was long, narrow, the lips classically rosebud. The ears were delicately formed, close to the skull, culminating in decided points. The effect of such Renaissance beauty in a Starfleet uniform seemed incongruous. If Leonardo da Vinci had ever sketched a saint or angel with Vulcan features, Picard decided, this would be the result.

Her expression was placid, beatific; Picard had never known a Vulcan to generate the peculiar quality humans termed "charisma," but that was indeed what this female possessed. She took in Picard, Ensign Luptowski, and the transporter room with a single, encompassing glance, one that shone with breathtaking intelligence and absorption of detail.

She stepped from the pad and gave Picard a low, respectful nod. "Captain Picard." Her voice was arresting, authoritative, larger than her physical form—a match for the captain's most commanding, sonorous tone. "Greetings. I am Counselor T'Lana."

Picard did not smile—he wished to be sensitive to her Vulcan distaste for displays of emotion—but her relaxed, gracious demeanor made him feel comfortable in exhibiting warmth in his expression and tone. "Counselor. Welcome to the *Enterprise*."

His warmth was genuine . . . but there was a slight discomfort hidden beneath it. He had requested another Betazoid, of course, but there were only a handful of them in the fleet and their empathic abilities were in high demand. He had grown used to the incredible advantage of being able to know what opponents were feeling, even across the vastness of space.

But Command had been swift to underscore T'Lana's qualifications. Her counseling skills had been honed after two decades of service to the fleet. She had spent the bulk of her career specializing in diplomatic counseling, advising commanders who found themselves enmeshed in negotiations with warring groups. As such, she had been transferred often, to the place where she could do the most good. More recently, she had had a permanent assignment aboard the *Starship Indefatigable*. When the ship had been destroyed in battle, T'Lana had earned commendations for rescuing wounded comrades. Afterward, she had specifically asked to be assigned to the *Enterprise* as soon as a position was available.

Her record was sterling. She had the Vulcan coolness needed to calm overheated antagonists; at the same time, she possessed uncanny insight into the intentions and character of beings far more emotional than herself. She had garnered commendation after commendation with each simmering conflict she resolved, each war she helped avert, each battle she brought to a halt.

And while she could never compete with Troi's ability to "read" another being on another ship, a distant world, T'Lana's talent as a touch-telepath was exceptional. Most Vulcans worked for years to enhance their telepathic abilities; T'Lana had worked for years to contain hers.

Picard was honored to have her aboard. And though he was certain she would serve the *Enterprise* impeccably, he was privately concerned about her ability to provide him with personal guidance. Deanna had been warm, nurturing, nonjudgmental—a friend with whom he could let down his guard, to whom he could express the most painful feelings. He could never have recovered emotionally from his experience as Locutus without Deanna's help.

How could he ever weep or confess his inadequacies to a Vulcan?

Picard brushed aside the question. Such a horrific incident was a once-in-a-lifetime occurrence. Besides, it was no longer time for such concerns; he had made his decision to accept T'Lana as his new counselor. Now it was time to adapt to the change and make the best of what was rather than what had been.

"Would you like to be shown to your quarters to rest?" he asked politely.

"No," she replied.

Ah, the first sign of Vulcan bluntness.

"I am well rested, Captain. I would prefer to report for duty."

"Very well." Picard gestured toward the door. "Then let's proceed to the bridge."

As he led her through the corridors, he began a discussion of the most pressing matter at hand. "I understand you have experience in dealing with the Trexatians." He had studied her file more than a dozen times and knew her history well. The Trexatians were marauders with recently acquired warp capability and a complete disregard for the rights of other societies. Some years ago, they had begun pillaging two other planets, T'hirada and Xochin, in a neighboring solar system. Their victims were even more technologically advanced than the Trexatians and fought back with a vengeance: a three-way war broke out, with none of the parties interested in a diplomatic solution—until the T'hiradans finally asked to join the Federation and requested Starfleet's assistance.

T'Lana had counseled Admiral Yamaguchi and his diplomatic team, and been present throughout the negotiations. The mission had met with resounding success, and the Trexatians, although they had refused to join the Federation, had signed a treaty agreeing not to prey on their neighbors. They had kept that promise . . . until now.

Now they were raiding a planet in their own system—Repok—for a rare ore, vadinite, recently discovered to cure a disease that had been ravaging the Trexatians. The raids had begun slyly, with Trexatians shielding their vessels and conducting secret mining operations, beaming the mineral directly into their cargo holds. But the Repoki soon discovered the losses, since they mined vadinite themselves, and they were resoundingly disinclined to be generous—vadinite was their currency.

An all-out war soon erupted. The Repoki were at a serious disadvantage. They possessed only a first-generation warp drive that permitted them to put up a limited defense. The Trexatians were far more technologically advanced and became more brazen in their efforts to seize vadinite. They used phase weapons to slaughter Repoki workers at the mines, which they seized; they quickly destroyed most of the Repoki defenses. The natives began forming land armies to try to resist the impending Trexatian invasion.

But the Repoki realized they had little chance against their enemies, and so they contacted Starfleet for help. They had resisted earlier overtures from the Federation, but they were now willing to ally themselves in order to avoid the devastation of their people and their world.

"Approximately seven years ago, I worked for a short time with Trexatian representatives to resolve a conflict," T'Lana said. "During that same period, I was also part of a delegation who visited Repok, at the invitation of a faction interested in joining the Federation."

Picard lifted his eyebrows. "Indeed?" He had not seen any mention of the latter fact in her file but, then, the document was massive, referring to hundreds of missions over a twenty-year period. "How did you find Repoki culture? What drives them as a people?"

He was curious; he'd found only a smattering of information on them in the ship's computers. There had been far more about the Trexatians because of the earlier war. They were a competitive race that embraced technology; physical appearance and abilities were enhanced by prosthetic eyes, limbs, cybernetic implants. Eye and hair color, as well as facial structure, were constantly changed; skin was colored and etched to create interesting designs and textures. Precious metals and gems were embedded in eyes, ears, and skin, woven into hair. The culture valued its notion of beauty above all else—except perhaps its ability to steal whatever it could from other planets.

The Repoki, on the other hand, were a gangly, orange-skinned people with opaque white eyes, blunted features, and little racial variation. Picard knew nothing more about them, except that their level of technology was behind that of the Trexatians and perhaps two centuries behind that of the Federation.

"They value social cooperation as well as financial independence so that the individual will not burden society; nonfunctional art is considered frivolous. They are isolationist but not xenophobic. They wish to exist undisturbed, with little interest in how their culture or technology could be enhanced by interaction with other worlds." She paused. "That was our greatest challenge seven years ago, when we met with their representatives. The only reason they have contacted us now is that they now desperately require our help. But there is a greater challenge to surmount now."

"Which is?"

Conversation ceased for a moment as they arrived at the lift and entered. "Bridge," Picard ordered, then turned his face toward T'Lana, who stood beside him.

As the lift began to move, she answered his question. "Bigotry. Since the Repoki place a high value on social cooperation, they frown on thievery and self-aggrandizement. They find Trexatian culture morally repugnant, the people vain and corrupt. This, added to their outrage over the murders of their citizens and the invasion of their mines—the very basis of their monetary system—will prove a most difficult obstacle in bringing them to peace and acceptance of Trexatian culture."

"I suspect," Picard said, "that the Trexatians find the Repoki backward and naïve."

T'Lana gave an affirming nod. "As well as physically repugnant. And they do not comprehend their lack of aesthetic appreciation. Each side, therefore, feels it is morally superior to the other. This is the greatest challenge to a lasting peace. Apparently, our efforts seven years ago were unsuccessful in terms of assisting the Trexatians in becoming more open to other cultures' perspectives . . ."

As Picard listened, a comment formed in his mind about the need for a swift resolution, since without vadinite, the Trexatian population would soon be decimated by disease. But as T'Lana continued, her voice slowly faded and became unintelligible, like the far-off buzz of an insect.

Pressure mounted in his skull; soon even the buzzing was silenced by the pulse of his own heart.

Picard blinked and scowled, trying to shake off the sensation, to concentrate on the words T'Lana's cherubic lips were forming, but he could hear only the sound in his own head.

A virus, he decided. Or perhaps some abnormal residual effect left from his early experience with Shalaft's syndrome. After hours, he would make a point of consulting Beverly.

T'Lana's lips had stopped moving and she was studying him with intent curiosity.

A muscle in his cheek spasmed.

Fierce, abrupt, and inescapable, the dread of the previous night's dream descended on him. The thrumming heartbeat that filled his ears transformed—or had it always been thus?—into a chorus of distant whispers.

This is not happening, Picard told himself

with infinite force, infinite fury. He would not permit a nightmare spawned by events long past to become reality. Whatever this was, it had nothing to do with the Borg. *Could* not have anything to do with the Borg. Any remnants of them were scattered, helpless, without a queen to direct their activity. He had had the pleasure of snapping her writhing, inhuman spine himself, with an impossible strength born of adrenaline and desperation. Admiral Janeway dealt them an even more crushing blow from the Delta Quadrant. Picard had read the reports following the triumphant return of the *Starship Voyager.* The Borg were scattered. Lost without access to a considerable portion of their network of transwarp conduits. They could not possibly have regrouped so quickly.

This was merely a symptom, the onset of a physical malady or neural malfunction. He would will it away, would escort T'Lana to the bridge, would notify Beverly at the first opportune moment.

T'Lana was speaking again—a short phrase—then she paused for a response. Fighting to ignore the chaos in his head, Picard watched carefully as she formed the words. He could not hear them, but he managed to read them.

Captain Picard. Are you unwell?

He opened his mouth to answer, to reassure, but no sound emerged, as if he were still prisoner in a dream, unable to find his voice.

Captain Picard?

With agonizing effort, he forced out the words. "I'm fine."

He could not hear himself utter the word "I'm." But with "fine," the sense of pressure evaporated as quickly as it had appeared; the whispers in his mind fled. His own voice emerged as startlingly loud. In a disconcerting instant, the world returned to normal. He let go a long breath of pure relief.

T'Lana was gazing at him with calm expectancy.

"Just a headache," Picard said, annoyed at himself for such a clearly crippled explanation. He could not imagine how he must have appeared to the Vulcan during the episode.

She appeared to accept his excuse but said no more. They rode in silence, while Picard mentally repeated the mantra:

This is not what it appears to be; there is a physical explanation. This is not what it appears to be. This is not the Borg . . .

2

———

BEVERLY CRUSHER WAS WAITING FOR THEM ON the bridge.

She was glad that she had no medical duties too pressing to keep her from welcoming the new counselor. Beyond that, she was glad for another chance to keep an eye on Jean-Luc.

Beverly had not shown it, of course, but she was concerned for his sake. The nightmare had unsettled him more than he had admitted, and earlier that morning, in engineering, he had seemed . . . off. Not himself. She had known him for decades, and their friendship had grown progressively more intimate over the years, until they had at last confessed their love for each other.

She recognized every nuance of his moods so well that she knew he was still troubled. But this was more than being upset over a dream, or over the memory of what the Borg had done to him long ago.

There was something else wrong, something neither emotional nor physical, nothing she could put her finger on. Something unusual had happened that he had yet to confess. Whatever it was, it so troubled him that he was hiding it from her.

She had done her best to ignore the fact that morning and kept her mind focused on her duties. When the time was right, he would speak to her about it; she knew she could trust him to do so.

In the meantime, she stood beside Worf, who sat in the captain's chair. The Klingon had never been one for idle conversation, but this morning, he was even more taciturn than usual. Beverly knew that Jean-Luc had already given the good news to Worf about his promotion to permanent first officer . . . but judging from the Klingon's dark mood, the encounter had not gone as the captain had planned. She had intended to congratulate Worf when she first arrived on the bridge, but one glance at him made her decide to keep her mouth shut.

So she stood, waiting with arms folded, staring silently along with Worf out at the stars. The rest of the bridge crew had picked up on the Klingon's mood; the tension hung in the air, blanketing everyone like heavy fog.

Beverly was relieved to hear the turbolift doors open behind her. She turned, ready and smiling, to greet the captain and the new counselor.

But the look on Picard's face made her smile freeze into place. Anyone who did not know the captain as well as she did would not suspect anything was wrong, but Beverly could see beyond his calculated, false composure. The small muscles between his eyebrows were taut and gathered, and while his expression conveyed warmth and welcome, she saw beneath it: saw the haunted, hunted look in his eyes. Whatever had been bothering him had just struck again, with a vengeance.

She decided at that instant to confront him as soon as possible. If she had to order him to sickbay on the pretext of a medical examination, so be it. She could no longer wait for him to come to her with an explanation. This was the face of a man who needed her personal and professional help.

Jean-Luc moved across the bridge—not with his usual brisk, intensely no-nonsense stride, but with his slower "diplomatic" pace, the one he reserved for showing visitors around the ship. The newest addition to the crew walked beside him; the two approached Beverly and stopped. Nearby, Worf vacated the captain's chair with unusual alacrity and stood at grave attention.

"Counselor T'Lana," Jean-Luc said, his voice gracious, showing no sign of turmoil, "this is my chief medical officer, Commander Beverly Crusher."

"Doctor." The counselor gave a graceful nod; her manner lacked the stiff formality of most Vulcans. She seemed uncommonly relaxed around humans. It certainly explained why she had received commendations for her diplomatic work and her counseling, this ability to adapt her mannerisms to put those from other cultures at ease. "It is my pleasure to meet you." She was a small woman—a full head shorter than Beverly—with a slight frame and possessed of a beauty humans would term "classic." Her eyes were heavy lidded, giving her a dreamy look incongruous with the rest of her Vulcan features.

"The pleasure is mine, Counselor." Beverly returned the nod, impressed that someone from T'Lana's planet would not shirk at using the word "pleasure."

Picard gestured at the flight control console. "And this is Lieutenant Sara Nave."

Nave swiveled in her chair, her pale, freckled face beaming despite the fact that she was being introduced to a being who supposedly disapproved of such displays of emotion. Yet T'Lana did not seem at all discomfited. Beverly liked Sara Nave, though she knew her only as a patient. Nave had come down with the Cardassian pneumovirus only a few months earlier, two days after she had returned from an away mission. The disease was rare in humans and often fatal, but somehow, Nave had held on. While she was recuperating, she managed to keep the sickbay staff entertained by her crackling sense of good humor and tales of her hijinks while at the academy—despite the fact that she was physically ill and miserable. Crusher learned afterward that Sara had a reputation among her *Enterprise* crewmates as a practical joker. But on duty, she was all business.

"Counselor," Nave said. "Welcome aboard."

"Thank you," T'Lana said. "I am pleased to be here."

Picard glanced in Worf's direction; neither of them directly met the other's gaze. "And this is my . . . first officer, Commander Worf." There was the slightest hesitation in Jean-Luc's voice. Beverly could guess at the word that had entered the captain's mind but that he had not uttered: *temporary.* She shot Worf a swift, surreptitious look; the Klingon's massive shoulders were tight, bunched. He was uncomfortable in the captain's presence, which meant that something unpleasant had indeed occurred during their meeting that morning, but she couldn't imagine what it had been. Surely Worf had no reason to turn down a promotion.

Worf directed his attention downward to the Vulcan. "Counselor T'Lana," he said stiffly. "It is an honor to meet you."

T'Lana looked him directly in the eye. She regarded the Klingon in silence. The ease and grace she had carried onto the bridge with her evaporated. Nothing overt in her posture or expression changed, yet without moving a muscle, without so much as narrowing her eyes, she managed to convey something approaching . . . disapproval. Beverly wondered if she had been too quick to commend the counselor's ability to interact with the crew. Either T'Lana wasn't as comfortable addressing Klingons as she was humans, or something else was transpiring at the moment.

"Commander," T'Lana said with a slow nod before turning to Picard. "I would like to meet the rest of the senior staff when it is convenient, Captain."

Worf couldn't help but think that the counselor had turned away from him in a pointed way. He would have chalked up her terse manner as being a typically Vulcan attribute, but there was something more there, something almost approaching emotion. He could not entirely mask his curiosity, particularly when he saw that Doctor Crusher seemed to have noticed something was off as well.

He had never known a Vulcan to be overtly rude, but Counselor T'Lana did not strike him as an ordinary Vulcan. As a rule, Worf did not like most members of the race: they were aloof, cold, unable to hide the distaste they felt in the presence of more emotional beings. T'Lana was different. Worf had watched her from the moment she set foot on the bridge. She seemed relaxed, free of her people's extreme self-consciousness. She was clearly comfortable being among a mostly human crew. And there was—or had it been his imagination?—something approaching warmth in her eyes. That is, until those eyes had focused on him.

Now, as she turned away, Worf noticed the fineness of her features. When he first began to serve alongside humans, he had found the faces of their females to be vaguely repulsive: their noses were too narrow and short, their lips too thin, their teeth too small and even. The smoothness of their foreheads seemed bland, unformed.

Over time, he had come to accept and finally to appreciate them. And all the things about Jadzia— things that once would have offended him, her straight, even, fine features—he came to see as delicate and beautiful.

Counselor T'Lana was beautiful in the same way.

The realization unsettled him, since Jadzia's death, he had avoided noticing such things. In fact, he had instructed Ensign Sara Nave in the use of the *bat'leth* and never once noticed that she was female. But he could not deny at that moment that he was drawn to the new counselor, in spite of her coolness toward him.

Beverly measured her reaction as best she could under the situation. T'Lana's subtle snub of Worf would have been lost on most of the bridge crew, but it did seem to the doctor that T'Lana had just turned her back on him.

Jean-Luc's manner remained smooth, though he blinked once, rapidly, in surprise. "Of course, Counselor," he replied. "Commander La Forge is currently completing a task in engineering. I'll introduce you to him when he's available. In the meantime, since you prefer to report for duty . . ." He gestured at the chair that had been Deanna Troi's.

To get to it, T'Lana had to move past Worf. Beverly watched with curiosity as the petite Vulcan sidled by him without even meeting his gaze.

Was it possible, she wondered, *that this person, whose Starfleet record indicated enormous respect for other societies, was a bigot when it came to Klingons?*

His expression one of thinly veiled puzzlement, Worf moved to Will Riker's old station and settled into the chair. T'Lana coolly took Deanna Troi's former position. She appeared oblivious to the awkward reactions from the three senior members of the crew, the ones who knew enough to realize that the first officer had just been slighted.

Beverly leaned toward Jean-Luc, who was still standing, and said in a low voice, "I'll be in sickbay if you need me." The undercurrent in her tone was intentional, one that she knew the captain would pick up on; she was inviting him to tell her what was wrong. And she fully intended to insist, the instant he was off duty, that he come to sickbay for an exam and a little talk.

She turned and headed for the turbolift but had taken only three steps when she was stopped by the mixed chorus of sound: a groan, Worf's urgent question, "Sir, are you all right?" and Nave's exclamation, "Captain!"

She whirled, intuitively knowing what she would see. Nave was already out of her chair; Worf was up and reaching toward the captain; T'Lana was sitting, staring calmly at the tableau.

And Jean-Luc . . . Jean-Luc had sagged to his knees a step from his chair, torso bent slightly forward, fists curled and pressed against his ears as if to blot out a painful noise. His mouth was still open, his eyes squeezed tightly shut, his brow contorted in agony.

She did not remember moving over to him. In one instant, she was standing a short distance away; in the next, she was kneeling beside him, hand on his shoulder, vaguely aware that Worf's massive bulk was hovering over them.

"Jean-Luc," she said loudly into his ear, "can you hear me?"

In reply, the captain gasped. His eyes opened, but he did not appear to see his surroundings. His gaze was focused on something far distant and terrible.

"Jean-Luc!" she said again, this time, almost a shout.

He did not hear. Whatever he was listening to was so deafening, so horrible, that it drowned out the rest of his world.

Beverly managed, with the help of Worf, to get the captain down to sickbay. Nave was left temporarily in charge of the ship. The Klingon had to support the captain's full weight in order to get him off the bridge. By the time they got off the lift and were moving down the corridor toward sickbay, Picard—not yet able to speak—had come to himself enough to wave away Worf's and Beverly's supporting arms and walk, slow and uncertain, on his own.

His face was slack, stricken; he was forcing himself to breathe slowly as he moved. And although he would not meet Beverly's eyes, she could still see what he was attempting to hide from her: horror, the same horror that had made him cry out in his sleep the night before.

"Jean-Lu—" Beverly stopped herself. Through an act of will, she forced herself to become distant from the distress she felt, as someone who loved the man who was now suffering. She was no more than a doctor now, concerned for a patient. As such, she asked calmly, clinically, "Captain. Can you hear me?"

Picard shot her a sidewise glance and nodded. Slowly, the terror that had come so swiftly upon him eased, and his breathing slowed. It took him a few more steps to say hoarsely, "Yes. Yes, I'm fine." As the three of them entered sickbay, he straightened and seemed to regain control of himself, then cleared his throat. "Thank you, Mister Worf." He directed a fleeting glance at the Klingon. "You may return to the bridge."

Worf shot an uncertain look at Crusher, who nodded. The Klingon turned and disappeared through the double doors.

Beverly led Picard to one of the diagnostic beds and gestured. He sat on the edge, his hands propping himself up. "So," she said, with feigned casualness, "shall we talk about it first, or should I just go ahead and start the exam?"

Jean-Luc looked grim, haggard, but there was no subterfuge in his gaze, his tone. "The exam won't show anything."

"Why not?"

He glanced down at the floor, miserable. "Because nothing . . . physical happened."

"*Something* happened, Jean-Luc. You collapsed. And you're not leaving here until I find out why."

Reluctantly, he looked up at her again. "I heard them."

It was the softness, the certainty in his tone that pricked the flesh on her upper arms, on the nape of her neck. She did not ask who *they* were, perhaps because she feared she already knew the answer.

His eyes focused on a distant point somewhere beyond her left shoulder. "I had tried to tell myself the dream was nothing more than that . . . a dream. But I heard their voices even after I woke up. It was so faint that I convinced myself I hadn't really heard them. But it happened again, when I was with Counselor T'Lana. Unmistakable. And now . . ." He paused and shook his head as if trying to clear away the vestiges of the experience.

"Now?" Beverly prompted, her own voice scarcely louder than a whisper.

"I can make out bits of what they're saying now." He drew a deep breath and stared at her so intently that he seemed to be looking through her. "It's different, though. They sound . . . almost frantic, if that's possible. Rushed. Urgent. One thing I know is clear: the Borg collective is regrouping. And they're here, in the Alpha Quadrant."

On the bridge, T'Lana sat silently beside Commander Worf and watched the shifting pattern of stars on the viewscreen. The Klingon was brooding, silent, clearly unsettled by what had just happened to the captain. Indeed, the humans on the bridge emanated a great deal of tension regarding the event.

But there was no purpose in speculating on Picard's condition. They would know more when Doctor Crusher gave her report.

T'Lana had been favorably impressed by Captain Picard's presence the first few moments after meeting him. She had expected him to be much more choleric in nature, given his history of relying heavily on emotion and intuition—as well as the fact that he had, in the past, brazenly ignored direct orders from Starfleet Command. Instead, he seemed extraordinarily self-possessed for a human.

But his strange behavior on the turbolift and on the bridge had concerned T'Lana. Admittedly, she was disturbed by the fact that Commander Worf was now in command of the ship. While Captain Picard's reliance on emotion had proved effective, Commander Worf's had not.

She was displeased with herself, however, for her behavior toward the Klingon; she should have greeted him as cordially as she had the others. She knew that the shifts in her behavior would be barely perceptible to most humans. But it was clear that, at the very least, the captain and chief medical officer had noticed something amiss. At the same time, altering her behavior would have been dishonest; her disapproval of Worf was solidly based in fact. And honesty, to Vulcans, was more important than manners. Even after serving for more than twenty years on Starfleet vessels, she was still more Vulcan than Starfleet.

T'Lana had to admit to herself that Worf's personal presence had not been what she had anticipated. She had expected to find the most Klingon of Klingons, one who emanated ferocity, instability, ill temper. Given her exceptional telepathic abilities, she had expected to sense the proximity of a disordered, chaotic mind.

She had found none of that. She had sensed a proud Klingon, yes, but also a disciplined officer, not a warrior, who had looked on her with respect and admiration. He possessed a trait unrevealed by the holographs in his Starfleet file, an attractive, intangible quality that had no counterpart in the Vulcan language but that humans referred to as *charisma.* And T'Lana had been astonished to find that her first instinct was to respond favorably to him . . . with interest.

Then memory had returned to her and left her unable to respond courteously to him.

Even so, she felt she had made the best possible decision, for the good of the service, by requesting a transfer to the *Enterprise*. If Captain Picard was in fact incapacitated, Worf would assume permanent command—a situation that could easily bring about disaster. The *Enterprise* had already come close enough to it before, courtesy of irrational command decisions. Her logical input as a counselor would be desperately required.

And T'Lana knew all too well what it was like to stand on the bridge of a starship blasted apart and ultimately destroyed, all for the sake of emotion.

Beverly reacted as Picard had anticipated: with a bright flash of fear, which she quickly dismissed and replaced with a healthy medical skepticism. His intimate friend and lover was gone, and his chief medical officer stood in her place. He would have expected no less of her. At the same time, he felt a very personal regret for what he had had to tell her, for what she would no doubt discover to be the truth.

"I realize you're convinced of this," she said carefully, "but I'm sure you understand that I can't rule out a physical or emotional component until I've had a chance to examine you."

"Of course." He hoped desperately that the whispers in his head were the result of illness; at the same time, he knew—with the certainty of the Collective to which he had once belonged—that they were not. Without being asked, he swung his legs onto the diagnostic bed and lay back.

As she began to run the scans, he sighed and closed his eyes, grateful for the silence, however temporary, in his skull. On the bridge, the Borg chatter had grown so thunderous that he had buckled beneath it. Words that had previously been inaudible whispers had roared in his consciousness: *Alpha . . . launch ship . . . attack.*

He had sensed anger beneath the words—or perhaps not anger, since Borg drones were incapable of feeling. But there was something. An outrage of a sort, one that had been brewing for some time now. It was the outrage of a race once consummately powerful, determined to conquer the universe. Now broken, the Borg were determined to seek justice, at last to have their revenge against the one group that had so steadfastly refused to be conquered—and had instead turned into the conqueror.

Humanity.

Picard knew there was no way to prove that what he intuitively sensed was fact, no way to validate it, to quantify it. He was going to have to ask his senior officers to trust him simply because he believed it was so.

And once it became evident to them all that the threat from the Borg was real, he was going to have to ask for even more of their trust.

Such was clearly going to be the case with Beverly. She kept up a sternly professional front during the scans, but in the end, she let go a small, barely audible sigh of frustration. Picard could have told her the results, but it was best to let her see them for herself.

"Nothing unusual showing up," she said finally, and in her voice he heard the same keen disappointment he felt. He had desperately wanted the sound in his head to be something treatable, something that would disappear, anything but the Borg. "No physical cause presenting itself. No tumors, no fever, no detectable infections. The auditory hallucinations aren't the result of psychosis . . . your neurotransmitters are well within normal range, same as your last physical."

She turned off the diagnostic panel and he sat up to study her. Her features were still carefully composed in the most professional of expressions, without so much as a glimmer of fright. "That's because the auditory hallucinations *aren't* hallucinations," he said.

She hesitated, clearly unwilling to admit that such a horrific thing might be true. "You know, this could be connected to your experience in the nexus. In a sense, you're still there . . . at least, a part of you will always remain there. So your past, present, future—all of it's jumbled together. Perhaps what you're hearing is an echo from an earlier time—"

"No," Picard insisted. It was his turn to be frustrated. If he couldn't convince his chief medical officer and closest friend, how was he going to be able to convince anyone else?

And it was imperative that others be convinced, and quickly.

He slipped off the table and stood. "I'm going to need your help, Doctor," he began formally, then his tone softened. "Beverly . . . I wish, more than anything else, that I was wrong about this. But as dreadful as this is, I can't ignore it, I can't run from it. I can't explain *how* I know—but I *do* know—that we must act swiftly, *now,* to stop the Borg."

"And if we don't?" Her voice was very quiet. She was listening at last, considering for the first time that he might be right.

"Then humankind will be assimilated," he answered flatly.

She regarded him in silence. For the first time, he saw a real fear in her eyes and imagined the reflection of Locutus there. She gathered herself quickly, then pressed. "But how can we stop them? Do we just wait for them to come looking for us?"

"No." He gave a grim, not-quite smile. "We don't wait. Because I know precisely where they are."

3

———◆———

IN HIS QUARTERS, PICARD SAT AT HIS COMMUNI-
cations screen and watched as the insignia of Starfleet Command faded, to be replaced by the image
of Kathryn Janeway.

The admiralty suited her. She had aged little, despite the trauma of years trying to get *Voyager* and
her crew safely home; her reddish chestnut hair,
pulled back from her face and carefully gathered
into a coil, was only beginning to show the first few
streaks of silver at the temples. Picard had always
liked dealing with her. Janeway was direct, plain-
spoken, with handsome Gaelic features arranged in
an open expression. Although she was capable of
guile if duty demanded it, she disdained it; you always knew where you stood with Janeway.

She smiled at the sight of him. *"Captain! To
what do I owe the pleasure of this subspace visit?"*

Picard could not quite bring himself to return the enthusiasm. "It's good to see you again, Admiral. But I'm afraid the circumstances are less than pleasant."

Her demeanor became at once utterly serious, her tone flat; the smile was now no more than a memory. She put her elbows on her desk and leaned forward. *"What's going on?"*

"The Borg are in Alpha Quadrant," he said. "They're regrouping. Forming a new Collective."

She tilted her chin upward at that, the only sign of surprise she allowed herself; in the space of a second, however, she had lowered it again, and narrowed her eyes, digging in for a fight. This was not, Picard knew, going to be easy.

"Where?" she demanded.

"In Sector Ten. On a moon . . ." He paused, frustrated with himself. He knew that he could not give her the details she wanted, which would make him sound irrational. "They're creating a new cube, a ship. It's nearly habitable and will be launched soon."

"Do you have the coordinates? We could send a ship to investigate." Her emphasis on "could" revealed a healthy degree of doubt.

Picard tried to shake off a sudden sense of awkwardness. "I don't know the *precise* coordinates . . ."

She scowled slightly at that and folded her hands atop the desk, abruptly formal. *"Are your long-range scanners malfunctioning? Or are you basing this on some sort of intelligence?"*

Picard did not allow himself to hesitate. He replied firmly, "We're not close enough for long-range scans, Admiral. I have detected Borg chatter. They're communicating with each other about the new Collective, about their intent to organize and make a fresh attempt to assimilate humanity."

Janeway grew very still, fixing her gaze on him so intently that a weaker personality might have withered beneath it. *"Would you mind explaining, Captain, how you detected this 'chatter'?"*

"I heard it. In my . . . mind. I was part of the Collective once, you know."

"Yes, I do know." Her tone and expression softened briefly, then she came down hard, with no effort to veil her skepticism. *"When* Voyager *emerged from Delta Quadrant, I saw the queen destroyed— as well as her vessel and all the progeny contained within it. More important, their transwarp corridors have been obliterated. The Borg are crippled, Captain. There might be a few surviving drones scattered throughout the galaxy, but without a queen or contact with the Collective, they're lost. The majority of drones that remain are no doubt still in Delta Quadrant. How could they possibly be a threat to us here?"*

Picard matched her vehemence. "Nevertheless, they *are* regrouping here. I've sensed it. My connection to the Borg is documented. And I know that they have grown frustrated with the fact that humanity has stood in the way of their goal of total assimilation. This time, they are determined to conquer us. It's more than just assimilation. The Borg want revenge."

Her gaze remained unwavering, unmoved. *"The Borg don't seek vengeance. Their actions aren't based on emotions. At least, the drones' aren't. You should know that better than anyone."* Her posture and expression suddenly relaxed. *"Jean-Luc, you're asking me to issue orders, to send a ship to who knows where, based on nothing more than your instincts. Put yourself in my position . . ."*

She sighed, and in that sigh, Picard sensed victory, however slight. *"But let's assume you're right—that the Borg are re-forming a Collective, in the Alpha Quadrant. I'm willing to give you the benefit of that doubt. If so, then the best person to deal with this is Seven of Nine. She's currently assigned to Earth. I'll contact her immediately, then forward any specific information you can give me. But I'll need to know more than just, 'We think the Borg are on a moon somewhere in the Alpha Quadrant.'"*

It was all Picard could do not to interrupt her. "Admiral, there's no time. You must trust my instinct, which is telling me that the *Enterprise* is the closest starship to the hive's activity. There's a chance we can stop them before the ship is finished and they launch an attack. They have to be destroyed *now.*"

Perhaps there'd been more heat, more shrillness in his tone than he'd intended; Janeway was studying him with concern. *"Let me be blunt, Cap-*

tain. You still have a score to settle with the Borg; you're far too emotionally involved. Seven of Nine will be impartial. But because I have respect for your instincts—and because it would be far better to risk sending a ship to investigate nothing than to risk not investigating what might be Borg activity—I'll send Seven of Nine by shuttle as quickly as possible to the Enterprise. *I can get her there in a matter of days. But you will have to follow her lead on this."*

Her words summoned the memory of his own, spoken years ago, to Will Riker, explaining why a different admiral had forbidden him to fight the Borg: In Starfleet Command's opinion, *a man once captured and assimilated by the Borg should not be allowed to face them again. It would introduce an unstable element to a critical situation.*

If that were the reason, Picard wasn't sure that Seven of Nine would be the best to place in charge of this situation either. Certainly the Borg had more of an effect on her life than they did his. He had never met the person who had spent more time as a drone than a free-thinking individual, but Picard was familiar with her file. All of Starfleet knew of Seven of Nine. Though everything Picard had read maintained that she could keep her professional cool, it was still disconcerting to think that he couldn't be trusted to handle the Borg. Particularly since he had bested them in every encounter. And especially since time was most definitely of the essence.

The frustration was agonizing. How did he *know,* with such infinite certainty, what he was saying was true? He could not explain even to himself how he knew what he did about the Borg's plans—so how could he prove they existed to Janeway or to anyone else at Command? Yet he was no less certain, no less urgently desperate. "Admiral, Earth is too far away; the Borg are moving swiftly. We don't *have* a 'matter of days.' By the time Seven arrives—"

She cut him off. *"You are to do nothing until Seven of Nine arrives, and she will be in charge of the investigation. You'll be contacted shortly with her ETA. Those are my orders. Janeway out."*

He found himself staring at the Starfleet Command logo as he whispered the words she would not hear: "It will be too late."

For several minutes, he sat looking at the darkened screen. Even now that his mind was still, and the voice of the Borg no more than a memory, he felt the invisible tendrils of the Collective pulling at his consciousness. He *knew* what they were doing, and although he did not know the coordinates Janeway had asked for, he knew what heading the *Enterprise* should take in order to find the mysterious moon.

He propped his elbows on the desk, leaned forward, and massaged his temples. Beverly had found nothing physically wrong with him. Was it possible that there was a third, less sinister cause for him to hear the echoes of the Collective's voice, to experience this gut-level certainty?

In his memory surfaced a familiar face, one cinnamon-skinned, beautiful, framed by close-cropped dark russet hair, a face from another century—Lily, Zefram Cochrane's assistant. He smiled faintly at the thought of her. She had lived in such a desperate, cruel time in Earth's history, surviving a war that had killed millions. It had toughened her, made her strong, made her cling desperately to the hope that Cochrane was going to convert an instrument of death—a nuclear missile—into a warp ship, an instrument of hope. The harshness of her life had also made her frightened, liable to lash out violently at anyone, anything she did not know.

Yet even she had seen beyond her own hurt to the depth of the psychological scar he had borne. She had called him "Ahab"—the crazed captain from *Moby-Dick*—willing to sacrifice his vessel, his crew, and ultimately himself for the sake of revenge on that which had wounded him. Lily had brought him to a moment of epiphany: he realized he had to let go of his bitterness before it destroyed him and those he loved.

He had thought he had finally freed himself from his angry obsession with the Borg. He had never forgotten the words from Melville, evoking Ahab's madness:

"He piled upon the whale's white hump the sum

of all the general rage and hate felt by his whole race; and then, as if his chest had been a mortar, he burst his hot heart's shell upon it."

Had it returned to haunt him? Was it possible that he was overreacting, that he had created a scenario after picking up on some fleeting, disorganized Borg chatter? That *he* was the one that had created the sense of urgency, not the Borg?

His instinct said no. But before he could consider disobeying orders, before he could in good conscience approach his crew about doing so, he had a responsibility to discuss his dilemma with a certain crew member.

He rose when T'Lana entered his quarters and gestured for her to sit across from him, with the desk between them. She sat, seeming relaxed enough— for a Vulcan. Picard was far from feeling the same: for one thing, he had never confided in her before, and he was used to the comforting warmth of Deanna Troi, not the cool, rational appraisal he was no doubt about to receive. Deanna had always been acutely aware of his emotions and therefore brilliant at helping him sort through them, combining both instinct and logic into the best possible approach to a problem.

He was uncomfortable with T'Lana for a second reason: although the all-consuming wave of Borg chatter had left him ill equipped to focus on his surroundings, he *had* noticed the subtle coldness she had displayed toward Worf. There could have been many reasons for the behavior. Certainly nothing worth discussing at the moment, but he would need to keep an eye on the situation. For now, he placed his concerns aside because he needed to hear the advice of an experienced counselor.

In unconscious imitation of Janeway, he folded his hands atop his desk and leaned slightly forward, forcing away all discomfort, all doubts about his ability to utilize T'Lana's skills effectively. There was work to be done, a decision to be made; he launched into an unrehearsed speech without hesitation.

"Counselor," he began, "you saw my . . . apparent collapse on the bridge."

"I did," she replied serenely. "You seem to be fully recovered. I trust that is so."

"It is." He paused, trying to explain much with an economy of words. "You are also familiar with my experience with the Borg?"

"Insofar as your Starfleet file records it. You have experienced two significant encounters with them: first, when they assimilated you; second, when you successfully stopped them from preventing the launch of Zefram Cochrane's warp-drive vessel."

"That's all correct," Picard said, marveling that such profoundly horrifying events could be condensed into such bland, emotionless phrases. "Perhaps you are not aware that I have retained the . . . ability to sense the Borg communicating with each other. I was, after all, once part of the Collective."

Neither her gaze nor her expression changed in the slightest, but she tilted her head to one side, causing the fringe of soft, black hair to spill across her forehead, revealing pale skin beneath. "I have not studied the personal logs concerning your ability. Has this been empirically documented in any of them?"

The question caught him off guard. He gathered himself and answered carefully, "It has been . . . noted by senior crew members, including Doctor Crusher. You might want to look at Counselor Troi's log in particular; she knew that I heard them. You can also check the records of the *Enterprise*'s encounter with the queen ship shortly before it was destroyed. Several starships had engaged the Borg, and many were destroyed, including the admiral's vessel. I took command of the fleet and directed all the surviving ships to lock in their weapons at a precise location on the Borg cube—with the result that the cube was destroyed. That is a recorded fact."

Her face returned to neutral position again. So cherubic and innocent were her features that it was too easy to forget the piercing intelligence behind them. "Was this the reason for your distraction during our initial conversation, and for your collapse on the bridge?"

"It was." He could not prevent his tone from

turning dark. "The voice of the Borg became over-whelming, so loud it blotted out all else."

"What did it say?"

"It said . . . they said . . . Well, I heard fragments. They're building a ship, a cube, near a moon in the far reaches of the Alpha Quadrant. They're prepar-ing to attack again."

"Who is their target?"

"Earth." He gave a single, rueful shake of his head. "They haven't appreciated our interference with their plans to assimilate and conquer all races. They apparently desire revenge." He drew a breath. "I . . . also have acquired an instinct about the Borg. I know—I can't explain why—where they are. At this very moment, I could give the navigator the course heading that would take us to where the Borg are constructing their ship. I *know*, with com-pletely certainty, that the *Enterprise* is the closest starship to the site, and that we have little time be-fore the Borg complete their vessel and launch their attack.

"I notified Admiral Janeway of this. Unfortu-nately, she has ordered me to wait until Seven of Nine . . ." He hesitated and shot T'Lana a question-ing glance.

"I know who Seven of Nine is," she responded.

". . . until Seven can arrive aboard the *Enterprise* in order to direct the mission. Admiral Janeway feels that my emotions are too involved, given my experience with the Borg. But here is the problem: I know, without doubt, that by the time Seven of

Nine arrives, it will be too late. The Borg will already have attacked." He fell silent, to give her time to absorb all he had said.

It took her no time at all to react. "You are asking me, if I understand correctly, whether you should disobey the admiral's orders and pursue the Borg without waiting for Seven of Nine."

"Yes," he said. It had been so easy to read Deanna. If she disapproved, there would have been a swift flash in her black eyes, accompanied by a carefully neutral expression before she began to speak in a low, measured tone. If she approved, there would have been an obvious look of sympathy. T'Lana's expression remained placid, maddeningly inscrutable.

Perhaps, in time, Picard would learn to read her.

"I would suggest," she said evenly, "that Doctor Crusher perform a psychological evaluation on you and run a series of tests to be sure there is no physical basis for the phenomenon."

Picard slowly released a breath and, with it, as little defensiveness as he possibly could. "Such an examination was conducted earlier today. You may feel free to consult with the doctor yourself, but I can tell you the results: no mental or physical abnormalities were found. This appears to be the same phenomenon that occurred during my previous encounter with the Borg and their queen."

"Interesting," T'Lana murmured. She hesitated, then added, "You are aware, Captain, of the Vulcan mind-meld."

"I am," Picard affirmed. "I have participated in one before." He had not mentioned it because the experience was intensely personal and he did not feel comfortable participating in one with someone who was still a stranger to him. In addition, he did not see the need to use such a highly intimate technique to prove himself to her, when she would most likely see the evidence soon enough.

"Good," she replied. "I suspected you might think that a mind-meld would allow yourself to 'prove' your position to me and justify your not following the admiral's orders. However, I can only sense what you are thinking and feeling. And it's clear that you are quite convinced that what you feel is right. I would experience that conviction—but ultimately I would still not be able, after the meld was completed, to say whether your conviction was based in fact or not."

"But might you not be able to hear the voice of the Borg for yourself?"

"Yes. But only filtered through your consciousness, with your convictions. I would not be able to judge whether I was hearing an outside entity or one created by the workings of your own mind."

"Understood," Picard said. "So let me be blunt. What is your opinion? Do I ignore what I know to be an imminent threat and obey Janeway's order? Or do I listen to my instincts and possibly prevent the death and assimilation of billions?"

"You have framed your questions in terms that show your bias, Captain. Let me ask a different question: is it worth your court-martial—and the court-martial of loyal officers who choose to support you in your insubordination—in order to substantiate a suspicion?"

He felt a surge of anger at her words but quickly suppressed it. He had asked her here, after all, in order to get another viewpoint. "This is far more than a suspicion," he said heavily. "If you look at the facts . . ."

"The one fact you have mentioned that could prove your assertion is the fact that the Borg cube was destroyed when you ordered several starships to concentrate their fire on one specific location. But that could be explained by the evidence that the cube had already sustained damage, and that the combined force of several weapons was enough to destroy the ship." She paused. "If there is another fact, Captain, that can be unemotionally verified, I would like to hear it."

He scanned his memory and found himself at a loss. So many things had happened . . . So many members of his senior staff had trusted his connection to the Borg, and not asked for such verification, that he had never before thought of other incidents that could prove it to an outsider.

Given his silence, T'Lana continued. "My opinion is that Admiral Janeway is correct in her assessment: it is important for someone other than you to investigate the possibility that the Borg have become active again. I know of your experience with the Borg; it would be impossible for a human to suppress hostile emotions and a desire for rash action in such circumstances. Therefore, you must obey the admiral's orders. It is the most logical and cautious course of action." She paused. "You must remind yourself, as well, that both you and Janeway herself killed two powerful embodiments of the Borg queen. The drones that remain are few, scattered, and directiveless. It would be against their established pattern for them to unite and make a group decision in the manner you suggest."

He had to remind himself that he was grateful for someone willing to take the opposite side; at the same time, her statement fueled his frustration even more than his conversation with Janeway. "Is it really cautious to ignore a conviction that, if I wait for Seven to arrive, the Borg will be ready to strike? Where is the logic behind that, Counselor? I would rather risk my career than countless inno- cent lives." He rose, signaling that the meeting was at an end, but he could not resist a final ques- tion. "T'Lana . . . have you ever encountered the Borg face-to-face? Have you ever seen firsthand the results of one of their attacks, or seen the transformation of an individual who has been as- similated?"

She had risen as well. "I have not," she an- swered. "You must remember, Captain, that I lack the empathic skills of Counselor Troi. I cannot be for you what she was, and I hope that you do not consider my opposing views as a lack of respect for what you have endured at the hands of the Borg. But I can be the voice of logic for you. I can help you consider your options in that light."

"I do appreciate your input, Counselor," he said, with all the sincerity he possessed, but her words had only made his decision more difficult, not less.

"Thank you. Dismissed."

In sickbay, Beverly was preparing to conduct a routine checkup on Worf. Her mind was anywhere but on her incoming patient. Jean-Luc's condition still worried her. At best, he was suffering some kind of psychosis, which her scans had all but disproved. At worst, the Borg were preparing another attack. No matter what, she couldn't stop worrying about Jean-Luc. This was nothing new to her. She had always worried about him in times of duress. But somehow this was different. More personal. She just hoped that when the time came, she could retain her professional composure. She shook off the concern, knowing that she was too much of a professional even to allow for the doubt. She finished recalibrating her scans for a Klingon and was ready for Worf by the time he arrived.

After years of working with him aboard the *Enterprise,* she had eventually learned to read his moods, despite his fierce-looking features—the furry, upward-slanted brows that cast a shadow over his dark eyes and converged at the bridge of

his nose to form a sharp V; the bony, ridged forehead that emphasized the severity of his eyebrows
and intense glare. His lips were usually fixed in a
grim, rigid line. All of the foregoing made him
seem to wear a perpetual scowl—to an outsider.
Though he rarely smiled, and his mannerisms were
gruff, Beverly now could detect his various moods:
playful, joking, serious, embarrassed, uncomfortable, furious, sad. The slightest quirk in the corner
of his lip conveyed a wealth of emotion.

She knew that Worf had felt awkward on the
bridge after T'Lana's snub, but he had covered it
well. By the time he entered sickbay, his mood had
again shifted; he was plainly melancholy. She did
not understand why, but she was not surprised to
see such emotion in him. Beverly had learned that
there was a great deal of insecurity and tenderness
lurking beneath the fierce Klingon exterior. She
knew that Worf had been married to a Trill during
his absence. Beverly had seen holograms of her—a
beautiful, delicate-looking woman. No doubt, her
death had devastated him, though he never spoke
of her; he worked to hide his grief from his crewmates.

Just as he was hiding something now, something
that deeply troubled him, something Beverly suspected had to do with T'Lana's behavior on the
bridge.

As his physician and his friend, it was Beverly's
job to find out what.

She'd said nothing to him at the beginning, just the usual conversation between doctor and patient during a routine physical. It was best to get him comfortable and somewhat relaxed with the procedure before starting to ask the sensitive questions.

Near the end of the exam—after minimal exchanges, with Worf answering most questions with an affirmative grunt—the Klingon rose and straightened his tunic, clearly ready to be dismissed after the usual brief affirmation that he was in perfect health.

Now or never.

Beverly drew in a deep breath and said, tentatively, "Worf . . . you know that as chief medical officer, I'm responsible for more than just your physical health. And I can't help sensing that something is bothering you." She paused. "You know that ethics require me to keep everything you say in strictest confidence."

Worf let go an abrupt, short sigh at that. His lips parted, as though he were about to answer—but then a look of uncertainty came over him, and he fell silent.

At least he hadn't dismissed her outright, which was a good sign. She pressed, her tone gentle, cautious. "Does this have something to do with the reason you turned down the promotion to permanent second-in-command?"

His russet eyebrows lifted swiftly. "The captain told you?"

"I'm one of the senior officers. Of course he told me. I would have learned about it soon enough, anyway."

He looked into the distance and released a sound between a groan and a growl. "I do not deserve the position."

The statement honestly shocked her, and she let go a gasp of disbelief. "Worf, I can't think of anyone more deserving, or more qualified!"

He pressed his lips firmly together, not meeting her gaze; his own was fixed on a distant spot beyond her shoulder. "I had a choice once," he said tautly, "between duty . . . or personal loyalty. I chose incorrectly. A starship commander does not have that luxury."

She thought a flicker of pain crossed his features. She suppressed the impulse to reach out and put a comforting hand on his great shoulder. He was uncomfortable with the notion of a gentle touch. Instead, Beverly decided that she had come this far and might as well get to the heart of the matter. Months ago, Jean-Luc had told her the story of how Worf's wife had been wounded during a mission. The Klingon had left her behind in order to fulfill his duty, knowing full well that she would die before he could come back to her.

In the end, Worf had aborted the mission and returned to save her. Beverly had found the fact touching, despite the fact that Worf had failed in his duty. She had asked herself: *If Jean-Luc were dying, would I be able to turn my back on him, even if I had direct orders to do so? Would I be able to leave him to die?*

Softly, she asked, "Does this have anything to do with Jadzia?"

He drew in a startled, silent breath and blinked rapidly, then his expression turned to stone. She'd hit a nerve—*the* nerve.

"I do not want to discuss it," he answered stiffly.

She had pushed too far; the wound was still too tender. Yet she had to do something to salvage the situation.

"The past is the past, Worf," Beverly said, hoping her words did not come across as trite. "We can't change it. But *we* can change. And it's clear to me that you would change what happened, if you could." She paused. "You're the best possible candidate for the position. The captain *needs* you."

His expression softened slightly; she was making an impression. "There are others just as qualified," he said, but all the vehemence had left his tone. "I will remain until a replacement can be found."

"Tell me," Beverly said, "if you were on a Klingon vessel, what would your job be, as second-in-command?"

The question took him by surprise. "To support the captain totally, of course. So long as he does not endanger the crew."

She gave a single, emphatic nod. "That's all you have to do, Worf. You don't have to dwell on the past, or punish yourself for it by denying the captain the first officer he deserves. Just be Klingon for him."

He lifted his bronze face and finally met her gaze directly. His eyes still bore lingering doubt, but he was considering very carefully what she had just said.

She was about to dismiss him with that thought when—at the same time that she heard the doors to sickbay slide open behind her—Worf's eyes grew round with alarm. He moved past her, toward the doors.

"Captain!"

She turned. Behind her, she saw an ashen apparition bracing itself in the doorway to keep from falling: Jean-Luc, his face pale and glittering with sweat, his mouth slack, his eyes wide and vacant, emptied of his shrewd intelligence. In its place was something *else* . . . another consciousness, cold, mindless, and mechanical, a consciousness that filled Beverly with dread, for she had seen it in his eyes many, many years before . . .

She cried out his name, but he was beyond recognizing it—beyond recognizing her or Worf, as they seized his arms and took him over to a diagnostic bed.

He would not lie still, thrashing like a man in the throes of a fever. Worf held him carefully in place while Beverly frantically raced to get a reading.

Nothing abnormal in the standard scans . . . but something was terribly, terribly wrong. She frowned at the diagnostic panel, but her attention was forced away from it by the haunting sound of a single voice that seemed to combine a thousand whispers. It was a voice she knew and had hoped never to hear again: the voice of the Borg.

And Jean-Luc's lips were forming the words.

A queen . . . We are birthing a new queen . . .

4

THE EPISODE LASTED NO MORE THAN A MINUTE,
but to Beverly, it seemed to continue for an infinite
length of time because there was nothing she could
do to stop it, no medical help she could render to
ease the horror of what Jean-Luc was enduring.
There was no point in sedating him; whatever he—
or rather, the Borg—said might be helpful.

It ended dramatically. One instant, Beverly was
staring down into the blank yet driven gaze of the
Borg, listening to the faint, eerie chorus of many
voices joined into one. The next, she was gazing
into the eyes of the man she knew as Jean-Luc
Picard, who was abruptly silent.

He fell, limp, against the bed, exhausted by the
wave that had overcome him. For several seconds,
he lay panting until at last he caught his breath and

said, "I heard it. Every word that I spoke . . . And all of it is true."

Beverly no longer had any doubt; no emotional trauma, no illness, could possibly re-create the voice of the Borg so faithfully. Worf, too, was leaning over the captain with a look of both dismay and conviction.

"The Borg have a new queen?" the Klingon asked. It was not a question so much as a request for confirmation.

Picard sat up slowly, waving away the doctor's attempts to support him. He pressed a hand to his temple as if it pained him. "Not yet . . . but they soon will have." He lowered his hand and looked pointedly up at his two officers. "With the destruction of the transwarp conduits, the Borg that remain in the Alpha Quadrant have been cut off from the Collective as a whole. When a queen is killed, the Collective eventually creates a new one. Now that these Borg are essentially alone, they have taken it upon themselves to create their own queen. One with a singular purpose."

Beverly folded her arms, as if warding off a chill. "To conquer us once and for all."

Jean-Luc pressed his lips into a grim line before answering. "No. Not to conquer us . . . to *destroy* us. They want to wipe all traces of humanity from the universe. They're building their vessel in order to accommodate the queen. Once she comes to consciousness, and is able to issue directives, the attack will commence."

Worf's expression had grown fierce, determined, the look of a Klingon ready for battle. "When will the queen be ready?"

"Too soon," Picard replied. "Too soon."

Seated in one of the *Enterprise* conference rooms, Picard rested his forearms against the cool, polished surface of the oblong table and studied the faces of the officers who looked to him for direction.

Beverly was seated on his left. Her face was carefully composed, her posture somehow managing to telegraph her full support, yet a furrow of tension had formed between her eyebrows, and her lips were taut, showing strain at the corners. Worf had taken a position at Picard's right. The Klingon was a solid, powerful presence, showing no sign of the discomfort from the earlier events of the day. Nave sat next to him, her youthful features emanating pure seriousness, but her eyes were wider than usual, the only hint of the trepidation they were all feeling. Although she was technically not a member of the senior crew, she had proved valuable enough to merit inclusion; she deserved a voice, given the seriousness of what the captain intended to ask of her.

Two other bodies new to the room sat across from each other at the end of the table. Picard was familiar with the recently promoted security chief, Lionardo Battaglia. The man had been with the

Enterprise during their last encounter with the Borg, though, like Nave, this was his first time in the briefing room. Picard was not surprised that Battaglia had taken the seat beside Nave. The warmth passing between the two crew members was evident, particularly in contrast to the stoic presence opposite them. Placid as the still surface of an untroubled pond, T'Lana sat on the other side of the table, her spine so immaculately straight it failed to touch the back of her chair. Nave was not particularly tall, but it was clear even across the table that she dwarfed the Vulcan.

Geordi was leaning forward, seated between T'Lana and Beverly, his fingers tightly interlaced, his expression one of frank concern. Of all the members of the crew, he had probably heard the least about recent events, but judging from his demeanor, the scuttlebutt network had clearly given him a good idea of what was going on.

The thunderous voice of the Borg announcing the nascent queen had silenced all vestiges of Picard's self-doubt; he knew what had to be done. Yet he could not ask his officers to blindly risk their lives and careers without explanation. He owed them that much.

"You all have some idea why you have been summoned here," Picard began. "You know that I have heard, as it were, the voice of the Borg, planning to launch an attack in Alpha Quadrant. I am utterly convinced that this is a fact, yet I have no way to prove this to any of you. I can only ask you to accept my word." He paused. "That is not all that I have sensed. Recently, I learned that the Borg are creating a new queen."

Beverly and Worf were already aware of the fact, of course, but Geordi let go a soft gasp, while Nave stiffened in her chair and exchanged a glance with Battaglia. T'Lana alone remained unruffled.

"This is a most distressing discovery," Picard continued, "as the queen can issue directives. I believe she is not yet conscious, but when she becomes so, she will oversee the attack. And everything that I have sensed indicates that they will be out for blood."

Geordi's crystalline brown eyes were wide, stunned. "You killed the queen, Captain. And Admiral Janeway killed one in the Delta Quadrant. Are you saying they just . . . rebuild her that easily? Construct a new body and somehow animate it?"

Picard directed a glance and the slightest of nods at the doctor.

"The structure of Borg society closely parallels that of Earth's insect world," Beverly explained. "If the queen in a bee colony were destroyed, for example, a male drone would be taken and fed a special substance that would transform it into a female queen. We're postulating that the same thing has been done here—that right now, one of the Borg drones is being transformed."

"What you do not know," the captain said, "is that I contacted Admiral Janeway at Starfleet Command when I first sensed that the Borg were regrouping for an attack. She gave me direct orders not to take any initiative but to wait until Seven of Nine, a rehabilitated Borg, could be sent to the *Enterprise*. I have since received a message indicating the time of Seven of Nine's arrival: four days."

"And how much time, sir, before you think the queen will be ready and launch the attack?" Nave asked.

Picard turned to her, his gaze piercing and grim. "Less than thirty-six hours. Again, I can offer no proof. I can only say that I *know* this to be so." He drew a breath, then looked at each officer in turn. "It is my intention, as captain of this vessel, to disobey Admiral Janeway's order and put the *Enterprise* on course to intercept the ship the Borg are constructing. It is imperative to destroy the queen before she is completely transformed and capable of launching an attack—because once that happens, the Borg will stop at nothing until all of humanity is extinct. However . . ." His tone, which had grown impassioned, now softened. "I cannot ask any of you to assist me in this. To do so puts you at very great risk of court-martial. Each of you has the right to register a protest and to refuse any involvement."

He had already made his plans for just such a contingency. Beverly had offered to help him navigate to within scanning range of the Borg vessel. Once he had gotten that far, he would take a shuttle and find a way to get to the queen, while those aboard the *Enterprise* retreated back to safety. It was a suicide mission, but he could think of no worthier way to die.

A tension-filled pause followed.

Worf was the first to speak. "You have no choice, Captain. You *must* disobey the admiral's orders. We have seen how swiftly the Borg can attack and assimilate an entire starship. They must be stopped before the queen can give them a new directive." He hesitated, then after a brief glance at Beverly that mystified Picard, added, "You have my complete support."

"And mine," Geordi said. "There's no way we can risk giving them another chance."

"The captain already knows I'm with him," Beverly said softly.

Nave glanced at the others; the uncertainty that had taken hold of her features melted away as she studied those of her fellows. "I've never fought the Borg before, but I'll follow any order you have to give, Captain."

Battaglia shared another glance with Nave. "Well, I have fought them," he said, "and I'm ready to take them on again."

Picard directed a warm glance at them all. It was impossible to put into words what such loyalty meant to him, and so he did not try. He was used to that level of loyalty from his former senior staff. But with old friends now gone, it was nice to know that the ones stepping up to fill their places had as much faith in him. Thus far.

T'Lana spoke at last, her features impassive and

unreadable. "You have asked for my advice as counselor, Captain," she said evenly. "It has not changed, nor has my position. For the benefit of the others, I will repeat it here: there is as yet no definitive proof that a threat from the Borg exists. You are asking these officers to prove their loyalty to you by risking court-martial—based on nothing more than a hunch. Even if you are correct about the existence of a Borg ship, you are still obligated to obey Admiral Janeway's orders."

"I shall note your objection in my log, Counselor," Picard said. He had expected no less of her. She was ruled by logic and had not developed the same level of trust his other officers had. "Thank you all for coming." He rose, giving the others leave to do the same. "Mister Battaglia, I wish you to remain a moment," he added as the rest of the crew filed out. Beverly gave him a questioning glance back as she crossed the threshold. He knew that she would not approve of what he was about to do, but he saw no other option.

Still standing, Lio moved up the table to take a seat beside Picard. He already suspected what the captain had in mind and was going through his mental roster of the security staff, ready to pull out the most logical choices for an away mission. He knew the *Enterprise* alone was no match for a Borg cube. Their attack would need to be smaller and more focused.

"I would like you to gather your most experienced security officers," Picard said, confirming Lio's suspicions. He simply nodded in response, having already chosen his team. The captain didn't need their names at the moment. "I will accept only volunteers for this mission," Picard added.

"I don't think any member of my team would shy away from this mission," Lio replied. "I know I won't."

Picard allowed himself a grim smile before he locked his steely eyes onto Lio. "Actually, I want you to remain on the *Enterprise* in case this first mission fails. I will lead this away team."

Lio did his best to cover his shock. He knew Picard was a fighter and should have anticipated the captain would assume this course of action. "But—"

Picard held up a hand to stop him. "I've been through this many times with any number of my officers in the past. I know all the arguments about away missions being a danger to the captain. I'm sorry, but this is too important to me to trust to anyone else."

Lio tried not to take offense. He knew the captain well enough that his comment wasn't meant to doubt Lio's abilities; it was a show of how seriously he took the Borg threat. At the same time, Lio knew that he needed to be heard, no matter what the captain believed. "I'm sorry, sir. I do understand what you're saying, but my concern isn't about your safety on this mission, it's for the success of the mission with you on it."

Picard's eyes narrowed slightly. "Go on."

"I mean no disrespect, sir," Lio said. "You say that you're hearing the voice of the Borg, but I have to wonder if they are hearing your voice as well."

"If they were aware of me, I would know it," Picard said calmly.

"Okay," Lio relented. The captain certainly knew more about this than he did. "But still, there's no guarantee that once you're on that Borg ship they won't be able to tap into your mind in some way. It's just too big a risk. As much as you may know about the Collective, they know just as much about you."

Picard gave a slow nod. "What is it you have in mind?"

In the *Enterprise* rec room, dressed in a unitard, Nave was warming up early with the *bat'leth*. She'd gone the instant she was off duty. Sitting around worrying about what would happen once they encountered the Borg vessel simply wasn't her style; physically working out was her preferred method of dealing with anxiety.

It wasn't that she was afraid, she told herself. It was more the fact that the Borg were an unknown, and she disliked uncertainty. She'd heard all the horror stories about them, but rumors were one thing; facts were another.

She felt tough enough to handle almost anything. She'd been born and raised on a starship; her mother and father had both been full lieutenants aboard the *U.S.S. Lowe,* so she was used to the requirements of duty, used to the fact that officers were often called upon to risk their lives.

Her parents had done so several times. Sara had grown up learning how to deal with the fear of them not returning each time the saucer had separated from the bridge of the ship to protect the children from battle. Distraction through physical exercise, games with friends . . .

They had been so proud of her when, at age sixteen, she was accepted early into the academy. Her mother had wept and touched her cheek the day Sara had left, and her father had hugged her so hard and so long, she'd thought he would never let go. She'd looked into their eyes one last time before boarding the shuttle and seen there a glimmer of fear. They were afraid—afraid because their only child would soon be facing the same risks they had grown to accept as part of serving in Starfleet.

It was at the very end of her first year as a cadet, when she was utterly distracted, studying for finals, that she'd been called to the commandant's office. She had absolutely no idea why—until she saw the haunted look in the silver-haired man's eyes, saw the meticulously composed expression that failed to entirely mask his utter dismay.

My mother, Nave had thought immediately. *Or is it my father?*

She had not been prepared for it to be both of them. She remembered only snatches of what the commandant had said. *Caught in an interplanetary war. The* Lowe *crippled. Bridge destroyed.*

It was very clean, very cold, very surgical. One moment, her parents existed in her consciousness; the next moment, they had been excised. And there was nothing left of them, not a single memento of the dead, not even someone to grieve with. All their belongings, all their friends, had been aboard the incinerated *Lowe.*

Nave had never bothered to find out the names of the warring factions. Even now, she did not know the details; she had not looked up the records. It was enough that her parents were lost: what point was there in learning anything more? It would only bring back the pain.

And so she had distracted herself from her grief by studying fanatically for her finals. She did not attend the memorial services; instead, she took her tests and aced them. That, she knew, would have pleased her mother and father best.

Now, distracting herself from the coming encounter with the Borg, she moved gracefully through the different moves Worf had taught her with the *bat'leth*—reversals, figure eights, spinning and thrusting—until she had worked up quite a sweat. She'd been honored that he'd been willing to teach her—even though she was still pretty lousy with the weapon and played with a formidable handicap.

When Worf's dark form at last appeared at the entrance, she broke into a smile, which quickly became a scowl.

"Worf! Why are you still in uniform?"

The Klingon's demeanor was awkward. "I came to tell you that we must forgo our lesson this evening. I am . . . preoccupied."

"But the best way not to think about the Borg is to work out," she protested good-naturedly. "Besides, honing your skills with the *bat'leth* will help you do more of them in."

He failed to respond to her humor; his expression remained stern, grim. "It has nothing to do with the Borg," he said.

"Really? There's something worse than a Borg with a vendetta?" she joked. "Well, you certainly can't go through something like that on your own. Come on, tell me what's up."

Worf's mood darkened visibly. "I do not wish to discuss it," he said, in the lowest possible tone, the one approaching a growl, the one that indicated anger and hurt.

"I'm sorry," Nave said. It wasn't the first time her lighthearted mood had been met with a chilly response. Yet there was something worse than coldness from the Klingon. "I didn't mean anything by it . . ."

But he had already disappeared from the doorway.

Nave finished her workout alone, then went, per custom, to relax at the Happy Bottom Riding Club, where she knew Lieutenant Lio Battaglia would be waiting for her. Commander Riker had christened the crew lounge shortly after the *Enterprise*-E had been commissioned. The name, she had since learned, harkened back to the early days of Earth's space exploration, when astronauts went to a similarly monikered watering hole. Nave liked the name, particularly because it seemed so out of place in the stately and modern starship.

Much like the ship's former first officer, Lio Battaglia also had a quirky sense of humor and entertaining eccentricities. His Italian mother had christened him Lionardo, using the original spelling of da Vinci's name. He occasionally referred to the "artistic temperament" and "erratic moods" he'd inherited with the name—a comment that always made Sara laugh, since Lio was utterly good-natured and easygoing. He uttered such nonsense with a half-facetious air, as if realizing the silliness of such a claim; even so, he would continue, stating that his scattered mannerisms came from an artist's way of focusing on so many things at once.

But he had spoken so passionately of Italian art and literature that she had agreed to learn more about his birth country's history with him. They had started out their exploration of the Italian culture by reading Dante's *Divine Comedy*. Nave had found the work particularly interesting, having never before understood or bothered to examine any religious beliefs. The fact that Lio insisted they highlight their studies with the original texts was an interesting challenge that she believed he had instituted largely so they could spend more time together, but that was just a feeling and she had yet to come up with concrete proof.

Now, in the Club, she walked toward their customary table and saw him waiting for her. His face lit up with recognition; she smiled in return. He was dark haired, olive complected, with eyes such a clear green they reminded Sara of the warm, pristine waters of the Mediterranean. He'd been sitting next to her at the bar one night, shortly after she'd been assigned to the *Enterprise,* when she was still head of security. They'd been formally introduced while on duty; at the bar, each of them had recognized a kindred spirit. Now they were at the point where their friendship was metamorphosing into something more. Nave allowed it because she was no longer Lio's direct superior—in fact, he'd received a promotion and had taken over her position as security chief. There were no longer any concerns about a personal relationship getting in the way of their professional one.

She stared down at the short glass in front of her, which held a few ice cubes, clear liquid, and a wedge of lime. "What is it tonight?" she asked. The first time he'd asked her what she wanted to drink, she'd said, "Surprise me." And so he did, every night.

"Gin and tonic," he said. "Ever had one?"

She shook her head, brought the glass of synthehol to her face, and sniffed. Her temptation was to wrinkle her nose, but she kept her expression non-committal. The ritual was a contest of sorts; no matter what Lio ordered, she drank stoically.

"What's that smell?" she asked carefully.

"Juniper berries."

"Like the tree?"

"Exactly. Now squeeze the lime and put it in the glass," Lio prompted.

She did so, took a gulp, and managed, through pure will, not to grimace. Clearly, gin was not one of her favorites. Her preference, when it came to synthehol, was a nice, soft merlot, nothing strong. But she was determined to handle anything Lio ordered for her.

"Interesting," she said.

"You hate it." Lio grinned, a perfect lunar crescent appearing beneath his long, prominent nose.

"I didn't say that." She held the glass to the light, sniffed it again, and took another swig. "Gin and tonic it is tonight. Only the next time, more lime."

"So," Lio said. "Petrarch. What did you think?"

Nave allowed herself a smile. "Talk about your artistic temperament," she said. "Though I'd like to meet this Laura woman he wrote about."

Lio took a sip of his usual glass of amaretto, then set it down emphatically. "Petrarch probably would have as well. Many people believe he had little or no real contact with the woman, because she was married, possibly to an ancestor of the Marquis de Sade."

"As good a reason as any to stay away from a woman," Nave said. Though she was enjoying the thinly veiled flirtation on romantic characters from the fourteenth century, her mind was focused on darker themes. Instead of continuing down the path of the mysterious Laura, she began, very tentatively, "You were here, on the *Enterprise,* when the crew encountered the Borg and their queen."

She didn't want to dwell in a negative way on whatever the encounter with the Borg might bring, and she had no intention of allowing herself to become afraid, although even reading through the dry texts of the *Enterprise*'s, and especially Captain Picard's, battles with the Borg had been harrowing enough. But Lio had survived that, Lio had seen and fought the Borg, and Sara felt it would be useful to learn from someone who had personal knowledge of the enemy.

Lio quickly pulled his head back, as if he'd been slapped; pain flashed in his eyes, so brightly Nave was sorry she'd asked the question. For the second time that evening, she had overstepped her bounds without meaning to.

But Lio composed himself with admirable speed, although he cast his gaze downward at his glass. In his expression Nave saw at last some of the dark, brooding temperament he had always claimed.

"I fought against the Borg." He steepled his hands around his glass, framing it in a triangle composed of his fingers. "I was an ensign. I had no clue what I was doing then. But now, I'll be leading any away team that boards their ship. I spoke to the captain after the briefing." He glanced up at her, all the humor gone from his tone. "What do you want to know?"

That gave her pause; she had assumed any combat involved would be ship-to-ship. She hadn't considered that Lio himself might be put directly in jeopardy. Even so, it was too late to back out of the conversation gracefully. "I want to know what they're like, in case . . . in case things escalate."

"If things escalate," Lio countered, "then I'll have failed at my job."

"You won't fail," Nave said firmly. "I just wanted . . . any tips you have, as someone who's been there before."

"Tips," Lio said, and his lips twisted with infinite irony. "Stay the hell away from them. That's the best tip I can give you."

"Lio . . ." She was gentle in her exasperation.

He threw back his glass of amaretto and emptied it in a single swallow, then slammed it down on the table. "What are the Borg like?" he asked rhetorically, gazing out one of the ports. "They're soulless. Mindless. Bent on taking from you everything that makes you a unique individual. If you're lucky, they'll simply kill you. If you're not, they'll assimilate you."

"How did you fight them?" Nave asked softly.

"We used phaser rifles, which killed a few, slowed down the rest—then they adapted. We had to keep changing the frequency . . . and each time, they adapted and took more of our people. You've seen the pictures, how their bodies, their limbs are fitted with prosthetic weapons. Razor-sharp hooks, vibrating saws, rotating blades . . ." He looked down at the empty glass, his expression bleak. "I had a friend. Another ensign, a buddy of mine in engineering. We were assigned to the *Enterprise* the same year. Joel Azaria from Delios VII, a great guy. He was . . ." Lio paused, ran a hand over his face.

"It's all right," Nave said. "You don't have to talk about it."

Lio recovered and continued. "We were with Commander Worf in one of the corridors, and the Borg just swarmed us. We kept firing the rifles; they kept adapting. I was standing next to Joel—he was on the outside flank. One of the Borg had a retracted blade built into his wrist. Joel was firing at him one second, the next he was down. The Borg advanced one step, and before any of us realized it, the blade had gone straight through Joel's midsection." He lowered his head and shook it slowly. "I wanted to take him with us, even though he was already gone . . . but we couldn't. They had us cornered. The only thing we could do was retreat. We had to leave Joel lying where he was . . ."

"I'm so sorry," Nave whispered.

"I wish that had been the end of it," Lio said. "Because we had to fight them again later, in another corridor. And Joel . . . Joel was there. But it wasn't really Joel. They'd taken him, changed him, defiled his body with these . . . these weapons and cybernetic attachments to his head, his eyes, his arms. He was no longer human." He drew in a long breath. "And the worst part was . . . I fired my rifle at him, again and again, but I couldn't take him down. I couldn't destroy the monster they'd made of him. I know he went on to kill his own crewmates . . . He would have wanted me to stop him from doing that."

Nave leaned forward and rested a hand on his forearm. He looked up at her, a hint of gratitude showing in his grim expression.

"That's what it's like to fight the Borg," he said tonelessly. "They're relentless. The only way we could stop them from taking our souls was to take theirs—to kill their queen. Captain Picard did it once; we'll do it again." He sighed. The darkness eased, and he gave her one of his wry Lio grins. "Look, I don't mean to scare you, Sara. *I'm* going to be fine this time. My team will be fine, because now we have the advantage. This time we'll get there before they have a new queen. Without her, the captain believes they're incapable of moving against us. We'll go in, get out . . . it'll all be over and we'll be on our way to Repok again."

Nave took two large swallows of the gin and tonic, and waited for the synthehol to produce the familiar tingling in her feet. "Promise me," she said. "Promise me that's exactly how it's going to happen."

"I promise." Lio took her hand and clasped it

firmly in his own. "Look, I was a jerk even to mention all that other stuff. That's all over now. I just . . . this stuff brings up a lot of unpleasant memories. But nothing like that is ever going to happen again." His tone turned mildly sarcastic. "Just my Italian sense of drama acting up."

"I'm sorry for what you went through, Lio."

For a long moment, they simply looked at each other. His eyes were so green, so clear, she thought again about the Mediterranean, about being pulled beneath the water by strong currents.

"Do you want another drink?" Lio asked suddenly. It was a simple question on the face of it, but Sara knew he was asking something more. She felt herself sliding, pleasantly, over the edge of a precipice. Things were different tonight: in the morning, he would be leaving to go to the Borg vessel.

She shook her head and rose. Without a word, he rose as well, and they walked arm in arm from the room.

In his quarters, Worf sat cross-legged on his bed, with the orange tabby, Spot, curled contentedly on his lap.

He still could not think of the cat as his own. Spot would always be Data's pet, a living reminder of the friend who had sacrificed himself to save the *Enterprise* crew. Yet Worf and the animal had come to understand each other, even though the concept of a pet—at least, the way humans interpreted it—was foreign to the Klingon. To his surprise, Spot had required more than just food and shelter; in fact, Spot had *demanded* more. It had taken Worf a good week to understand why Spot persisted in rubbing herself against his ankles, his hands, and called out plaintively in her strange little voice.

He had consulted Geordi about the phenomenon. The engineer had laughingly explained it to him. "She wants to be petted, Worf. That's all."

"Petted?"

"You know, stroked, with your hands. She just wants a little affection. She'll let you know where."

"Affection?" Worf was aghast. This was something to be shared with a lover, a child; he could not imagine showing it to an animal.

But Spot was insistent. Worf was clumsy at first and received small scratches and bites as a result, but he remembered how Jadzia had taught him to be gentle. He applied the same principle to Spot, who showed her approval by purring loudly.

Now she sat with her eyes closed, her expression one of pure bliss as she purred, featherweight and warm, on his lap. He stroked her with a practiced hand, but he did not look down at her. His gaze was on the holograph of Jadzia beside his bed. It was his favorite image of her, captured shortly after she had challenged him with the *bat'leth*—and won. There was victory and a hint of fierceness in her smile; her eyes were shining, exhilarated, her face flushed.

She looked like a warrior.

"I cannot be what the captain wants me to be," Worf told her softly. "I am not worthy to command a starship. You remember what Captain Sisko told me, after Lasaran was killed."

She would have remembered, of course. He had gone to her afterward, bitter, full of regret, and confessed everything that Sisko had said. Their bond was far too strong for him to have hidden such a thing from her.

She had agreed that Sisko had been right—in a way. But she had also asked, *Knowing what you know now—that Lasaran would be killed, that many people would die—would you have acted the same? Would you have come back for me?*

No, Worf had answered firmly, then paused. *I don't think so.* He sighed. *I don't know . . .*

None of us knows for certain how our actions will affect others. She had looked on him with infinite kindness; she knew how deep and bitter his guilt was. *We can only do what we judge to be right at the time. You acted from your heart. You couldn't have done anything else and remained true to yourself.*

"I had to be Klingon," Worf said aloud, then fell silent again, remembering what Doctor Crusher had told him. And he knew that, so long as he had been bound to Jadzia, he would have acted in the same manner. He would have gone back to her. "And I am still Klingon, so I cannot be trusted with a command."

J. M. DILLARD

That's ridiculous, Jadzia retorted in his imagination. *Are you saying, then, that no Klingon is ever fit for command?*

Worf considered the question, then heard himself echo what he had told his wife long ago: "No. I don't think so . . . I don't know . . ." Had he never bonded with a woman, the choice between love and duty would never have arisen. Perhaps now that he was again alone . . .

He thought of the startlingly attractive Vulcan counselor and flushed, unable suddenly to look into his wife's holographic eyes.

In the end, the answer again escaped him, as haunting and elusive as Jadzia's ghost.

In her quarters, T'Lana sat cross-legged on the cool deck, meditating.

Memories often surfaced during such times. She had learned not to suppress them, merely to observe, then let them go, without reaction or analysis.

The ones that emerged now in her consciousness were no doubt triggered by the meeting today with Picard. They came in singular, vivid images:

Aboard the Federation *Starship Indefatigable,* the face of Captain Karina Wozniak—intensely determined, framed by short silver curls. T'Lana had greatly admired and respected her. Wozniak had been deliberate, cautious, receptive to her counselor's advice.

But the first time they had met, Wozniak had been anything but receptive; she had, in fact, been challenging.

Less than an hour after T'Lana's arrival on the *Indefatigable*, she had been summoned to the captain's ready room, where Wozniak sat, waiting. Her skin was dark bronze, contrasting sharply with her ice-colored eyes, her pale hair.

The captain was keenly blunt. It was a trait T'Lana admired, one that most humans failed to appreciate. Wozniak's tone was good-natured but forceful. "I had requested a Betazoid counselor. I got you instead. Your people are not renowned for their interpersonal skills, yet Command sends me a *Vulcan* counselor."

"True. However a Vulcan counselor gives you a distinct advantage," T'Lana had replied.

Her answer had the intended effect: Wozniak did a slight double take, then lifted a brow and opened her mouth to pose a question.

T'Lana did not give her time to ask it. "I am a talented touch-telepath, of course," she said. "My ability is so strong that I can sometimes sense the presence of minds even without direct physical contact—though I cannot decipher any thoughts. But it is not to that skill I refer. I know that in most cases, your 'enemy' will be standing on the bridge of another vessel, separated from you by space. They will see what you see: a Vulcan, giving you the 'upper hand.'

"I have years of diplomatic experience. I have

worked with beings from many cultures . . . and as a result, I have developed a skill that most Vulcans despise but that you humans seem to prize."

"Which is?" Wozniak interjected, her gaze intense but also amused, curious.

"Intuition."

Wozniak broke into a broad grin. "Finally . . . a truly honest Vulcan. I like you, T'Lana. I think we'll do well together."

Back on the *Enterprise,* the image in T'Lana's mind shifted: The *Indefatigable*'s bridge viewscreen, filled with Jem'Hadar warships—three tiered, evoking bugs with head, body, wings.

Wozniak had asked her: *What does your intuition tell you about the Jem'Hadar?*

That in their case diplomacy fails, T'Lana had answered. *That they are single-minded creatures whose sole focus is killing. That they cannot be reasoned with.*

Yet she would have made an effort, if there had only been time.

Next, she saw a series of images, starting with the face of a Jem'Hadar commander reptilian with skin that seemed carved from stone, his temples and jaw covered by rows of osseous projections. His voice, harsh and gloating: *You are surrounded by a dozen of our warships. Prepare to be destroyed.*

The screen had gone black. A bolt of light bright as Vulcan's sun blinded T'Lana for seconds, even with her inner eyelids squeezed shut.

Acrid smoke, the stench of burned circuitry and flesh. The thick haze blanketed the bridge, forcing T'Lana to grope for the captain's chair, only to find it empty.

On the deck, partially obscured by smoke and the afterimage from the blast, Wozniak, wide-eyed and unseeing, slack jawed, half her face incinerated, revealing ivory bone beneath papery remnants of blackened skin.

Instinctively, T'Lana had moved to lift her, but logic halted the action, with the painful realization that Wozniak, if she were not already dead, would not survive long enough to flee the ship. Others might, and her duty lay with the living. That reasoning propelled T'Lana swiftly past the corpses of her crewmates, past the smoldering consoles and nonfunctional lift, down the nearest auxiliary shaft.

She crawled, gasping for air, down to the next level, then the next, and the next, then ran coughing down the corridors toward the shuttlebay. Along the way, she encountered three crew members still living. She carried and dragged them with her into one of only two shuttles still operational.

The final image: from space, the sight of the *Indefatigable,* scorched and lifeless, as the massive warships moved off.

T'Lana took a deep, controlled breath, then slowly let it go.

Such was the price of a decision rooted in emotion, such was the cost of heeding intuition.

T'Lana opened her eyes and rose slowly. As always, the image of Wozniak's charred face remained and rose with her.

After hours, Beverly sat in the captain's quarters—in *their* quarters—barely touching the glass of synthehol cabernet in her hand. She longed for a glass of *real* wine, fine wine from Picard's private stock, but tonight was not the night for indulgence. The lights had been dimmed, in honor of *Enterprise*'s night; a single lamp burned nearby on Jean-Luc's desk, casting sharp shadows.

They were five hours out from their dreaded destination. Sleep was out of the question, and she would need all her energy and wits to face what was coming. This was the hardest part of any mission where lives were at stake—the wait before the storm. It was hard, too, not to stare obsessively at Jean-Luc, to worry when he might next become overwhelmed and collapse.

Seated beside her, Jean-Luc no doubt sensed her worry. It had become their custom, at day's end, to sit in his quarters, talking and looking out at the stars. Tonight, they were both doing their best to be casual and talk about anything but what was on their minds: the Borg.

"So," Beverly said, "what do you make of your new counselor?" She knew that Jean-Luc would understand her question. He, too, had noticed the Vulcan's odd reaction to Worf.

Jean-Luc had chosen to forgo even the synthehol. Without a glass in his hands, he seemed not to know what to do with them tonight. He let go a small sigh. "I'm not at all sure what to make of T'Lana. At first, she had seemed almost genial. And it wasn't like she had outright snubbed Worf on the bridge, but her reaction was definitely . . ."

"Cold." Beverly shook her head and set down the unfinished wine. "She seemed so relaxed, so gracious with everyone else—"

"A perfect diplomat," Picard interjected.

"Exactly." She paused, then stated carefully, "She hasn't exactly been supportive of you or your decision."

He quirked his lip at that. "Far from it. She's told me straight out—once she was convinced that you had examined me and that I wasn't floridly psychotic—that she believes my conviction about the Borg is nothing more than an emotional delusion."

Beverly frowned. "Frankly, that's hardly helpful advice from a ship's counselor. Do you think she's going to fit in with the crew?"

"Give her time," Jean-Luc said. He began to speak again, then fell silent. She saw the shift in his expression, as if he were listening to something far away. Though his face was half obscured by shadow, she caught his eye, and he managed a faint and unhappy sheepish smile.

Determined to show no alarm, she kept her tone even, neutral. At the same time, she needed to reach out to him. She placed a reassuring hand on his arm. "You're hearing them now, aren't you?"

Jean-Luc shrugged. "Nothing new. Just more faint chatter. Boring stuff, actually. And certainly not as bad as it could be. The majority of them are sleeping, waiting for a directive to wake. A skeleton crew is tending the queen and readying the ship."

And when they finally wake . . . Beverly did not permit herself to finish the thought.

He sighed. "I just don't like them . . . being in my head again."

"I understand," she answered softly. She had been worried not just about the physical threat from the Borg, but about the psychic damage to Jean-Luc as well. "It's a violation . . . *another* violation . . ."

Before she could think of something comforting, therapeutic, to say, Picard spoke first, his tone and expression consummately resolute. He pointed to his brow. "But I'm glad they're here. Glad to be able to sense them. The alternative . . ."

He left the alternative unspoken, but Beverly shuddered mentally. The memories she had of the Borg still entered her dreams from time to time: the Borg breaking down the walls of sickbay, forcing her to flee, panicked, with her patients and the utterly terrified Lily; witnessing the carnage left in their wake, seeing crew members she knew assimilated or killed.

Worst of all was the memory of the day she had stood on the Borg cube. She had been the first to see Jean-Luc as Locutus. She had worked for years to rid herself of the image, of all the other memories, but now they were all resurfacing.

He laughed abruptly, bitterly. "You know, I keep hoping I'm mad, that this is all some sort of psychotic delusion. It'd be easier to deal with."

"I know," she answered gently. "But all your scans checked out, Jean-Luc. I'm afraid you're sane . . . unless this is some new, rare disease, or some strange form of metaspace we've entered . . . in which case, we'd all be affected."

"I keep wishing it was something else, anything other than what it appears to be," he confessed. "I'd hoped never to have to do this again. It's like cutting the head off the Hydra; another two take its place." He rubbed his face, and she caught the glimmer of frustration in his eyes. "It seems like it will never end."

"But this time is different."

He looked up at her, his faint surprise mixed with even fainter hope. "How so?"

"This time," Beverly said firmly, "we're stopping the Borg before they can start. This time, thanks to your connection to them, no one will have to die. No one—except the Borg."

His expression grew grim. "I pray you're right, Beverly. Too many have died under my watch, far too many. Now I've not only put my crew's lives at risk, I'm asking them to risk court-martial as well."

She faced him, her gaze and words pointed. "Do you have any choice, Jean-Luc?"

He looked away at the stars and in a low voice uttered, "I don't."

"And *we* don't," she insisted. "We know you, Jean . . . Captain. We trust you. You wouldn't do this unless it was absolutely necessary. Can you think of a single one of your officers who wouldn't make the very same decision you have?"

His lip quirked wryly again. "Counselor T'Lana."

"She doesn't know you. Yet. But she'll come around."

"When she sees the Borg ship," Jean-Luc said heavily.

The words made them both lapse into silence. Beverly settled back into the couch beside him and waited for the encounter that would come before the *Enterprise*'s dawn.

5

———

PICARD SAT THROUGH THE NIGHT, OCCASIONALLY rising to stare out at the stars streaking by. He felt no fear for himself, only for what his crew might have to endure, only for what he had asked of Beverly, now curled, dozing, beside him.

Instead, he felt anger: anger that he was again called upon to fight a nemesis he had thought conquered, an even greater anger that he again had to subject his crew to a horror no one should be called upon to face. Worse, he felt a mounting fury—one he believed he had overcome but that had apparently lain long buried. It was the rage of a man embittered by an intolerable violation, and with it came infinite grief. He had never forgotten that the Borg had used his knowledge to kill: the crews of forty starships, half as many Klingon warships, assembled near the star called Wolf 359 . . . all dead, because of the contribution Locutus had brought to the Collective. He had known many of the perished; at night, he saw their faces more distinctly, saw their graveyard: ships blackened and battered, helplessly afloat, their hulls rent, leaving twisted bridges open to space . . .

He'd had enough counseling—enough time spent with Deanna—to know that it was not his fault, that the Borg had committed these crimes. Rationally, he understood that well. But thoughts and emotions were two different things.

What had Beverly said?

A wound as deep as yours won't ever heal completely . . .

He had thought her wrong; he had believed that Lily's admonition had helped him form a scar too thick ever to be pierced. Now the wound was exposed again, raw: T'Lana was correct in that regard. But he had made a silent promise to himself, to the long-dead Lily, to his crew. He would never again let his fury against the Borg color his command decisions.

The Borg chatter had become progressively louder throughout the night, though the few phrases that were comprehensible gave him no further insight. Yet he could sense himself, his ship, moving steadily closer to them.

He was not surprised when, at last, his communicator chirped. He pressed it at once. "Picard here."

Beverly stirred, then sat forward, instantly alert.

The voice was Geordi's. His tone managed to

convey an incongruent mix of excitation and grimness. *"Per your orders, Captain, we're not in visual range yet. But our long-range scanners have found the moon we're looking for."* He hesitated. *"And, sir . . . you're right. There's a structure resembling a Borg cube in orbit. And it's massive."*

"Of course," Picard murmured. It was, after all, a queen vessel.

"It doesn't seem to have detected us yet."

"They have no reason to use their long-range scanners. I doubt they're expecting visitors." The captain paused, doubting himself for the first time. He couldn't be sure of that fact, or anything he suspected about the ship. Everything that he had heard so far led him to believe that the Borg cube was not yet fully functional, that all the systems would come online at once when the queen was awakened. But there was no way to be sure of that information. He had put a great deal of faith in his intuition already, but what came next was a tremendous leap. It was the one part of his plan that required his crew to support him without question, even though he already questioned himself.

On the bridge, Picard sat surrounded by his crew: Worf, Geordi, T'Lana, Nave. He could not help but think of Shakespeare's *Henvy V* in the moment: *We few, we happy few, we band of brothers . . .* Never before had he felt so alone against an enemy.

The Vulcan counselor had expressed polite interest in the fact that the *Enterprise* scanners had detected *something,* but she was still unwilling to yield the fact that it was a Borg vessel. He had avoided another confrontation with her over their difference of opinion on the definition of proof, but just barely. Picard could not help noticing that she had scrupulously avoided eye contact or conversation with Worf during the encounter. It was only logical that any counselor would approach the first officer for further discussion once she had exhausted all options with the captain. Not that she would want to undermine Picard, but her level of objection would naturally lend itself to further discussion. For the moment, Picard was thankful for what he perceived as a self-imposed distancing between T'Lana and Worf. Regretfully, that distance was beginning to extend to the other members of the bridge crew as it became clear that T'Lana was singular in her objections.

Beverly alone was absent from the bridge; she'd gone to sickbay. During her half-dozing state the previous night, she'd become inspired to reexamine the many years' worth of biomedical data collected on the Borg. She would not state what she was hunting for, only that she had a "hunch." Picard had learned to value those hunches a great deal over the many years he had known her.

The Borg cube was too distant for them to get an image of it on the viewscreen, but Picard knew it was there.

Picard turned to his navigator. "Lieutenant Nave, on my command, I want you to take us to the Borg ship at warp one. Plot a direct route. No diverting course."

"Aye, Captain."

"Mister Worf, I want you in control of the weapons system," Picard said. "Take it off-line but ready to bring it back up on a moment's notice."

"Sir, you wish to engage the Borg with our defenses down?" Worf asked skeptically.

"If the Borg do not determine us to be a threat, we may not have to engage them at all," Picard reasoned. "Minimal power to the shields, however, and be prepared."

"Sir . . ."

"The cube's systems are not fully online yet," Picard reasoned. "We should be safe." Picard knew that he was taking a huge risk, but it was the only option. There was no reasonable way a ship like the *Enterprise* could sneak up on the Borg cube. His only hope was that the Borg would assume they were on an exploratory mission. Surely they would know it was ludicrous for the *Enterprise* to take on a Borg cube on its own.

Picard looked over to T'Lana, who met his gaze. He had expected her to protest, but she merely looked resigned to the knowledge that her concerns would fall on deaf ears. When she remained silent, he turned his attention to the conn. "Lieutenant Nave, take us in."

Nave complied.

Before twenty minutes had elapsed, the neighboring star, a superhot blue giant, appeared on the viewscreen.

"Slow to impulse," Picard ordered.

The solar system came into view. A ring of rocky, atmosphereless planetoids appeared on the screen, followed by a pair of multiringed gas giants.

They were headed farther in, toward the terrestrial planets. At the first of them, Picard lifted his hand; Nave caught the silent signal and slowed the ship further.

In the planet's orbit hung a solitary moon, reflecting the brilliant blue-white light of the sun.

This stunning backdrop was half eclipsed at its center by something dark and ungainly, something that pricked the hairs on the back of Picard's neck.

The Borg cube was a hideous thing: an exposed latticework of thousands of metal conduits haphazardly bracketed by panels and laced with black tubing. Infinite rows of conduits and panels were visible beneath, dotted with the glowing lights of internal machinery. To Picard it looked as if someone had taken the inner workings of a ship and turned them inside out. The vessel had been constructed with no regard for aesthetics, design, grace; even in moonlight, the random accretion of dull gray metal failed to gleam.

Picard had seen his share of Borg cubes, but this one dwarfed them all. It was monstrously vast: next to it, the *Enterprise* was a gnat, a tiny annoyance easily slapped down.

Of course, Picard realized. This vessel had to be the greatest of them all, for it housed not only the queen but also all the Borg's determination to finally conquer—no, *obliterate*—every humanoid race that had fought back, that had prevented the Borg from achieving their ultimate goal of total assimilation. This ship was designed to crush, forever, all resistance.

He glanced at his crew. Nave's eyes were unabashedly huge, and though T'Lana's expression remained impassive, she exhibited subtle gestures that, in a Vulcan, were tantamount to a startled gasp: a slight lean forward in her chair while fingering the edge of her console, as if she were fighting the urge to clutch it tightly. The captain felt no sense of satisfaction that she at last saw the empirical proof that he had been right.

As for La Forge and Worf, their faces reflected what Picard himself felt: grim determination and hatred at the sight of an old foe.

Geordi directed his attention away from the ship and back to his console. "Only minimal systems seem to be online. Short-range scanners. Partial weapons. Propulsion is still off-line." There was relief in his voice.

Picard stared at the screen. Even partial weapons were too much of a threat. "What about shields?"

"Nonoperational at this time, sir."

"Lieutenant Nave," Picard said, quiet in the presence of such an awesome and deadly sight, "take us to just within transporter range and no farther. I want to keep as much distance as possible from that vessel."

"Understood, sir." The task calmed Nave at once; her wide-eyed astonishment vanished, replaced by focused intensity.

"Mister La Forge." Picard swiveled toward him. "How long will it take you to locate the queen's chamber?"

Geordi frowned slightly at his readouts. "I'll need a few minutes, Captain. That's a lot of ship there . . . but she *is* the only female on board."

"There are no more than a few dozen drones awake at present."

"True, sir," Geordi agreed. "But *she's* sleeping . . . and so are a few hundred drones."

"Understood." He pressed his combadge. "Picard to the Armory."

"Battaglia here, sir."

"Lieutenant. Assemble your team and prepare to beam over to the Borg vessel. Commander La Forge will be transmitting a schematic of their ship's interior to you shortly; we'll try to get you directly into the queen's chamber." He paused. "Most of the drones are asleep—hibernating, if you will—and you should encounter no resistance from the others. As we discussed, Lieutenant, no more than four people. It shouldn't take more than that to accomplish your goal." *And no point in risking more . . .*

"Aye, Captain." The edge in Battaglia's tone was unmistakable. It was the sound of someone who had done battle with the Borg before and knew what to expect now.

As Picard closed the channel, Nave looked up at him expectantly.

"Yes, Lieutenant?" he asked.

"It's . . . it's nothing, sir," she said, flushing as she turned back to the conn.

Picard knew what question had gone unspoken. It would have been unthinkable for her to ask, even more so for Picard to grant the request. But the captain had been in this position before. He knew what the away team was facing. Furthermore, he knew that Nave was friends with them all, and possibly most of all with Lieutenant Battaglia. What Picard was about to do was not exactly within protocol, but then no part of this mission fell within Starfleet standards once he had ignored Admiral Janeway's orders.

"Counselor, please take the conn," Picard instructed. This was met with a questioning look from T'Lana and one of great relief from Nave.

"I promise to make this quick," she said as she stood.

"I will hold you to that, Lieutenant," he replied. "Five minutes and no more. I need you back at the conn by the time our people are transporting over to the Borg vessel."

She flushed even more deeply. "Thank you, sir." And in an instant, she was gone.

Nave was striding down the corridor just as Lio and his team were heading into the transporter room. He caught sight of her behind him.

They were a fearsome-looking group, with the largest, most powerful, and most sophisticated of the phaser rifles strapped over their shoulders and around their torsos. There were two men, new assignees, whom Nave had recently met—one of them twice her size. And there was Amrita Satchitanand, her former workout partner, a small woman with blue-black hair and full, rounded cheekbones beneath golden eyes. Amrita acknowledged her with a nod, but no one, including Lio, was smiling.

Lio gave her a quick glance and gestured for the rest of the away team to head inside the transporter room without him. He looked different from the man she met every night in the club; his easygoing manner was replaced by deadly seriousness. Even his features seemed sharp, stern: his lips were thin, compressed, his eyes full of a hardness behind which lurked grief. And his body—normally lanky and relaxed—seemed taut, strong.

Certainly he appeared different from the man who had lain in her arms only hours before. Then, his pose as the brooding intellectual had been entirely stripped away. He had looked younger, vulnerable; his manner had been sheepish, sweet, and endearingly awkward. His uncertainty had given

Sara confidence; she had taken the initiative, and he had responded resoundingly.

She looked at him now and remembered how his skin had smelled: warm and clean, and masculine. She hadn't wanted to leave his quarters—as if by staying she could somehow stretch time and keep the Borg and their ship at bay.

"Shouldn't you be at the conn?" Lio's tone was urgent but not unkind. He had a mission to accomplish, and Nave realized abruptly how foolish she had been to leave her post now, of all times—especially when she had no idea what she had come to say.

"Good luck," she said awkwardly, then stopped, disgusted. "No, that's not it." She squared her shoulders and stared at him dead-on. "I forgot to say it last night: I love you." Hardly the most romantic delivery: she had issued orders with more gentleness, more feeling.

It was like watching a Japanese paper lantern suddenly illuminated from the inside. Lio's face and eyes brightened, and he graced her with one of his brilliant crescent-moon smiles. "Then kiss me," he said.

She did, swiftly, because there wasn't time and because this was the most unprofessional thing she'd ever done—while on duty, at least. And then she turned her back to him and headed for the nearest lift.

"Sara."

She turned.

He was half standing in the entry, his expression once again urgent, serious. "If I don't make it back, just consider me dead. It's easier that way."

His words made her furious. "Don't say that. Don't even *think* it!"

"I'm sorry," he said. "But . . . in my quarters, on the desk. I left you something. Just in case."

"I don't understand," she called. "What? What did you leave?"

He shook his head to indicate he had to go. "You'll know. Just in case."

His words made her inexplicably furious. "There won't *be* any 'just in case,'" she insisted, but he had already disappeared behind the door.

Lio Battaglia materialized on the Borg cube and drew in a breath. Before his eyes could focus, his body tensed at the changed environment. The air was hot, suffocatingly humid, evoking memories of those terrible patrols down the *Enterprise* corridors, when the Borg had seized the starship and adapted it to their comfort.

He gazed out at a vertiginous view: he and his team stood on the uppermost deck—or, rather, a catwalk with metal conduits that served as railings. The interior of the ship—which looked very much to Lio like its exterior—was a vast, open maze of decking, panels, and exposed circuitry and pipes. Below was an infinite spiral of more decks, more conduits. Beneath them in the metallic jungle, row after row of alcoves held a hundred motionless drones, their bloodless white faces marred by black cybernetic implants, unblinking inhuman eyes, tubing that encircled their hairless skulls. The sight startled Lio as much as it disgusted him: how had so many of them managed to survive?

The sight also evoked the memory of his friend Joel. He had met Joel in the Happy Bottom Riding Club the first night the young ensign had arrived aboard the *Enterprise.* Joel had had a wicked sense of humor, and he had brought with him a bartender's guide which, Lio believed, listed every mixed drink (cocktails, Joel called them) ever created. Joel was working his way through the list, and he insisted that Lio join him.

The first night had featured gin and tonics. It was where Lio had first heard of juniper berries. It was the reason he had introduced Sara to the drink the day before.

Lio had lied to Sara: when Joel—or, rather, the *thing* he had become—had attacked, Lio had fired. The Joel-Borg had stayed on its feet, impervious, until Commander Worf shouted an order for his officers to change the frequency of their phasers. Lio had recalibrated and fired again, this time taking the Joel-Borg down with a blazing, killing blast to its midsection.

It had writhed a second, no more, on the *Enterprise* deck, then died. And any hope of retrieving whatever remained of Joel had died with it.

Lio had spoken of the incident to no one; all of

his fellow survivors had suffered similar traumas when the Borg invaded the *Enterprise.* Others had certainly been forced to destroy former crewmates. Lio had dealt with it by reminding himself that his hurt was not special.

Yet when he had tried to confess the truth to Sara, he had choked on the words; he had found it easier to lie. He could not bring himself to voice the fact that he had murdered his friend. Picard himself, filled with rage, had ordered them to shoot any assimilated crew members.

But Lio would deal some vengeance to the Borg today; he intended to take no small amount of pleasure in destroying the queen. And then he would return to the *Enterprise,* and Sara, where he would begin a new and better phase of his life. He had not thought, before he met Sara, that he would ever let himself become entangled in a permanent relationship. She, of all people, should understand the dangers of family life aboard a starship: her own parents had died serving aboard the *Lowe,* though she never spoke of it. He had learned about their deaths not from her but one of their crewmates.

For Sara, he was willing to live dangerously. But he was not willing to live without her.

He refocused himself immediately. It took him a minute to gather his bearings; they'd materialized some thirty meters from their destination. He nodded to his team. "This way."

He'd assembled a good group. Amrita Satchitanand was the most experienced, with the steadiest nerves he'd ever seen; she was his backup in case his attempt to destroy the queen somehow failed. Jorge Costas—lumbering and extraordinarily tall, yet with brilliantly fast reflexes—and Noel DeVrie, a deadly shot, would provide cover.

"Remember," he said, hefting the phaser rifle as they began to move, "no firing unless attacked. We can move freely among them so long as they don't perceive us as a threat."

Their steps rang hollowly against the metal decking. It was eerily silent, save for the faint, distant hum of engines. There were no voices here, no movement; a dim grayish light strobed overhead, emphasizing the profound lack of color, of life. Lio focused and suppressed his fear, his memories of Joel. It would all be over quickly: one shot, and the queen would be destroyed and all the Borg rendered harmless. All so easy . . .

Their destination was the only enclosed chamber in the vessel. At the open entryway, Lio paused.

Inside the vast interior, the light was even dimmer, with a greenish cast.

Lio pressed his combadge and breathed, "Captain Picard . . . We have found the queen." He closed the channel.

On a table, encased in a gleaming gelatinous substance, lay a pale monstrosity: a bald head and shoulders, and a spinal cord that emerged, bloody and serpentine, from the incomplete mass of flesh. The features were bland, regular, utterly androgynous, but nearby, a Borg drone worked on a shiny black form set upon a pedestal, the missing two-thirds of the body, which bore decidedly feminine attributes.

Above the queen's table, dark tubes extended downward—one inserted directly into her/its flesh, the second excreting more of the gelatinous medium. Two drones oversaw the procedure. A third drone was just finishing grotesque surgery on the supine figure encased in the gel: the amputation of a cybernetic arm.

An easy thing, to quickly kill . . . Lio was about to lift his rifle when he heard a scream behind him.

He should have continued the motion. He should have pressed the trigger—should have, but the instinct to protect his crewmates was too strong. He turned.

Borg drones had moved in *behind* them. A quartet, one for each member of the away team. It was DeVrie, leading up the rear, who had screamed. He had already dropped his weapon and fallen to his knees, dead—a whirring saw at the end of a drone's prosthetic arm had gone straight through his chest. At the same instant that DeVrie dropped forward into the spreading stain of his own blood, a second Borg lunged forward, piercing through Costas's midsection with a spiraling blade that split the man in half. Lio paused for the briefest moment as he realized that the Borg weren't assimilating, they were butchering.

The moment was short. Both Lio and Amrita

fired at the Borg who had so swiftly killed their friends. The drones dropped, but two more were advancing. Lio fired again, only to watch the beam bounce harmlessly off its target. With echoes of Worf's voice in his head, he shouted to Amrita, "Recalibrate the frequency!"

She did so but too late. The drone was upon her, and Lio's assassin was again advancing, slightly more than an arm's length away now. In his peripheral vision, he realized that the drones tending the queen were also moving in to intercept the intruders.

As he struggled to ignore the sounds of what the Borg were doing to Amrita's body, Lio had a dark thought: *At least I won't become one of them.*

Before he could prepare himself for death, he knew that his first and last duty was to the *Enterprise,* and he had critical information for those who survived him.

The drone reached for his shoulder. In the final moment, everything slowed. Lio looked into the face of his attacker—the chalky flesh surrounded by black—and thought, with an odd sense of bemused detachment, how Terrans had so often personified Death as pale-faced, cloaked in black.

At the same time, he studied the Borg's features—so colorless, so devoid of character or individuality—and felt pity.

Most of all, he felt sad for Sara. She would weep when she went to his quarters; he felt deep regret for the sorrow his death would cause her. He had wanted so badly to return to her, to love her, to make her life happy.

Enveloping it all was mortal fear—and its opposite, fearlessness, at the realization that others would follow him, that Captain Picard would never permit the Borg to win. His death would be avenged.

Calm acceptance washed over him as the Borg took him by the throat. But the fear was renewed when instead of a violent death, he felt only the cold metal of a Borg tubule piercing his neck. At the same moment, Lio punched his combadge and shouted . . .

"Enterprise! They attack on sight! Repeat: They now attack . . ."

6

———

"ENTERPRISE! THEY ATTACK ON SIGHT! REPEAT:
They now attack . . ."

Picard was on his feet, but only briefly. The lieutenant's voice was replaced by a shrill sound that knifed through the captain's brain and brought him to his knees. At first, he thought the sound was only in his head—like the song of the Borg—until he saw that the entire bridge crew was similarly doubled over.

"Sever the connection," Picard called out to the communications officer, but the young man had already dropped to the floor in agony.

In two leaping steps, Worf reached the communications console and worked the controls. "The Borg have piggybacked a signal onto the lieutenant's comm," he shouted over the whine. "I cannot terminate the . . . *Incoming!*"

The bridge rocked as the *Enterprise* was hit by a tremendous blow. The few officers still on their feet fell to the ground. Nave and T'Lana had both been thrown from their chairs.

"Shields are down," La Forge reported as he pulled himself back up to the console.

"Lieutenant Nave, take us out of weapons range!" Picard ordered as a second burst hit the ship.

The lieutenant struggled back to the conn, squinting in pain as the piercing sound grew impossibly louder. With a few commands, she brought the ship around and punched in a course that would take them as far away from the Borg ship as they could allow. As they sped away, the noise finally stopped.

"I've cut the connection to Lieutenant Battaglia's combadge," Worf reported.

"We've got shields," La Forge said.

Picard looked to his two officers. They had been through this before—and much worse—yet he knew the looks of shock on their faces as they continued to work at their stations mirrored his own. The Borg never lashed out so quickly, unless they were in attack mode. "I want a full—"

"The cube beamed something into sickbay while the shields were down," Worf said. "Readings are unclear."

Beverly!

Picard was immobilized for a fraction of a second. Though the rest of the bridge crew would have hardly noticed, to the captain, it felt like an eternity. The Borg were after Beverly. Somehow, they had sensed the connection and read his thoughts. They were hitting him personally, going for blood.

"Bridge to sickbay," Picard commanded.

Worf and Picard both went for the turbolift, when Beverly's voice filled the air. *"Sickbay to the bridge."* There was something hollow about her voice, calm yet emotionless. The tone stopped Picard.

"Yes, Doctor?"

"The Borg," she said, halting.

"We're on our way," Picard said with a glance to Worf. He knew they both shouldn't leave the bridge, but he'd be damned if he was going to stay behind.

"No," she said. *"It's not drones. It's the away team. The Borg have returned their bodies . . . or, rather, what remained."*

Picard felt a flush of relief. The Borg hadn't noticed the connection and sent a personal attack. They had merely sent the bodies to the most logical location on the ship.

The bodies.

He had failed them. He had done the one thing he had sworn he would never do: lose even one more of his crew to the Borg. With his eyes focused on the bridge personnel, his mind finished Battaglia's last utterance: *They now attack on sight.*

He had assumed that the Borg would react to the

away team as they always had to humans who posed no direct threat—that they would ignore them. He had assumed . . . and been wrong. How had he not known? He had been correct on everything else; he had known about the existence of the unborn queen, the location of the Borg cube . . .

But he had not known about the Borg's new tactic of attacking all intruders. Or their murderous intentions. His imperfect connection to the hive mind was a defect, a flaw, that had to be corrected, and swiftly.

Sickbay was filled to capacity, and yet there was none of the chaos typical in triage. The brief attack on the ship had resulted in about a dozen minor injuries to the crew, the most serious being Ensign Wahl's broken leg from a fall from a ladder in engineering. As in any emergency situation, the entire medical staff had reported for duty and were tending to the patients. And yet the room was almost as quiet as it would be when it was empty. The reason was clear to Beverly as she conducted her autopsy on the remains of the away team.

The attack had been particularly vicious, far more so than anything she had seen the Borg inflict previously. Their bodies had been destroyed . . . desecrated. It was almost like their attackers had taken joy in the killing. There seemed no clear reason why the Borg would send back the dead instead of assimilating them. It ran counter to everything she had experienced when dealing with the Borg in the past. Her scans revealed nothing beyond the horrific way the away team died. There were no clues to what the Borg were planning.

As she continued the examination, Beverly did her best to compartmentalize her emotions. That was always the most difficult part of her job. She needed to remain focused on her task and treat it just like that: a task, a chore. She had to forget the lives these people had been living barely an hour earlier.

To help herself deal, she allowed her focus to split and busied her mind with the information collected on the Borg that she had been reviewing when the ship had come under attack. She regretted that they had collected few details on the queen herself. Even with all that Data had stored in his positronic circuits after his encounter with her, or what *Voyager* had collected in the Delta Quadrant, there was little of use. Certainly there was nothing to indicate how the queen had come into existence. But the more Beverly's mind worked to compare the Borg to Terran hive insects, the more possibilities occurred to her.

She suspected that the loss of the queen had triggered a survival mechanism in the race, that perhaps one of the drones had adapted into a temporary "leader" and issued a directive to the surviving Collective: *create a new queen.* So the queen had not existed from the beginning of the Borg. That would be the easiest explanation for the fact that the Federation had already encountered two versions of the queen. In fact, perhaps this was a natural part of the cycle—of a queen dying and the colony creating a new one. This survival mechanism might also explain why the Borg behaved so violently toward the away team.

To continue the analogy, Beverly theorized that a queen might possibly be created from an adapted drone. *But how would such a transformation be accomplished in the cybernetic world of the Borg? Was it a simple matter of attaching the right prosthesis, or of altering the DNA of a drone in much the same way Jean-Luc's had been altered when he'd been assimilated?*

Beverly was so engrossed in her train of thought that she barely heard the doors to sickbay open. Figuring it was another minor injury, she glanced up briefly to see Jean-Luc approaching. His arrival had been anticipated, though she had expected him sooner.

Picard walked directly toward her, but even with his single focus, she could see the slight falter as he saw the remains of the away team lying out on the examination tables. She knew that he would blame himself. Any captain would. But they both knew that this was not the time for that discussion.

"What have you learned, Doctor?" he asked,

almost coldly, as he reached the examination table with the remains of Noel DeVrie.

"There's nothing out of the ordinary," she reported, "beyond the brutality of the attack itself. The cuts and . . . dismembering were accomplished by the usual Borg weaponry." Her voice softened. "Lieutenant Battaglia's body was not among the dead."

Jean-Luc looked down at the three bodies laid out beside each other on the tables. "Who would have thought these would be the lucky ones?"

Beverly could see Ensign Wahl's body tense as her leg was being worked on. The doctor knew that the reaction wasn't due to the pain. Wahl had heard what the captain had said.

Beverly nodded toward her office and walked with Jean-Luc to continue their conversation in private. She also wanted to get them both away from the gruesome reminder of their losses. Not that there was anywhere on the ship they could go that would be far enough. The death pall clung to both of them with every step.

"What I don't understand," she said as she took a seat at her desk, "is the Borg aren't like this. They aren't vicious. They're systematic. Violence is a means to an end. It's never done for show. The Borg certainly don't taunt."

Picard's lips twisted bitterly. "They are scattered across the galaxy, cut off from one another. And time and time again the Federation has shown them something they've rarely seen: defeat. In this case, the Borg have done what they do best. They've adapted."

Beverly tried to ignore the full depth of what that statement could imply.

"You should also know," he continued, "that the Borg killed the away team without any provocation. A skeleton crew, which should have been too busy completing the ship, attending the queen . . . yet they murdered our people without hesitation."

Murder. It wasn't a term she associated with the Borg. Certainly they were killers, but murder implied an emotional state, one that wasn't usually present in the drones. And to kill without provocation . . .

She recoiled at the notion. She had walked among the Borg herself without being harmed, although it had been an inexpressibly eerie experience. "But I thought—"

"So did I," Jean-Luc replied heavily. "I was wrong. Obviously, my connection to the Borg is incomplete, imperfect. They are different now. Bolder. Vicious. I can't afford to be wrong again."

"Do you think it was a trap?" she asked.

"I don't believe so," he said unsurely. "I don't think they know that I can hear them. I hope that they cannot hear what is in my mind."

"Perhaps they're more aggressive because they're protecting the developing queen." She paused, knowing her words did nothing to ease Jean-Luc's sense of responsibility for the lives lost. "I have a theory that they're transforming one of the drones into the queen," she said as she brought up the files she had been studying. "What I don't understand is *how* they're doing it."

"That will be your next priority," Picard ordered.

"What are you going to do?" Beverly asked. Something about the way the captain's eyes had fallen on her told her that he already had a plan. The *Enterprise* could never survive a battle with the cube; retreat seemed the only answer. Yet she knew from looking at Picard's set expression that he had not even considered the option.

"The rules have changed," Jean-Luc said. "We have fought against the Borg—and they have adapted, grown impervious to our weapons, and forced us to fall back each time. Now it's our turn to adapt." There was an odd defensiveness in his tone, his eyes, an unflinching sense of determination; he knew that she would disapprove strongly of what he was about to say. "The drones react aggressively to humanoids. But they would not react at all to another Borg."

She stared blankly at him. Only her desk was between them, but she suddenly felt very far away from him. A muscle in Picard's jaw twitched subtly; she caught the glimmer of inward-directed loathing in his expression and felt a flash of understanding, of pure horror.

"No." She stood up, shaking her head as if to

dislodge the very thought. Jean-Luc reached toward her, but she pushed his hand away. "No! I won't permit it."

"Doctor." His tone was formal, gentle, utterly reasonable. "You have the knowledge and the technology—and we haven't any option. If we are to destroy the queen, I must become Locutus again."

Picard saw the shock and revulsion in her green eyes, her expression, even her posture as she stood behind her desk. She folded her arms tightly about herself and shook her head, red hair swinging gently.

The idea—that he would have to become Locutus again—had come to him swiftly, harshly as he had stood on the bridge listening to Lieutenant Battaglia's anguished screams. After their retreat, Picard took a moment alone in his ready room to contemplate the situation. It was one that he could not entertain lightly, but there was no other option. During the ride on the lift, the walk down the corridor to sickbay, Picard had felt the same horror he now saw in Beverly. But he'd had the time to overcome it, to yield to the necessity of the situation. And now, standing in her office, he was resigned to the fact that it was the only possible course of action. Beverly would have to come to that conclusion, too.

"What else shall we do, Doctor?" he pressed.

"Retreat, so that the queen can direct an attack against Earth? You've seen the vessel; it's even more formidable than the last. Shall we allow another battle like Wolf 359, permit thousands more to die in vain?"

"But Seven of Nine—" Beverly began.

He cut her off. "Seven will arrive too late to be of help. Even if she were here now, she's become too human. The Borg would never accept her as one of their own."

She had calmed; her arms were still folded, indicating her unwillingness to concede, but she was listening carefully. "I've been doing a great deal of research. Obviously, the queen is a drone who is being transformed into a female. My hunch is that it's far more than a simple surgical procedure, that biochemistry is involved. The Borg are half organic. There has to be a biomedical way to halt the transformation process—"

Picard interrupted. "This is still conjecture? You haven't yet discovered a method?"

She shook her head. "I need more time."

"Then your line of research will have to wait." He paused. "Even if you *did* find a way of halting the metamorphosis in time, someone would *still* have to get past the Borg in order to do it."

"Jean-Luc," she began softly. He heard the unspoken plea to find any other way.

"*Someone* must be transformed," he said, his tone hard. "Someone with special knowledge of the

Borg, their ship, their queen. Can you offer a more logical solution?"

"No," she admitted. "But what happens if we do this and something goes wrong?"

"That is a question we can't yet answer. But we already know with certainty what will happen if we *don't* do this." He sighed and lowered his voice. "Look, I'm no more pleased about this than you. I would prefer any other option—if there was one. But all personal feelings must be put aside. I am the best candidate. And I *must* have a perfect connection to the hive mind." He fought to keep the pain and anger from his tone. "I won't lose anyone else because of my ignorance."

Her shoulders relaxed slightly; the emotion left her face and tone, replaced by the intent look of the scientific mind at work. "I have all the records, and Borg nanoprobes. I can adapt them for our purposes." She paused. "And we'll implant a neutralizer chip, of course, to protect you from total assimilation. You'll hear every directive the hive does, be privy to all the Borg's information. But you'll still be yourself—capable of free thought and action."

Picard gave her a grim smile of gratitude; he knew it wasn't easy for her. "How long before I can be ready?"

She directed her eyes up and to the right as she calculated. "The actual work on you won't take more than fifteen minutes. But give me an hour to prepare."

"Make it less," the captain said. "We haven't that much time."

Picard sat in his quarters, listening to the haunting strains of Berlioz's *Symphonie Fantastique* and trying to quell the evil specters evoked by the knowledge of what was to come. There were flashes of the Borg operating room . . . of the terror of being a small mind closed off, imprisoned by the thundering voice of the Collective . . . the agonizing frustration of being encased inside a body no longer his own to control, of hearing his own voice speaking on behalf of the Borg while he, the individual trapped inside, could do no more than scream silently with outrage.

Each Borg drone represented just such an individual mind—trapped, forced to watch its body behave mindlessly, against its will . . . The magnitude of the tragedy was incomprehensible.

Now one of the drones was being altered, changed into a new creature—one with her own will and her own individuality, one bent on crushing those of others. He shuddered at the thought of himself as Locutus, supine in the operating theater while the queen, her skin moist and glistening, leaned her face close to his and whispered to him of their joint future as she stroked his cheek with cold, inhuman hands . . .

He quashed the unpleasant memories, replaced them with the one memory of pure triumph, unrivaled relief: the instant he had divorced himself from Locutus and the hive mind, and reached out, as Jean-Luc Picard, to grasp Data's arm.

Sleep, he had said. The utterance brought unspeakable satisfaction, for it was his own voice, so long silenced, that was speaking. It was his restitution for the crimes wrought by Locutus; he was giving his crew the information they needed to stop the Borg, to save Earth. Data had heard and had understood.

Those positive memories, he knew, would give him the strength to become Locutus again, to walk among the Borg as one of their own. He would be with them but apart from them; never again would he permit them to steal his or anyone's individuality.

He was staring out the window, lost in the past and the swelling music, when the door chimed. "Music off," he said, and then, "Come."

He turned as T'Lana entered.

"Captain Picard," she said formally. "I would like to state that I recognize you were correct about the existence of the Borg vessel. I realize that such validation is important to humans."

He smiled faintly at that. "So. Are you withdrawing your objection to my order to bring the *Enterprise* here without Seven of Nine?"

"No, sir," she replied calmly as she came farther into the room. "While I acknowledge that you were right about the existence and location of the Borg ship, you were incorrect in your judgment that the

Borg would passively accept the presence of the away team. Therefore, I have no way of verifying which of your assertions is correct. I do not know for a fact that Seven of Nine would have arrived too late to have been of help."

Picard felt the defensiveness welling up in him, especially at the mention of the lost away team. He wanted some physical distance between himself and the Vulcan and made a sudden move for his chair, brushing T'Lana's arm as he passed. "I'm all too aware of the fact that my connection to the Borg collective is imperfect. It was a regrettable mistake but one that had to be made to learn what we know now."

As he sat, he saw a look on T'Lana's face that could only be described as . . . curious. "Yes?"

"You intend to become Locutus again."

There was no anger in her tone, no question either. She knew this as fact. This was the benefit—and the challenge—of having a highly sensitive touch-telepath as a member of the crew. He hadn't intended to tell T'Lana his plan yet, but there was no reason to deny it.

"No humanoid can safely accomplish our mission," he explained. "So, yes, I will become Locutus again. I will wear a neutralizer chip so that my assimilation is not total. The Borg will accept me as one of their own, and I will be able to destroy the queen quickly."

T'Lana digested this, showing no sign of surprise save for a slight lift of one eyebrow. At last she replied, "There is a significant chance that your plan will go awry and you will be captured. Starfleet would lose an asset and the Borg would gain an invaluable one."

"I need not be reminded," Picard answered heavily. "Counselor, I was unaware of a single detail which, tragically, led to the loss of four crew members. Now I am pursuing a course of action that will allow me unlimited access to the Borg hive mind and give us our greatest chance of disabling the Borg before they can launch a deadly attack against us. Why are you so unwilling, after the evidence you have seen, to trust me?"

"Your emotions," she said bluntly, with a slight lift of her chin—which, were she human, Picard would have taken as a sign of defiance. "When you first announced that you sensed the Borg collective, I read all the relevant logs and reports concerning your encounters with them. During your last, when the Borg invaded the *Enterprise*-E, your anger brought you very close to allowing the Borg to destroy every member of the crew. Your actions jeopardized your ship and the future of the Alpha Quadrant. You behaved irrationally, Captain. As counselor, it is my responsibility to remind you of such facts. I would be remiss if I did not mention that I have sensed a great deal of emotional turmoil in you regarding this decision. I urge you to reconsider your actions, to change your strategy, and report back to Admiral Janeway for instruction."

Picard, careful to contain any trace of heat in his tone, said, "I can hear them, but they are different now. I misunderstood how the Borg had been changed. But now I do have a better understanding. Without the voice of their queen, the hive mind has become a mob mentality. At this moment, there is no logic within the Borg. If I can walk among them as Locutus, we can end this before it starts."

"You are working off a supposition that has no basis in fact," she reminded him.

"As is my prerogative as captain," he countered.

"Intuition." T'Lana almost whispered the word.

Picard wanted to see her relenting as a break-through, but he feared that this would merely be the first of many conversations where they butted heads. "Counselor . . . we obviously have read each other's files. You requested assignment to the *Enterprise;* you wanted to come here. May I ask why?"

Something subtle flickered in her dark eyes, not outright emotion but perchance an uncomfortable memory. At last she answered, "I deemed it logical to go where I was needed most."

"I see." Coming from anyone other than a Vul-can, the remark would be the most pointed of insults; Picard struggled not to take it as such. "Dismissed."

He turned his back to her and once again faced the window. Against the backdrop of space and stars, he saw her faint reflection before the doors closed behind her.

Sara Nave could not eat. She could not think. She could not even consider performing her regular duties. If Lio had simply been killed like the others, it would almost have been better. But knowing he was out there, knowing what he was going through at that very moment—it was all too much for her.

She stood at the entrance to Lio's quarters, unwilling to enter. Stepping over the threshold seemed to be an admission of the finality of Lio's loss. And she was not willing to let him go so easily. He was still on the Borg vessel, most likely still one of them. And if he was alive—in any fashion—there was still hope. Stubbornly, she had refused to cry. She would not allow herself to grieve. Not yet.

She had lost her parents cleanly; she'd been far removed from them, from the final explosions, the death cries, the torn, bleeding bodies. One moment they were alive in her consciousness; the next, irrevocably gone. She'd spent her life avoiding attachments, afraid of another moment this terrible.

But she had made an exception for Lio, had let herself care . . . She had done so for two reasons. One, she had yielded to hope; she had found someone worthy who had broken her resistance, who had made her love him. She'd known that together, they would have been good. Two, she had been afraid, afraid that if she did not take advantage of her opportunity to be with Lio that very moment, another chance would never come.

Nave shuddered, grasped her elbows tightly. She'd heard Amrita's garbled keening, the soft, subtle sound of human flesh being ripped asunder . . . then Lio's panicked report.

And his scream—quickly extinguished by the whip of metal through air.

She squeezed her eyes shut and heard her own exasperated retort. *There won't be any "just in case."*

But here it was.

Nave drew a breath and stepped inside. The doors slid shut behind her.

She opened her eyes. What had once been standard-issue quarters was now a pure reflection of Lio. The simple, streamlined cot was covered in linens in a variety of earth tones. The walls had been draped with faux leather covering, evoking the feel of a Tuscan villa. One wall had been turned into a larger-than-life-sized holographic picture window that looked out on an ancient village that Lio had told her still stood near the place he had been born. On a nearby wire rack sat a dozen bottles of real Italian wine, not synthehol. Lio had once threatened to share one of those bottles of real alcohol with her. She'd politely declined, stating that the cocktails he ordered up in the club were challenging enough.

The desk, she remembered; he had mentioned leaving something for her on the desk.

He had added a hutch with shelves to the desk; they were lined with a dozen or so real paper books—ancient, leather-bound, with Latin and Italian writing on the spines. Awed, Nave reached out and put a hand on one. Lio had spoken of collecting nineteenth-century Italian literature, but she had never imagined that he actually owned such priceless volumes. She leaned forward to draw in their smell of musty paper and aging leather. She would associate that earthy scent with Lio for the rest of her life.

As her mind filled with images of her lost love, she remembered why she had come to his room in the first place. He had left something for her.

Sara looked down to find a delicate-looking model airplane resting on the desktop. As she carefully picked it up, she recognized the design from her academy history lessons. It was a replica of a flying machine designed by his namesake, the artist and scientist Leonardo da Vinci. Sara was impressed by the simple detail on the handmade model. Nothing on it appeared replicated. It had a genuine feel to it. She immediately loved it for its imperfections as well as for the fact that it was the perfect gift for a flight controller.

She gently placed the model back on the desk and picked up the note it had been resting on. It was parchment paper, with lettering written in calligraphic script.

For Sara—

My mother made this for me as a gift that she gave me on the day I was accepted to the academy. It was a fitting enough gift, but now I wonder if maybe there was a bit of premonition about it, that she knew I'd fall in love with someone who dreamed of flying, like yourself.

I never thought you'd give me a chance, Sara. Since the first day I saw you, this model inspired me to take a chance. Leonardo da Vinci never successfully got off the ground, but with you, I could soar.

You gave me hope; you gave me yourself. Borg or no Borg, I leave this room a happy man. Remember that. It's the only thing that really matters.

> *Lio*

She read it over several times, numb at first, but with each successive reading, her defenses slowly melted, until they could no longer contain the torrent of grief. She put down the paper, put her hands to her face, and wept.

She thought of the terrible moment when Lio had faced the Borg, when he had first realized he was going to die. The physical pain must have been horrible enough, but the mental must have been unbearable for him. She thought of the anguish he had felt on seeing his friend Joel as one of the Borg. How much more anguished had Lio felt realizing that the same fate now awaited him?

Just consider me dead. It's easier . . .

When she was finished, she said, as if Lio himself were standing in front of her, "As much as I love the conn, I'm going to transfer back to Security. They'll need a new chief, and I'm the most experienced." She paused, then added, bitter and vehement: "The Borg will never win. I'll board that ship, Lio. And I'll find you."

7

IN SICKBAY, BEVERLY WAS PERFORMING MICRO-
surgery, staring down at computerized enlarge-
ments of Borg nanoprobes.

Unaltered, they would infiltrate Jean-Luc's neu-
rons, twisting and intertwining themselves around
the double helix of his DNA, corrupting its chemistry, supplanting it, until it became something new
and inhuman.

Beverly was subtly changing them so that they
would mask, not replace, Jean-Luc's humanity. The
process made her recall their last encounter with
the Borg—but her memory ran not to the harrowing
battles aboard the *Enterprise* but rather to the moment she had first gazed upon Zefram Cochrane's
ship, the *Phoenix*.

She'd seen old pictures of nuclear missiles, and
there was no mistaking the *Phoenix*'s genesis. If

ever there had been a plowshare hammered out of a sword . . .

Which was precisely what she was attempting to do now. If the nanites were successfully implanted, and the captain's neutralizer chip functioned correctly, the technology the Borg had used to enslave billions would finally bring about their downfall.

She glanced up, then turned at the sound of the door opening behind her. She expected to see Jean-Luc and was prepared to tell him to be patient a little longer.

Instead, standing just inside the door was Counselor T'Lana. Beverly rose and faced the Vulcan, who stood primly, hands clasped behind her back. Beverly had to direct her gaze downward. She was not a tall woman, but T'Lana was exceptionally short for a Vulcan.

"Doctor Crusher," T'Lana said by way of greeting.

Beverly was surprised to find herself repressing an instinctive dislike. It was hard to feel gracious toward anyone who challenged the captain at a time when he most desperately needed the support of his entire crew, but her reaction did not really suit the situation. Beverly realized that her emotional response was more that of a lover than a chief medical officer. T'Lana was only being logical in her doubt. Secretly, the doctor wished she had a better handle on her own reservations.

"Unless you're experiencing a medical emergency, I'm afraid I'll have to speak with you another time," she said, hoping that she didn't come across as overly dismissive. "I'm working on an extremely urgent project for the captain."

T'Lana took a step closer. "He is precisely the reason I have come to speak with you. I would be grateful if you would hear me out before you continue your efforts to transform him into Locutus."

Beverly lifted an eyebrow in surprise. "You've spoken to the captain recently."

"I have just come from his quarters. I realize that you have an intimate relationship with the captain. At the same time, you hold the most crucial position aboard the ship: that of chief medical officer."

"I'm aware of my responsibilities," Beverly replied coolly. In one statement, T'Lana had put into words the same internal conflict the doctor had been trying to avoid for the past hour. "If there's a point to this conversation, please make it. I have a job to do."

"I submit that transforming the captain into a Borg and sending him over to their vessel is a reckless and dangerous act. The risk is high that he will again be assimilated, and I need not remind you of the countless Starfleet personnel who died when he was last Locutus." She paused, tilting her head to study Beverly more closely. "You Earth physicians have a saying: First do no harm. At the very least, you are harming the captain . . . and the potential harm to others is extremely great."

Beverly felt herself start to color. She was not

about to explain herself to the new counselor. It would be impossible for a Vulcan to fully understand why she was going along with Jean-Luc's questionable plan. In order to keep from showing anger, she began to turn back to her monitor. "I have my orders."

"That is the point," T'Lana persisted. "You are chief medical officer. If the captain makes an irrational decision, you can relieve him of duty."

Beverly whirled to face her. "So *that's* why you've come."

"You have the power, Doctor. Someone else could take command and follow Admiral Janeway's orders."

"That is not an option," Beverly replied coldly. Too coldly, she realized. T'Lana's suggestion was only logical, from the counselor's point of view. But still, Beverly couldn't help what next came out of her own mouth. "I've always heard that Vulcans were extremely loyal to their commanding officers. What makes *you* the exception?"

Only the most observant eye would have seen T'Lana start, seen her posture stiffen, seen the single flash as she blinked, the infinitesimal lift of her chin. "That is an inaccurate assessment. My loyalty to Captain Wozniak of the *Indefatigable* was noted by Starfleet Command."

"We're talking about Jean-Luc Picard," Beverly said. "You asked to come here, Counselor. You asked to serve *him*. And right now, you've shown him nothing but distrust; in fact, you're doing everything in your power to undermine his authority. Why? Does it have something to do with the *Indefatigable* being destroyed? Are you so afraid that the same thing is going to happen to you again? Is that why you refuse to put your confidence in Captain Picard?"

She'd struck a nerve. T'Lana moved not a muscle; her face was set as stone, but the intensity in her eyes was breathtaking. "Vulcans do not experience fear," she said woodenly. "My actions are based in logic. I question whether yours are as well."

They studied each other in silence for a time.

T'Lana was the first to speak. "I suspect that you are wondering the same thing about yourself."

Beverly would have smiled if the nerve that T'Lana had just hit weren't already so raw. "I don't have time for a counseling session," she said. "I have work to do. I will thank you to leave me to it."

She directed her attention back to the monitor and did not look up at the sound of the doors closing.

After waiting an unendurable hour for the summons from Beverly, Picard at last made his way toward sickbay and transformation. These were the same *Enterprise* corridors he knew so well, yet today they were filled with ghosts: black-and-white killing machines, both the slayer and the slain, who had roamed here. Efficient, fatal, and silent. The screams that echoed in Picard's memory were human, those of his perished crew.

His stride was brisk, yet the walk seemed uncommonly long. When he finally arrived at sickbay, Beverly, wearing her blue surgeon's coat, was waiting, not busy at her monitors and scans as usual, but standing facing the door, arms folded, posture conveying determination. Yet Picard saw the tension in the muscles of her jaw, her neck, saw the narrowing of her eyes.

The doors closed behind him with a whisper of finality.

They nodded at each other in grave silence. There were no words appropriate to the situation, capable of expressing the horror of the duty each was now going to perform. There was no point in discussing the harrowing memories the imminent act was about to evoke.

With barely a glance to the two security guards pointedly stationed inside the doorway, she turned and led him to surgery. Next to the waiting bed stood a table bearing ominous apparatus: black tubing, a black carapace designed to fit above and beneath his eye, then curve around his skull; nearby sat a Borg optoscope and several neatly placed hyposprays, holding the nanites that would change the essence of what he was.

One object on the table made him recoil: a black prosthetic arm composed of thick serpentine coils rather than muscle, terminating in pincers and a many-petaled rotating blade. He recognized it with gut and instinct more than mind; it was the exact arm worn by Locutus more than a decade ago.

Beverly saw his reaction and said, with taut professionalism, "I saved as much as possible for research purposes." She paused, then spoke again, her tone abruptly softened. "It was a part of you, once."

And so it would be again. Picard did not respond to her statement. Instead he drew a deep breath, settled onto the bed, and said, "Let's get on with it."

Complete sedation had been unnecessary; Beverly could easily have used a local while injecting the neutralizer chip, then fitting the arm, the carapace, the optoscope, the tubing that ran from his cheek and jaw to the crown of his skull. It was, Picard later decided, an act of mercy on her part.

Beverly woke him when it was time for the injection of the nanites; this required him to be conscious so that she could better monitor the results.

He sat up on the bed, half blind from the facial carapace and optoscope, feeling heavy and awkward from the weight of the tubing on his head and the long, protruding mechanical arm. He could see the two guards stiffen, standing at the ready should anything go wrong.

The doctor was blessedly swift in her work,

devoid of any emotion. She injected the hypos into Picard's shoulder one after the other, then stood back to observe her patient.

Picard fought to still the rapid beating of his fleetingly human heart. The first sign was strength: the sense of heaviness vanished, as if someone had gently lifted the weight of all the prostheses from him. He found himself sitting stiffly, perfectly erect. The second was sight. He blinked as his own eyes ceased their functioning, as the optoscope took over and the colors surrounding him faded to dull monochrome. The blue of Beverly's coat, the copper of her hair, were rendered now in shades of gray. Her image was distorted, abruptly looming one instant, receding the next.

He drew a breath; the air seemed suddenly chill, drier than any desert. In the midst of his discomfort, he realized that Beverly was leaning forward, speaking to him, the horror in her eyes not entirely masked.

"Jean-Luc. What effects are you experiencing?"

He swiveled his head slowly to regard her, struggling to make sense of the distant, muted sounds she was making. They were almost eclipsed by something much louder: the thunder of the Collective. He could hear it now—indeed, every word that had once been an unintelligible whisper now permeated his being.

He strained and managed to reply. "All of them. We are now the Borg."

His voice was no longer his own; all inflection

and naturalness were gone, leaving his words clipped and toneless. It was Locutus who spoke.

Yet it was Picard who remained transcendent, Picard who had composed the answer, who had observed the changes with trepidation, who did not permit himself for an instant to consider the consequences should his mission go awry.

"How is the neutralizer chip working, Jean-Luc?"

"Well," he said, and to his own relief, was able to add, "I'm here, too. Picard is here." He climbed stiffly, deliberately from the bed. "And it's time for me to go."

On the bridge, Worf sat in the command chair and studiously ignored Counselor T'Lana when she returned. He could not permit thoughts of self-blame or inadequacy to mar his focus. He had been contemplating what Doctor Crusher had said about his being Klingon for the captain. Now was the most critical of times, when the captain needed his loyalty the most—especially when Picard's own counselor was outspokenly critical of his decision.

Instead, Worf waited for Doctor Crusher's summons and stared at the viewscreen image of the Borg cube. The Borg were completely without honor. They did not kill cleanly, granting their victims noble deaths. Instead, they stole the souls of the living and subjected them to mental slavery.

Worf mourned the fact that Lieutenant Battaglia had just been so thoroughly dishonored, while he silently celebrated the valiant deaths of the rest of the team. It was something the rest of the crew would never understand. For as horrific as the murders had been, Satchitanand, Costas, and De-Vrie had all died with honor.

Behind him, the lift doors opened. Nave emerged and paused to face him before she replaced the officer at the helm.

"Commander," she said softly. Her normally pale face was flushed, and her eyes red rimmed; she had been weeping.

Worf noted the fact with profound discomfort. The tears of women—especially Jadzia's—had always produced a sense of helplessness in him. He never knew what to do to stop them. In the case of Nave, however, he at least knew their cause. Nave was formerly chief of security—a position with which Worf himself was familiar—and she knew the four crew members who had died or been lost. Worf suspected that one of them, Battaglia, had been a heart friend; he had seen Nave with him many times in the crew lounge. Worf refused to call the bar by the odd name that Captain Riker had christened it.

"Yes, Lieutenant?" Worf replied, uncomfortable. He was glad that Nave had at least stopped her crying and seemed to have gained control of herself. She reminded him, in a way, of Jadzia. She was impatient with herself when she failed to repress her emotions.

"Will the captain be reporting for duty again soon, sir?" Nave's tone was distinctly formal, quite the opposite of the friendly way she spoke to him during workouts with the *bat'leth*. "I . . . have a request to make of him. I went by his quarters just now, but he wasn't there."

Worf lowered his voice. "The captain won't be . . . available for some period of time."

"Ah," Nave said. She lowered her face, crestfallen, then summoned her determination and looked squarely at Worf. "Then . . . perhaps I could make the request of you, sir."

Worf answered with a stern look.

"I'd like to volunteer for the position of security chief, sir. We just lost our chief and three of the highest-ranking officers in security. Of anyone on this ship, I have the most experience for the job."

Worf considered this. "A security chief is critically necessary, especially in the emergency situation we are in. But we also require an experienced conn. Evasive maneuvers can often protect us better than armed officers."

"Ensign Nguyen is experienced," Nave said, referring to the officer who was just leaving the seat vacant for her. "And there's Lieutenant Krueger." Both officers shared conn duty with Nave, each working different shifts.

"I suppose, if our situation grows more dire, we

could let you fill the position and ask Nguyen and Krueger to pull longer shifts of duty." He paused. "Very well. If we have need of a chief of security, I will call upon you when the time comes."

"When the *time* comes . . . ?" Nave repeated, aghast. "Sir, the time is *here*. I'm volunteering to lead an away team *now* onto the Borg vessel."

Worf lowered his voice, though he had no doubt T'Lana, sitting nearby, would hear every word. "No away team is needed. I will be making an announcement to the crew shortly: the captain is beaming over to the Borg vessel."

"The *captain?*"

"He will be safe," Worf countered. "Doctor Crusher is transforming him into a Borg. But he will be wearing a neutralizer chip, which will protect him from being assimilated. The Borg will accept him, and he will be able to proceed unhindered to the queen and destroy her."

"And if he doesn't?" Nave asked outright.

Worf felt the Vulcan's disapproving gaze on him. "I don't know," he said quietly. "I will have the opportunity to consult the captain shortly and will ask him."

"Thank you, sir," Nave said, clearly crushed. She turned away slowly and took her seat at the conn.

"Lieutenant," Worf said softly. He understood and liked Nave; she had a warrior's heart. He wished very much that he could allow her to seek justice for her friends.

Nave glanced over her shoulder at him.

"If anyone else needs to beam over to the Borg vessel," he said, "I shall make sure you accompany him."

Nave did not smile. "Thank you, sir," she said.

Picard/Locutus walked through the corridors of the *Enterprise* with Beverly Crusher by his side. The world was gray, leaden, distorted—and cold, so very cold.

"So this is how it looked," he murmured, in the low, hoarse voice of Locutus; the sound of it still unsettled him.

Beverly turned her face toward him. "How *what* looked?"

"The ship. The way it appeared to the Borg when they invaded her. The deck, the bulkheads . . ."

"How *does* it look?" Beverly asked. She was distracting him, Picard knew, distracting them both from the fear of what was about to happen.

"Very odd. Without color; everything is varying shades of black, white, gray. And it's rather like being in a fishbowl looking out. When I close in on something, it grows alarmingly large—it's all I can see. And when it recedes, it's gone immediately." Speaking was an effort, yet he forced himself and was relieved when he could hear Jean-Luc's intonation and choice of words assert themselves. Gray and immediate, he decided, that was the Borg world. There was no right or wrong here, only directives, only stimulus and response. He understood now how they could kill so easily, without compunction: action was simply mindless action. They saw no difference among nourishing themselves, building a cube, or killing.

We are building a queen. Remain in your regeneration chambers and await the directive. He would have said more, but the single thunderous thought overrode all others, and he fell silent. The voices were tinged with emotion and an urgency that nearly overwhelmed him. It was different from the voices the last time he had been Locutus. Indeed, when Beverly spoke, he had to strain to make out the words.

"It sounds hideous," Beverly said softly.

It is, he thought, but the words proved too difficult to form beneath the chorus of Borg voices. He turned away and focused on walking; his gait seemed stiff, clumsy, as if he wore another man's body. Silently, he chided himself: he would have to adjust to the mental noise. If he could not speak quickly, coherently with his crew once he beamed over to the Borg vessel, all might be lost.

Beverly glanced at him. He could see in her eyes that she noticed his struggle, but she said nothing.

He forced out some words. "You were right—they will protect the queen at any cost. They will kill. It is not a directive. It springs from something . . . deeper."

They arrived at last at the transporter room.

Commander Worf and Counselor T'Lana stood side by side at the transporter console. It was growing increasingly harder for Picard to judge expressions. He could not read T'Lana's reaction to the appearance of Locutus at all, but he caught a flicker in the Klingon's eyes.

Picard turned his attention first to the Vulcan. He could only imagine that she had come in order to make a final argument against his course of action. "Counselor T'Lana?" He forced himself not to react to the sound of his own voice rendered hauntingly alien, and he forced himself, too, to ignore the mental chatter and speak fluidly, without halting. "I presume you're here because you wished to have a word with me."

"Yes, sir," T'Lana said. She stepped from behind the console in order to face the captain directly. While such body language was generally ignored by Vulcans, T'Lana had come to realize that humans valued it. Her action hinted at respect and directness.

She wanted to show him such things. While she did not approve of his choices, he was still her captain. And she could not look on him thus, as Locutus, and not consider his loyalty to his crew—a value equally prized by Vulcans and humans. It was difficult even for her to see him so changed: she had never stood in the presence of a Borg drone, though she had seen many images, and the experience was unsettling. One of his eyes was completely obscured by an optical device;

the other was dulled, devoid of emotion, of the spark that had made it human. His skin was as alarmingly pale as that of a bloodless corpse, and the black prosthesis fitted to his arm was equipped with an ominous and deadly looking metal blade.

T'Lana of course did not react outwardly to the change in his appearance, but Doctor Crusher and Commander Worf could not entirely hide the keen distress they felt. It must have been extremely difficult for them, given their experiences with Locutus. T'Lana was impressed that Picard was willing to endure what to him must be a horrific experience—again to become part of the Borg. Most important, he was willing to sacrifice himself in order to spare his crew and—he believed—the rest of humanoid civilization.

Captain Wozniak would have done such a thing. She drew a breath and pushed the image of the dying Wozniak from her mind.

"I have come for two reasons, Captain," T'Lana said. "First, I wish to tell you that I regret I was unable to be of use to you in my role as counselor—"

Picard interrupted immediately, in the grating, unsettlingly inhuman voice of the Borg, though the mere act of forming the words seemed to require enormous effort. "But you were of service. You gave your opinion. I value that."

"Thank you, sir."

"And the second reason you have come?" Picard asked.

T'Lana drew a breath. Whether the captain was

right or wrong was, at this moment, immaterial. "To wish you success in your mission, sir."

The Borg face could not quite smile, but she saw the very humanlike glint in the single exposed eye. "I appreciate that, Counselor. It is definitely something to be wished for."

As T'Lana exited, Picard turned to his second-in-command. "Commander Worf." His words came out harsh, stilted, uninflected, Borg. "You are now in command of this vessel."

He paused, meaning to say more, but the Klingon spoke first. "Aye, Captain. I will do my best, sir. As an emergency backup, I am assembling another away team—"

Picard cut him off, gesturing with the prosthetic arm, an action that made Worf and Beverly wince. "There will be no more away teams, even if I fail." It was nearly impossible to speak quietly while someone else was shouting in his brain, but he forced himself to maintain his focus, to make the words come. "Now that I am fully part of the Collective, I understand that the Borg's entire arsenal is almost online. And their engines will be ready in just under seven hours. Do you understand?" He paused. "If I am unable to neutralize the queen, your orders are to take the ship out of here and warn Starfleet Command immediately. We will risk no further lives."

Worf's expression grew stoic. He gave a single, curt nod. "Aye, sir."

"I'll stay in constant contact. If for any reason

my communicator fails, or the Borg taps into my comlink, you'll be able to get my coordinates from the transponder. If we lose contact, notify Doctor Crusher immediately; she will be monitoring the neutralizer chip to be sure it is functioning properly. I want you to remain just within transporter range. No closer." He let go a small gasp, drained by the effort of so much speech.

If Worf saw, he did not show it. "Yes, Captain."

That's it then, Picard told himself silently—a small, barely discernible thought amid the collective's babble, phrase layered over phrase layered over phrase.

Nutrient uptake successful.

Prosthetic body now available for use by the queen . . .

The queen's gestation is nearing completion. Prepare for the coming directive.

Maintain ninety-five percent humidity in gestation chamber. Construction completed on Levels Three through Twenty-one Alpha. Raising internal temperature . . .

Picard lumbered to the transporter pad, then turned and faced Worf and Beverly, both of whom stood at the console.

How distant they looked, how gray; how cold and grim and lifeless the *Enterprise* herself seemed. Weighed down by the cacophony of the collective, Picard made himself a silent, solemn promise: he would return again to a world warm and vivid and bright.

"Mister Worf," he said, "beam me over to the Borg vessel."

The world shimmered, sparks of light illuminating the gray. The edges of reality softened, melted into each other, then abruptly, relentlessly dissolved.

8

EVEN AS PICARD MATERIALIZED ON THE BORG vessel, he gratefully sucked in air. The atmosphere aboard the *Enterprise* had become so cold and dry to him that it pained his throat and lungs. Here it was obligingly hot and so moist a fine mist veiled his surroundings.

The voice of the Collective was clearer here, utterly pervasive yet somehow less intrusive, as quietly a part of him as his own breathing or the beating of his heart. The part of him that was Locutus found it welcoming. At the same time, he felt his level of anger increase. At first, he thought it was a natural reaction to being back aboard a cube. But slowly he came to realize that Jean-Luc Picard wasn't angry. It was the Borg.

Emotion was not typical of his connection to the Collective. The Borg were systematic. Even with all the added voices, Picard remembered that the last time he was Locutus there was an overall sense of calm. Of reason. The Borg did not see themselves as evil. They were merely performing a function of their superior biology. They had never attacked with malice; they were simply fulfilling their natural prerogative to expand their race. The sense of preservation was still there, but now it was mixed with a need for vengeance. And a feeling of satisfaction.

The queen's gestation is nearing completion. Prepare to receive a directive . . .

He found himself on the uppermost deck. Overhead hung exposed circuitry and conduits. Beneath his feet lay exposed metal scaffolding above a hundred other scaffoldings just the same, spiraling downward into infinity, and row after row of honeycomb alcoves filled with inanimate drones. To the human Picard, the sight was dizzying. To Locutus, it was unremarkable; the Borg's vision focused on what was closest to him, the better to detect intruders or beings to be immediately assimilated. Distant objects receded into near invisibility: height meant nothing. Only an individual could be afraid of falling.

Only individuals would desire to see colors, to appreciate aesthetics; Borg vision detected shades of gray because those were the functional colors of the Borg cube.

Levels Twenty-two A through Thirty-nine A now at acceptable life-support levels, ready for habitation.

Picard began to move slowly, deliberately, at the Collective's steady pace. He was keenly aware that he had beamed onto the precise spot where Battaglia and his search party had started out. Unlike them, he needed no coordinates to guide him.

He had grown sufficiently accustomed to the Collective's steady patter in his mind to focus on his own thoughts. He let Locutus guide his feet and let his mind recall each individual of the lost away team. He wanted to remember them separately; it fell to his responsibility to notify their families when he returned to the *Enterprise*.

If he returned, the thought whispered, and he corrected it quickly, firmly. *When.*

He could not let himself forget the cost of his own reluctance to face the Borg alone. The lost were not faceless officers, aware of the dangers of service aboard a starship. Each one had a history, loved ones, dreams. And Picard fought against the Collective to remember them as such.

There was Lionardo Battaglia, of course—a sharp, ambitious young man, but one with depth. When duty had brought him to the captain's quarters, Battaglia had immediately recognized the music Picard had been listening to: Puccini. He had spoken knowledgeably of the composer's life.

Though Battaglia was still alive, Picard had to think of him as lost. He could not cloud his mission with thoughts of rescue. Saving Battaglia could mean the loss of more than just Picard.

Instead, he focused on the dead—the truly lost. There was Amrita Satchitanand, whom he had met only briefly when she had first reported to duty aboard the *Enterprise*. He remembered her as a lithe, diminutive woman with skin the color of coffee with cream and an elegance to her movements that reminded him of Hindu temple dancers.

There was Jorge Costas, tall, dark eyed, and proud, who had come from a large family in Starfleet, all of whom would feel his loss. There was Noel DeVrie from Holland, painfully young, with an eager attitude and hair the color of sunlight, as pale as Costas was dark.

He moved past a row of darkened chambers, each one housing the silhouette of an upright, sleeping Borg. *The sleep that is not sleep,* he thought. The Borg did not dream. Their presence made him wary, but as he passed by, they remained silent and still, adrift in mindless existence.

Footsteps coming toward him. Locutus took no notice, but Picard tensed at the sight of a drone looming swiftly in his vision—coming, he knew with Collective instinct, from the birthplace of the queen. The drone had once been humanoid, though its original sex and species had been so long submerged that they had been washed away, like the tide wearing down stone, leaving smooth, bland features in its wake.

No alarm was sounded in the group consciousness, no call to action given, but Picard froze nonetheless, remembering how swiftly Battaglia and the others had been taken. The drone neared and lifted an arm terminating in a single, viciously sharp blade. Picard rested a finger on his communicator badge, ready to touch it if need be, to warn those on the *Enterprise,* just as Battaglia had done with his last breath.

The Borg moved within an arm's length, the arm still raised. And then he walked on, brushing against Picard as he passed.

Picard let go a long breath, then stilled his human mind. He allowed the Collective to become ascendant and resumed his steady pace.

He let the mind of the Borg draw him over the metal scaffold, beneath pulsing lights that might have dazzled human eyes. In the ship, all was silent. Locutus felt safe, nestled in the bosom of the Collective, a part of hundreds of others. Picard felt horribly alone.

It was not far to the single enclosed chamber on the ship. Picard paused in the open entryway and stood in the pulsing light—a longer wavelength than that in the rest of the ship, though his Borg's eyes could not identify the color.

The chamber was vast, high ceilinged, fogged with humidity; in the far misting shadows, an exoskeleton of conduits hung on the walls, pumping in specially warmed and dampened air, filtering the environment. Small, slickly shining nutrient tubes dangled down unused, a tangle of black snakes.

Captain Picard, Battaglia had whispered, *we have found the queen . . .*

T'Lana had just boarded the lift that would take her up to the bridge when she spotted Commander Worf in the corridor. He caught her eye and lifted a finger, a signal, she decided, for her to wait for him.

Out of courtesy, she did so, though she did not relish the opportunity to be alone in his presence.

He entered the lift and gave her a nod in thanks as the doors closed behind him.

"Bridge." For a few seconds, they rode in silence. And then Commander Worf said, "That was most gracious, Counselor. What you said to Captain Picard."

The remark caught her off guard, but she realized that the Klingon was attempting to be professional, courteous. To his credit, he was trying to establish a good working relationship. He had made the comment because he was loyal to Captain Picard, and he wished to show his support of T'Lana's sentiment.

Even flawed instruments, she told herself, could sometimes give correct readings.

She knew that she ought to respond positively; it was paramount, at such a critical time, that the crew function together effectively. But something in his demeanor made her hesitate to reply. He broke off eye contact a bit too quickly, and his tone bore a hint of shyness; he even took a step back, failing to maintain the normal physical distance between colleagues.

He was behaving so, T'Lana realized, because as a male he had noticed that she was a female. He was attracted to her and attempting to suppress it.

This alone would have been enough to unsettle her. But there was further reason: she had noted the powerfulness of his build and the fact that his fierce profile could, even by Vulcan terms, be considered handsome.

She did not approve of her own reaction. She lifted her chin, realizing that the gesture might be read as defiant but unable to prevent it in time. "I did what I deemed logical." She kept her tone cool.

"I saw no logic in it," Worf countered. "I saw loyalty and kindness."

T'Lana did not answer because she knew of nothing appropriate to say. She stared steadily at the seam in the lift doors and told herself that she felt no emotion: no longing and no outrage.

They rode in silence to the bridge.

In sickbay, Beverly Crusher glanced up from her work at the glowing legends on an overhead console. One steadily moving line in a graph, accompanied by numerical data below, represented Jean-Luc's brain activity; a green blip nearby indicated that the neutralizer chip was working properly. The blip was accompanied by a softly pulsing chirp, so that she need not monitor it visually, but she found it increasingly difficult to tear her gaze away.

She knew it should take the captain less than an hour to accomplish what he needed to do; ideally, it should take him a matter of minutes. Even so, she did not care to spend a single moment waiting anxiously, which she would certainly do if she did not find a way to occupy herself. It was hard enough just to blot out the image of Jean-Luc as Locutus, to intentionally disremember the nightmare of the first moment she had stood on the *Enterprise* bridge and seen Locutus on the viewscreen—of the first moment she had looked into Locutus's eyes and seen that Jean-Luc wasn't there anymore.

It had been hard enough to walk beside him to the transporter room in his guise as Borg; she had kept reassuring herself by looking into his eyes and verifying that the man she knew and loved was still there. But he had moved with a stiff, inhumanly mechanical gait, and each time he had spoken, the sound chilled her: the inflection belonged to Locutus, not the captain.

It was difficult to remember, too, the rage that had consumed him when the Borg had invaded the *Enterprise*-E. When he had first confessed that he heard the voice of the Collective, she had wondered whether that rage—so mindless, so fierce that he had been willing to sacrifice everything, including his crew, his sanity—had been rekindled. But to her relief, he had remained relentlessly rational. He could not bear the loss of even four officers, and when he asked that she re-create Locutus, she had hardly questioned the decision. But now, sitting alone in her sickbay, watching the effects of that decision play out over a graph of colored lights and numbers, she allowed herself to acknowledge what she had done.

T'Lana had certainly hit a nerve earlier. Beverly wondered herself if she had made her decision based on the emotions of a lover over the objections of a doctor, just not in the way T'Lana had thought. Logically, Beverly knew that her reaction to the captain's plan would have been the same prior to their admitting their feelings for each other. It would have been the same for anyone in her charge. That wasn't at issue. Neither was the question of whether she was blindly agreeing with a lover, as T'Lana had seemed to imply. Beverly knew she was a strong enough person that she would not lose herself just because she was seeing someone. But that was tied into her confusion now.

Beverly did wonder why she had not put up more of an argument. The only explanation she had was that she was trying not to look like the worried lover. If she debated Jean-Luc more on the issue, would she have come across as the chief medical officer or as his partner? Now she'd never know, because she hadn't allowed herself the question at the time. She hadn't given anyone—but most of all herself—the chance to wonder if she had stopped the captain, would it have been out of concern for his importance to the ship or his importance to her? Had she given in because she didn't want to come across as unprofessional? Her gut instinct told her that wasn't the case. She and Jean-Luc had been close long before they ever got together. But at the same time, the perception that her decisions might be based in emotion rather than logic was now there. T'Lana had proved that. Beverly knew that she was, above all else, chief medical officer, but it was the perception she was battling—largely with herself.

She was not feeling particularly logical at the moment. She had, for the most fleeting of instants, allowed herself to consider the possibility that the worst might happen. That the Borg . . .

She pulled herself up short. She had the proof in front of her in the blinking green light: Jean-Luc's neutralizer was functioning perfectly. And Worf and Geordi were monitoring the captain's physical movements aboard the Borg vessel; if anything went wrong, they would notify her immediately. The worst would *not* happen. Even if it did, there were solutions. There were *always* solutions.

And, she had decided, the best way for her to remedy her anxiety was to work on finding one of them. With luck, it would never be needed, but would be added to the scanty volume of research on the Borg.

Beverly forced her attention to the monitor in front of her. It displayed a rotating model of a double helix: the DNA molecule from a Borg drone.

How was an androgynous drone linked to the group consciousness transformed into an individuated female capable of independent thought?

She fingered a toggle and brought up the information they had on the Borg queen. For a long moment, she stared at it. The composition of the queen's flesh and blood did not differ from that of a drone's in any significant way, and the structure of her DNA differed not at all—the fully assimilated Borg lacked the X and Y chromosomes that produced males and females in most humanoid species. In terms of the queen's body chemistry, there was a slight amount of a hormonal compound that paralleled a human female's estrogen, but the question was, what initiated the process that brought about the transformation? What caused the hormone to appear in the first place? Was it something buried in the DNA?

"No difference," Beverly whispered to herself. No difference in the DNA. A slight difference in the blood, unaccounted for by a transformation in bodily organs, which might supply the estrogenlike hormone. So what caused the difference between the queen and the drones?

There was the difference in appearance, for one. Feminine features. The lips flushed with color, the skin not quite so pale, and . . .

Beverly hesitated and frowned. She pressed a control and enlarged an image of the queen that had long ago been imprinted by Data's positronic brain.

The queen's skin glistened. Jean-Luc had told

her, long ago, of the revulsion he had felt at the Queen's touch. It had been damp, sticky . . . coated with some sort of viscous semiliquid compound.

Beverly drew in a breath, then pushed another control and enlarged the image still further.

"Royal jelly," she said in a tone of wonder. It was the compound secreted by the pharyngeal glands of worker bees, fed to all bee larvae. But one special larva received *only* royal jelly—and this exclusive diet produced a queen for the colony.

Could this nutrient trigger the development of the hormone? Or might the nutrient itself be broken down into the hormone in the bloodstream?

Beverly could not help glancing up at the blinking green light—showing that Jean-Luc's neutralizer chip was still working—before putting the computer to work on the answer.

As he sat in the captain's chair with T'Lana beside him, Worf studied the image of the Borg cube on the main viewscreen. Like all the others on the bridge, he was unable to tear his gaze from it for very long—as if by staring at it hard enough he might be able to see where Captain Picard was and what he was doing.

Geordi La Forge, of course, knew better than all of them. He stood at the engineering console behind Worf, monitoring the readout that tracked the captain's position aboard the Borg vessel. The Klingon had instructed him to alert them if the captain veered off course or stalled in his progress to the queen's chamber. In the *Enterprise* transporter chamber, an operator was ready to beam the captain aboard at the first sign of trouble.

At that moment, Worf was also thinking of the past: of the moment he and Captain Picard had stood, in magnetized boots, on the gleaming white outer hull of the *Enterprise*. It had been like standing on the curving surface of a small, dead moon against the dark backdrop of space. He and Picard had gone in order to stop the Borg from finishing work on a transmitter. More specifically, Worf was remembering the instant he had wrested himself free from an attacking Borg, only to glance up and find one about to kill the captain.

Worf had reacted smoothly, without hesitation or thought. He had blasted the drone into eternity with the epithet, *Assimilate this.* And he had watched with pleasure as the impact of the blast had caused the drone to lose its footing and go sailing backward into space, receding swiftly in the frictionless vacuum until it could no longer be seen.

He did not regret killing the Borg that day. If he had not, it would certainly have killed the captain, an act that might eventually have brought the Borg victory. But Worf regretted the attitude that had seized him, the sense of satisfaction and smug triumph at destroying an enemy.

Now he looked at Lieutenant Nave, stone faced and grief stricken, at the conn. She sat, rigid and stiff, in her chair, one hand clutching the console as if it were the only thing supporting her. Her eyes were wide and vacant, reminding Worf uncomfortably of how he had functioned after losing Jadzia. Clearly Nave had cared more for Lieutenant Battaglia than the Klingon had realized.

He stared at the Borg cube and thought of the four crew members who had recently been lost to the Borg. He thought, too, of the captain and the enormous sacrifice he was making—embracing the specter of Locutus again, going alone onto the Borg vessel. He had seen the bitterness in the captain's eyes. It was one thing for one's body to be vanquished by a foe, but to allow one's mind and spirit to be degraded was unthinkable. Yet such extreme situations called for personal sacrifice.

Worf knew that if he had to face the enemy again, he would kill without question, so long as it was necessary. But this time, he would take no pleasure in killing, find no sense of victory or pleasure. This time, he would remember that behind each Borg was an assimilated—and tormented— individual who yearned to be freed, one like Captain Picard or Lieutenant Battaglia. And he indulged in a most un–Klingon-like thought: *Would it not be better to be cautious, to avoid killing, to save as many Borg as possible with the thought of rehabilitating them?*

Worf released a sigh. His life with humans, especially his marriage to Jadzia, had softened him greatly. And perhaps—just perhaps—the presence of the Vulcan counselor was influencing him, too.

He shot her a sidewise look. Poised and impassive, she sat beside him, her blue-black hair and brows contrasting starkly with her pale skin, her dark blue eyes fixed steadily on the image of the Borg cube. Unlike the others on the bridge, however, she showed no hint of turmoil or revulsion. *Admirable,* Worf thought, to be so cool and efficient under such pressure. Were they not averse to fighting, Vulcans would make greatly effective warriors.

Jadzia, he decided, would have liked her.

T'Lana's lashes flickered. She had detected his gaze; her expression hardened very faintly as she looked back at the viewscreen. He could not know the truth at that moment: that she was looking at the Borg ship and remembering what she had told Captain Wozniak about the Jem'Hadar.

In their case, diplomacy fails. They are mindless creatures whose sole focus is killing. They cannot be reasoned with.

Worf forced his gaze and his thoughts away from her, and stared back at the Borg cube. He hoped that he would not have to test his newfound resolution not to kill the Borg unnecessarily; he hoped for the captain's swift success.

But he had learned, when Jadzia had died, that hope was sometimes thwarted and that the very worst was indeed capable of happening.

At the helm, Sara Nave was holding on.

She was staring out at the Borg ship trying to

focus on her duty, on her ability to react swiftly the instant she was needed, just as she had forced herself, after her parents died, to focus on her finals at the academy. The problem was that this time there was nothing to study, nothing to learn, nothing to distract her. She had nothing to do other than sit and wait . . . which made it extremely difficult not to imagine what was occurring there, on the ship in front of her eyes.

Holding on, her father had called it. When things were so impossible that all you could do was keep breathing, keep taking that next step, keep going until finally you were somewhere else, where things weren't so terrible.

Her dad's mother had died long ago, in a skimmer accident, when Sara was still a girl. He had just gotten the news and was still dazed when she had hugged him, crying, and asked him how he was.

Holding on, he had said dully, no doubt feeling the same emptiness, the same disbelief, the same helpless anger Nave felt now.

Duty was her only link to sanity at the moment. Without it, she would have to think about Lio and what was happening to him aboard the Borg vessel this very instant.

Assimilate. Such an innocuous-sounding word for such an unspeakably monstrous act. If he had simply been killed, it would have been awful enough. She had assumed that his broken body was transported to sickbay. When she found out that Lio was still out there, she was temporarily awash with joy and hope, until she realized that he was being forced to suffer a far worse violation.

Despite her efforts to suppress it, Lio's voice spoke unbidden in her mind. *But it wasn't really Joel. They'd taken him, changed him, defiled his body with these, these weapons and cybernetic attachments to his head, his eyes, his arms. He was no longer human . . . And the worst part was . . . I couldn't destroy the monster they'd made of him . . .*

When her parents had been killed, Nave had not remembered the names of the two warring planets; she had not wanted to know which side was responsible for the destruction of the *Lowe*. In her mind, her parents' deaths were a faultless tragedy. She had been too stunned to think about blame.

Now it took near-impossible effort not to think of the Borg, not to be filled with venom at the sight of their ship, at the utterance of their name.

When Commander Worf had told her that there would be no second away team—that Captain Picard would be going alone onto the Borg vessel—Nave had been frustrated beyond tears.

There were only two things she desperately wanted. The first was to go onto the Borg ship and rescue Lio. Even though he had not been there to hear, she had promised him, standing in his quarters, that she would go to the Borg vessel and find him and bring him home. And she did not intend to break that promise.

The second thing she wanted was to go onto the

enemy ship and kill as many of the Borg as she could find. She did not want rehabilitation for them, or even justice. She wanted vengeance and blood.

The queen was beautiful and grotesque.

"You," Picard breathed, so quietly he could scarcely hear the word himself. He knew the face all too well: distinctly feminine, high cheeked, ageless, elegant.

It was the face of the queen who had desired and pursued Locutus; it was the face of the queen Picard had fought, in Earth's past, and killed with his own hands. Here she was reborn, her features in easy repose, her eyelids shut as though she were sleeping, trapped in a deep and vaguely pleasant dream.

We were very close, you and I. You can still hear our song.

But her voice was silent now. She was no more than a bust: a lifeless head and shoulders. They sat atop an exposed snakelike spine fashioned of bone and steel and blood. The whole of it, from the queen's neck down, was enveloped by a translucent, glistening cocoon . . . nutrients, Locutus knew. The nectar allowed only the queen.

But her sculpted body, of dully gleaming black metal, awaited her nearby, tended by two dead-eyed, ghostly drones. The body stood in a gruesomely alert fashion, legs and arms animate and slightly twitching, almost as if impatient for the absent head to come and rest upon its shoulders.

Picard moved over the threshold into the chamber and was relieved that neither drone glanced up from its task.

He had allowed himself an instant's reaction to the queen's familiar face, but now he was determined to waste no more time. He stepped cautiously toward the bed where she rested. So great was Picard's loathing that Locutus's impassive features began to contort from the emotion.

He kept his prosthetic arm—the arm the Borg had, ironically, given him so long ago—lowered by his side. He did not intend to strike until the last instant, when he stood directly beside her. He did not want to give the drones enough time to understand what was happening, to move in to protect her.

He stared down at her throat, its delicate veins throbbing with the first signs of life beneath a layer of glistening gel. One quick stroke, and that life would be snuffed out and the universe safe. He moved in, so close to her that his thigh brushed against the edge of the bed on which she lay. With a single thought, he activated the neural circuits that controlled the prosthetic arm and lifted it. The deadly blade at its tip, where a human hand had once been, began to whir.

He bent down.

As he did, her eyes opened, stark and wide, quicksilver, with no iris, no pupil. Yet she saw. In less than an instant, she saw—as if she had always known he was coming, as if she had been biding her time in order to startle him—and she shrieked, beauty transformed into a gorgon's rictus.

The cry roared through the Collective, so powerful and shrill and outraged that it blotted out every other sound, every thought. Picard closed his eyes at a mental pain so intense he feared his skull would shatter. It was so much worse than the sound that had come over the *Enterprise*'s comlink earlier. He staggered, only an agonized burst of will keeping him on his feet. Miraculously, he opened his eyes again, steadied his arm, tried to bring the whirring blade down to meet the tender skin of that feminine throat.

It was too late. The galvanized drones were on him now. One stood behind him and gripped the prosthetic arm as Picard tried to raise it. Picard cried out as the upper part of the arm was wrenched up, then back at an unnatural angle, snapping the human base of bone.

The second drone approached from the side, his limb terminating in a double-edged rotating blade. He aimed it menacingly at the center of Picard's chest.

Instinctively, the captain flinched at first. And then he set his jaw and straightened.

"Yes," he croaked. "Kill me. Go ahead." Better to die than to give them access to his mind, and the location of the *Enterprise,* and critical data about Starfleet. Better to die than to become one of them again; he would not be the cause of another Wolf 359, would not be used against the *Enterprise*. Worf would see the ship safely home; humankind would rally and defeat the enemy yet a third time.

He bared his chest and moved forward, embracing the blade, wondering whether it was capable of penetrating Locutus's molded black carapace.

It was. Its bite was stunningly painful, even to his transformed Borg body. His muscles, his internal organs spasmed intensely; his eyes widened at the accompanying fleeting flash of light. He fought to draw in air and found it tainted with his blood. Even so, he found the will and strength to press forward, to force the blade in deeper, to his heart.

Before his vision dimmed entirely, he sensed the drones moving around him, catching him as he fell. He lifted his face and saw that of the Borg queen, frowning.

He surrendered to darkness, praying the blow had been fatal.

9

PICARD WOKE LYING ON A BED. THE BORG CARAPACE covering his chest had been removed, and the chalky skin beneath it was pristine, unscarred, as if it had never been pierced and torn. There was no pain at all, not even from the broken arm.

The worst possible thing had happened. He had failed, this just as Janeway and T'Lana had predicted. Had he let his desire for revenge blind him to the inevitability of this outcome?

The fact that he had not died filled him with unspeakable frustration, unspeakable fury. He tried to rise and found himself bound by heavy restraints. Vainly, he thrashed against them, near weeping with rage and self-loathing. The one promise he had made to himself—that he would never allow himself to be used again to hurt his own kind—was about to be broken.

He took only a small degree of comfort to find that the neutralizer chip was still functioning—for the moment.

He was no longer in the birthing chamber but in an open area, next to a single white, solitary wall. Macabre surgical instruments—drills, saws, scalpels, useful for fashioning flesh as well as metal—hung ready for use. Their chilling significance was not lost on him.

And he had exchanged positions with the queen. He was now supine while she stood looking down at him. He was all too aware that the bed was in fact a diagnostic table; he glanced up and saw the monitors tracking his life functions.

The queen had assumed her body and wore it gracefully, naturally, with a dancer's bearing. Her face and eyes—so unlike those of others of her race—were utterly alive, shining with humor, confidence, pride, rippling with subtler nuances of emotion. *High-spirited,* he might have called her, in another century, under different circumstances.

Her features wore a thick layer of shimmering gel, remnants of the chrysalis.

He yearned to reach out, as he had only a few years before, and with his own hands snap her lovely neck, watch as her shining eyes flickered and dimmed. He had the strength of a Borg now. He could do it so easily, if only he could lift his arms . . .

"So," she said, the corners of her lips curving upward with dark amusement. Her tone was playful, her voice feminine, alluring, the whisper of thousands speaking as one. "There's a human expression, isn't there? The third time is the charm . . . ?"

She reached down and laid a glistening hand upon his shoulder. Her touch was cold and moist, a toad's; he recoiled from it. She gave a small, easy laugh.

"You've come back, as you were always meant to. I sensed you, you know. Even before I was born. I came to life before I was quite ready, just for you.

"Have you come willingly to me, now? It's how I've always wanted you: willing, eager."

His expression hardened, and he turned his gaze away.

"It doesn't matter. Come to me as the individual Jean-Luc Picard . . . or as a drone." Her amusement returned. "You've already done most of the work for us this time, very thoughtful. Is this the work of your talented Doctor Crusher?" She stroked his arm. "You see, I learned many things from you when you were last Locutus. I knew you loved her, even then, though you would not admit it even to yourself. But in the end, you will come to me."

"Never willingly," he snarled. "As you saw, I would rather die."

Her tone cooled abruptly; she lifted her chin, regal, haughty. "It doesn't matter. Either way, the destruction of your ship and your world is assured."

"It is *your* ship," he said with venom, "*your* world, that will be destroyed."

She gave a short, harsh laugh at his bravado, but the liquid metal eyes flashed with anger. "Did you not learn from Wolf 359? Do you want to see it repeated to understand?"

"We are wiser," he countered. "My people know you are here. Even if you were to kill me, they know what to do. They won't stop until you are destroyed."

"Ah, yes." She tilted her head, her tone mocking. "The brave crew of the *Enterprise.* We expect them to follow you, of course. And *you* will help us to be ready for them. I have created a special directive just for you. You will be my guardian, my protector."

Her voice softened, grew soothing. "Come willingly, Jean-Luc. Make your people lay down their weapons. All this thrashing, all this fighting, all this resistance is so . . . futile." She leaned down and ran her finger along the line of his jaw; he shuddered at the act. "We could make this pleasant, you know." She paused and brought her lips close to his ear; her breath was cool and soft. "It *is* pleasant for you, isn't it, Locutus? To be home, with no cares, no decisions. To truly belong . . ."

His lips twisted with disgust. "Locutus is not here."

Unruffled, she tilted her face and studied him with gleaming eyes. "Oh, but he will be." She straightened. "Make your decision, Jean-Luc Picard. You could be with me willingly and retain a degree of autonomy. Once I am sure of your loyalty, you could even rule beside me. You humans speak of pleasure, of ecstasy, but you cannot imagine the thrill of such power, the utter joy that would be yours . . ." Her tone flattened. "Or you can be another drone. You can have your will stripped from you and suffer, as you did before, with your poor little mind 'violated' by mine."

"Go to hell," Picard said.

Her chin lifted sharply at his words, her eyes narrowing as she took a step back from the table.

"You thought to kill me, fool. Do you think I am so stupid as to let it happen again? That was your first, greatest mistake, and your decision now will be your second. I must finish my genesis, but when I and my ship are ready, I will rise. And when I do, you will be waiting for me—as Locutus. Together, we will tear apart your beloved *Enterprise,* killing your crew—except your precious Beverly. She, I will have you turn into a drone. Then, together, we will tear through the Alpha Quadrant. We will not bother pausing to assimilate a single being. We will head straight for Earth and annihilate your planet. And when your Federation manages to regroup and comes to render aid—too late to do any good—that is when the fun will really begin."

She did not need to gesture or call to the drones. She drew them to her side with a thought. Even Picard felt the pull—and with it, a spasm of pure horror in the pit of his stomach. He looked up to see a pair of drones, one on either side, above him; he could not have said whether they were the same ones that had attacked him in the birthing chamber. One reached for the wall and retrieved a metal instrument: a long, needle-fine drill. The other held a pair of delicate pincers.

Picard closed his eyes as the tip of the drill found his right temple and for a fleeting instant rested there, cold, unrelentingly sharp.

Not again, not again.

He did not let himself scream. The sensation was that of a pinch, then a sting as the drill found its way through the skin; when pierced, the bone reacted with an intense, dazzling burst of pain that faded quickly.

The brain, of course, felt nothing at all. The pincers followed, cold and swift; he knew the instant that they found and locked onto the neutralizer chip and slowly began to draw it out.

His mind was like a blaze. It raged at first, angry and wild, determinedly ascendant. And then his will was slowly bled from him, escaping like oxygen from a breached hull. He struggled to hold on to it, to fight, but he was a single flame struggling in a relentless vacuum. In the end, he could not hold out; his resistance was extinguished. Only a feeble blue glow remained, flickering, bitter. Watching. Waiting.

In sickbay, Beverly was finally lost in thought.

It had not been easy. With each passing minute

that Jean-Luc was gone, her anxiety increased, but she was determined to find a solution to the mystery of a Borg drone's metamorphosis into a queen. Her doubts and concerns were in the past. There was nothing she could do now but prepare for the future.

Her research indicated a fairly simple solution to the introduction of the feminizing hormone: a complex form was no doubt present in the gelatinous nutrient, which could easily be absorbed through the skin or administered intravenously, then broken down in the future queen's equivalent of a humanoid bloodstream.

The question was whether the Borg produced the feminizing hormone artificially, or whether, like human bees, the drones naturally created the nutrient gel and somehow collected it for the queen.

If it was the latter—

Beverly frowned slightly as she directed the lab's computer to produce a tissue sample taken from the Borg Locutus. The frown deepened to a scowl as a shrill beep interrupted her train of thought. She glanced up, distracted, and stared for a half second at the blinking red light on the monitor screen before she realized what it was. Perhaps her mind had not *let* her understand what she saw because it was the one thing she had never wanted to see.

"No!" she said, at the exact instant she

instinctively struck her combadge. "Crusher to bridge! Worf! The neutralizer chip has malfunctioned!"

Doctor Crusher's anguished cry galvanized Worf; he did not waste an instant in reflection or remorse. He rose and leaned over Sara Nave at the helm. "Evasive maneuvers," he ordered. "Set a random course, as far distant as possible while keeping us within transporter range." Her fingers moved swiftly over the controls—but not quite swiftly enough.

Worf glanced up just in time to see the bright ball of light emerge from the Borg cube's underbelly and streak toward the *Enterprise*. It was followed by another . . . and another . . .

The deck beneath his feet heaved; thunder roared in his ears. Nave was slammed back against her chair, then forward against the helm. Worf was forced to his knees; the side of his cheek struck the edge of Nave's chair.

He pulled himself up as the ship shuddered. Pressing his combadge, he shouted over the background chatter of incoming damage reports. "Transporter room. Keep your lock on the captain's signal and prepare to beam him to the holding cell."

"Aye, sir."

Worf closed the channel. Sara Nave, still working at the helm, kept her focus on the viewscreen, doing her best to dodge the volley of fire aimed in their direction.

He tapped his combadge again. "Doctor Crusher," he said, "report to the holding cell. We're beaming the captain there."

"Already on my way," she replied.

Worf turned to La Forge. "Shields?"

"Still holding," he reported.

For now, Worf thought as Nave took them out of the Borg's weapons range. It was a fine line she was dancing, keeping them out of the line of fire but within transporter range. It wasn't clear how long until the Borg's long-range weaponry would be active, but Worf sensed it wouldn't be long. Once the immediate threat seemed over, Nave allowed for a half turn in his direction. Her eyes were lit with an emotion—*hope* Worf might have called it had it not had such a dark edge to it.

"Lieutenant," he said, "you are acting chief of security." He paused. "For the moment, however, *you* are critically needed at the helm. Keep the ship's course completely random. We can't allow the captain to anticipate the *Enterprise*'s next move before we retrieve him."

He watched as the light went out of her, so that only the dark remained. "Yes, sir," she answered quietly and returned to her work.

As he turned to move toward the door, he caught T'Lana's defiant glare in his direction. If she had been of any other race, Worf would have sworn he saw a look of smugness as a reminder that she had anticipated the worst. She said nothing as Worf swept past her to the turbolift, but the condemnation was still there. As if she was blaming *him* for what was happening.

By the time she arrived in the holding area, Beverly was numb. She had forced herself to be so, allowing herself to think only of what needed to be immediately done. She had prepared a hypo of nanites that would reverse Jean-Luc's transformation into a drone, and while she would inject him with it immediately—along with a strong sedative to prevent him from attacking—she intended to repair or replace the neutralizer chip as quickly as possible. It would immediately free Jean-Luc from the influence of the Collective so that she would not have to restrain him while the nanites did their work.

Worf and three armed security guards stood waiting for her beside the bed that had been placed in the cell. The Klingon's expression was one of fierce determination. Crusher didn't ask whether he intended to put any distance between the *Enterprise* and the Borg ship—especially after the attack— but she certainly didn't see any signs of retreat in his eyes.

He directed a single sharp glance at Beverly by way of acknowledgment. "Do you have a sedative ready, Doctor?"

Beverly silently produced the hypospray from the pocket of her lab coat and displayed it.

"Phasers on stun," Worf told the security team and raised his own; the four took aim at the empty bed. The Klingon tapped his combadge. "Ensign Luptowski . . . ?"

"Ready, sir," the young voice replied. *"The captain's communicator is disabled, but the signal from the transponder is clear."*

"Beam him aboard."

As the transporter beam began to shimmer, Beverly braced herself. She would be prepared, she told herself, for the dull, inhuman look in Locutus's eyes.

But she was not prepared for what she saw.

The glimmering miasma of the beam cleared . . . but no one lay on the bed. Worf spoke into the air again. "Ensign? Was there a malfunction?"

"No, sir," Luptowski answered.

Beverly and Worf approached the bed. Beverly leaned in and reached a hand toward the three items that lay there, arranged in a neat row: the transponder she had placed in Jean-Luc's right temple; his communicator, mangled and scarred, as if someone had tried to saw it in half; and the neutralizer chip, marred by a single dark drop of blood.

She failed to touch them. A sudden roar, so loud she could not hear her own cry of pain and surprise, reverberated in her skull; a millisecond later, the deck pitched sideways. Her ribs struck the edge of the bed, her outstretched hand flattening against the now-empty bed. She was aware, in the chaos, of Worf beside her, struggling for purchase, his legs tangling briefly with hers.

The ship righted itself with a lurch. Beverly pushed herself up and scrambled across the platform to retrieve the items so freshly removed from Jean-Luc's person. As she did, Worf got to his feet and pressed his combadge.

"Worf to bridge!" Silence. Clutching the precious chips, Beverly turned toward the Klingon. Worf scowled and thumped his combadge again. "Worf to bridge! Commander La Forge, report!"

Silence again, and then static.

The blast blinded Nave and hurled her sideways from her chair onto the deck. She tried to draw in air and couldn't; her ribs responded with a sickening jolt of pain.

Don't panic, don't panic, just got the wind knocked out of you . . .

Her first instinct was to get back to her station, back to the conn. She blinked hard, but the strong afterimage left by the nova-bright blast faded only slightly; she had to feel for her chair and use it to pull herself up.

She let go a hitching cough, so painful it brought tears, then sucked in air in a rush.

It smelled of smoke and scorched circuits, and left her dizzied. "Counselor!" she shouted. "Commander La Forge!" The blast had affected her hearing as well; her voice sounded muffled, distant. She stood an instant and listened carefully for a reply—and realized that the life-support alarm had been buzzing, low and harsh, all the while.

"Commander La Forge! Counselor!" The acrid air made her cough again. As her vision began slowly to clear, she saw the bridge through a film of smoke. It was dark except for the blinking consoles and the low-level emergency lights on the deck, which served as her guide. Eyes streaming, she staggered the few steps back to the conn and leaned heavily against it.

Weapons were off-line. The conn had gone off-line as well, but she doggedly kept punching controls until she managed to bring it up on manual. The ship had just started to drift; she set it back on its random course. At the instant she finished, the klaxon fell blessedly silent.

She heard a sudden spasm of coughing to her right. "Allen?" she called. Ensign John Allen was stationed at security communications. She glanced in his direction and saw his shadowy form bent over in his chair.

"I'm all right," Allen gasped, though he protectively cradled one arm. "My board is down." And then he let go a sound of pure amazement. "Good lord. *Look . . .*"

He was staring overhead. Nave followed his gaze and saw it: the narrow crack in the hull that revealed, beyond the mists of smoke and the faint glimmer of a force field, blackness and stars. It was, Nave thought absurdly, like staring up at a sliver of night sky.

"Hull breach requiring repair. Oxygen levels have dropped to substandard levels," the computer reported calmly. "Toxic particulate matter detected. Filtration systems off-line and in need of repair. Temporary evacuation required."

Someone behind her shifted and groaned. "Commander?" she called.

"I'm okay," Commander La Forge mumbled, but his tone—and the fact that he was still huddled on the deck beneath the engineering station—said otherwise. A waft of smoke rose from his console, which spewed red sparks and sizzled ominously.

"Take care of him," Nave said to the ensign.

"Aye, sir, I've got him," Allen said and rose stiffly.

But T'Lana was still unaccounted for. Nave scanned the area around the counselor's chair and saw, behind it and to its left, the Vulcan's still form, supine on the deck.

"Counselor." She knelt down at once. T'Lana was pale, motionless; her eyes were closed. There was a gash at her throat, just beneath her left jaw, and dark green liquid had spilled down her neck and soaked the shoulder of her uniform.

Nave reached out with an unsteady hand to feel for a pulse. At her touch, T'Lana's eyes snapped open.

"Counselor. You've been wounded." Instinctively, Nave pressed her combadge and said, "Sickbay."

T'Lana's lips parted; she struggled to speak.

"It's okay," Nave soothed, even as a voice filtered over the comm channel.

"Sickbay. Nurse Ojibwa here."

"This is the bridge. We need medics up here *stat.* I've got a Vulcan who's losing blood, and I think Commander La Forge is injured—"

"Sending them up now . . ."

Commander Worf's voice overrode Ojibwa's. *"Worf to Nave. Lieutenant, what's happening on the bridge?"*

"Hull breach, sir, conn is online, but we have wounded . . ." Nave looked down at the growing stain on T'Lana's uniform. The Vulcan's eyes were wide, her gaze distant. "Counselor!"

Nave reached for the wound and gently fingered it until she felt the small puncture, probably caused by a piece of shrapnel, she decided. She pressed her hand firmly against it until she felt certain she had stanched the flow. T'Lana's blood was feverishly warm.

"We're sending medics. Transfer control to auxiliary bridge. Evacuate as soon as you can. Worf out."

Nave absently touched her combadge, cutting off the channel. "Medics are coming!" she called to Allen. The ensign had helped Commander La Forge up into his chair; La Forge held a hand to his brow, dazed. One of his cybernetic eyes had gone ominously dark.

T'Lana tried again to speak. Nave studied her and saw something she had never before seen in a

Vulcan's eyes: horror. The counselor could not quite manage a full whisper, but Nave watched her lips form the words.

Your face is black.

Nave was momentarily confused; she ran the back of her free hand across her forehead and glanced at it. "Soot," she said. "Don't worry, Counselor, it's just soot."

T'Lana struggled and formed another word. *Leave.*

"Not on your life," Nave said.

The Vulcan's chest hitched as she emitted a soft hiccup; a bubble of blood appeared on her lips, followed by a sudden rush that flowed down her chin and joined the stream on her neck. Her eyes rolled back until not much more than the whites were visible.

"Damn," Nave whispered. "Oh, damn, Counselor, don't you dare. Don't you *dare.*"

10

———

IN SICKBAY, CRUSHER WITHDREW THE SURGICAL
stimulator from Geordi La Forge's temple and
watched with satisfaction as his left cybernetic eye
flickered, then began to glow reassuringly.

"Whew," La Forge said. He was sitting up on the
diagnostic bed, looking much better than he had
when Nave and Allen had arrived with him. He
blinked and studied Beverly appreciatively. "Now
that's more like it."

"Just some pressure on your optical circuit.
That's what comes of hitting your head so hard."

La Forge rubbed his scalp ruefully. "Good thing I
have such a thick skull."

Crusher could not quite bring herself to smile.
She was operating numbly, mechanically now. She
could not allow herself to feel, to think about any-

thing other than the present moment, until Jean-Luc was finally back safe aboard the *Enterprise*.

Both she and Geordi glanced up as Worf entered, his customary scowl even grimmer than usual.

"So, Doc . . ." La Forge slid off the edge of the bed to his feet. "Can I go? I've got things to do."

Beverly gave a nod. "You're good."

Worf stepped in front of him. "Commander La Forge, Nelson reports that the bridge should be habitable within the hour. In the meantime, all operations are being run from the auxiliary bridge."

"Are we out of the cube's weapons range?" La Forge asked.

Worf gave a curt nod. "And we should soon be out of scanning range as well."

"We've abandoned the captain?" Beverly asked, trying to keep the accusation out of her voice but knowing she had failed.

"The damage to the ship is extensive," he explained. "There are several hull breaches in the saucer section. The docking bays are all inaccessible. Our shields are still down. The Borg have left us no options."

Worf and La Forge shared a grim look. Beverly understood all too well: *Jean-Luc* had left them with no options.

"So we just give up?" Beverly asked.

"That is what we were ordered to do," Worf acknowledged, but there was something behind his words, something other than defeat. Worf was handling the decision far better than he should have been. Beverly doubted he had any intention of leaving the captain behind.

As such, she decided to play along. "Before he left, the captain said that the Borg cube's engines would be online in less than seven hours." She paused. "That was two hours ago."

Geordi's tone was grim. "That gives us five hours."

"Four," she countered, "to be safe." It was hard not to hold her breath while waiting for Worf to react.

"Understood," Worf said. He paused and glanced at Crusher. She realized that he was waiting for La Forge to leave so that he could speak to her privately.

Geordi took the hint. "I'll be in engineering, then."

Worf nodded. "I'll be in touch with you shortly, Commander."

"Your report, Doctor?" Worf asked as Geordi left sickbay.

"Two dozen injured," she reported without emotion. "Ranging from minor to critical. I had to induce a coma in Ensign McGowan to preserve his higher brain functions." She stood in awkward silence with the Klingon a moment before finally breaking the silence. "If we continue out of the area . . ." she began.

"The captain *did* order us to do so," Worf said. She had guessed right: he had wanted to discuss precisely this matter. And given his uneasy relationship with the Vulcan counselor, he could hardly discuss it with her.

"But you know what would happen if we did," Beverly countered. She could not be neutral on the subject; she could not even try. She had worried earlier about questioning her professionalism, which led to where they were in this moment. She would not let appearances keep her from speaking her mind. She was a Starfleet officer, and Worf was now her commander. She would abide by his decision, but she would not shy away from the conversation this time.

Worf sighed. "The Borg's engines will come online. They will be able to attack and to pursue us and any other vessel or planet they choose." He paused a long moment; his gaze dropped as he uncomfortably shifted his weight. "I . . . made an error of judgment once before, because I followed my heart instead of my orders. My decision cost many lives." He looked up at her. "I do not want to make the same mistake again."

"I understand completely," Beverly responded. "But, in all honesty, this is not the same situation, Worf. It's true you're the captain's loyal friend—"

He began to speak, but Beverly waved him silent.

"I know, *my* heart is involved here, too," she said. "I want to save him more than anyone. But I think that, when the captain gave the order to leave him behind, he was thinking only of the good of the crew."

Worf gave a slow, thoughtful nod. "But I must consider the greater good. If we do not stop the Borg now . . ."

Beverly let the question hang in the air between them. At last, she asked quietly, "And if the ship can't handle another encounter?"

"We will have tried," Worf said. His gaze was confident now that he had made his decision. "I do not relish disobeying a direct order from the captain. But I have an idea of a way we can . . . circumvent his directive."

Beverly's lips broke into a grin.

Worf did not return the smile, of course, but the lines in his face softened. "Thank you, Doctor." He paused. "Is Lieutenant Nave recovering?"

"Yes. She just had a few cracked ribs. I expect to be releasing her back to duty in the next half hour."

"Good," Worf said. "She will be heading security for the away team to rescue the captain."

"I'll tell her to contact you," Beverly responded. As the Klingon turned toward the exit, she added, "Before you go, Worf. Since it looks like we're headed back to the Borg ship, I've been doing some research, and I think I can come up with something to neutralize the queen and give us a chance to destroy the cube."

He frowned. "Neutralize?"

"It's . . . a theory I want to test. I'm sure the queen has metamorphosed from a Borg drone because of a feminizing hormone. If I can develop a chemical to counteract that hormone before we

reach the Borg ship, then we might be able to transform the queen back to a drone . . ."

Worf shrugged. "There is a simpler way, Doctor."

Killing, of course. Beverly briefly averted her
gaze. "I know. But . . . I can't help thinking I'm on
the verge of a breakthrough here. Call it instinct. If
we can transform the queen back into a drone,
then . . . then there might be a way to prevent the
transformation from occurring again. Ever. It would
send the Borg into disarray. Weaken them."

Worf's brows raised; she had caught his interest.
"That," he said, "sounds like a very worthy pursuit, Doctor. If there is any assistance that you
need . . ."

"You'll be the first to know," she said. "Thank
you, Worf." She was referring to more than just his
offer of help; she was thinking of Jean-Luc as she
said it.

He seemed to understand. He hesitated for a moment, then awkwardly, quietly said, "Thank *you,*
Doctor." Then he turned and was gone.

Impatient, Sara Nave ignored the doctor's orders to
remain on her diagnostic bed and wait until
Crusher came to release her. Instead, Nave sat up—
gingerly, because her two cracked ribs, although
healed, felt stiff—and swung herself around so that
she could stand. Holding her tender side, she
headed out toward the lab, where she could hear
Doctor Crusher speaking to someone.

Whoever it was left. The doors closed and Crusher turned around and almost collided with Nave.

"What are *you* doing up, Sara? I thought I was pretty clear that you weren't to budge until I came for you. Those ribs are still knitting. If you don't hold still, they might not heal properly and we'd have to start the process all over again."

"I have to get to the helm," Nave insisted. "It's critical that I monitor the ship's course—"

"You're not the only competent helmsperson on this vessel," Crusher said. "The helm's being taken good care of. Commander Worf will let you know when you're needed. *Unless* you want to go some-where now—and wind up having to come back to sickbay for twice as long." She gestured toward Nave's diagnostic bed. "Now, shall I escort you, or can you find your way back?"

Nave sighed in defeat. "I'll go . . ."

Crusher turned back toward the lab. Nave moved toward her bed, but as she did, she caught sight of Counselor T'Lana lying in a nearby surgical alcove.

She'd been quite worried about the Vulcan. When the medics had carried T'Lana to the lift, Nave had overheard one of them mention she was in shock from blood loss.

Careful not to draw Crusher's attention, Nave moved silently to T'Lana's side. The Vulcan skin was pale, sallow. With her long lashes and cherubic lips, she seemed very, very young—*As young as me,* Nave thought, though she had no idea how to gauge a Vulcan's age. T'Lana's eyes were closed as if she were sleeping, but when Nave stepped up beside her, her eyes snapped open at once.

"Counselor," Nave said, a bit startled. "I didn't mean to disturb you."

"It is not a disturbance." T'Lana was sharp, thoroughly alert. She pushed herself up on her elbows, as if she found it unsettling to be lying down in the presence of someone standing. "It is fortunate that you have come. I was aware that, on the bridge, you applied manual pressure in order to stop my bleeding."

"Yes," Nave said.

"Doctor Crusher said that the action saved my life. Thank you."

Nave felt herself flush. "It was nothing. You would have done the same for me."

T'Lana gave a single grave nod. "Yes. You are a valuable officer. It would be logical."

Nave shook her head and allowed herself a smile. "Naturally."

"I'm glad you are well, Lieutenant," T'Lana said. "What is our course heading? Are we returning to a safe location?"

"I have no idea," Nave said. "I just got out of bed myself; I haven't had the chance to talk to anyone. Frankly, I hope we're returning to the Borg vessel."

"Why would you wish such a thing? It would put the ship and crew in great danger."

Nave's temper flared, and she did not try to keep

the heat from her voice. "Because my friend is there. Because the *captain* is there. Do you think we should just leave them there—to be Borg drones? So that they can fight against us later? So that other Starfleet officers, on some other starship, can come and kill them without even knowing who they are?"

"I would regret losing the captain and a fellow officer," T'Lana said softly. "But leaving would be the logical thing to do."

"What is logical about betraying your friends and crewmates to keep yourself safe?" Nave countered. "If that's logic, then the hell with it. I'll take loyalty any day."

She turned on her heel and—ignoring her aching ribs—went back to her bed.

Half an hour later, Worf stepped off the lift onto the bridge. The air had been filtered and brought up to standard oxygen levels, and all systems were back in operation, but there would be no time to repair the damage to the hull.

Worf had seen hull breaches before. This one did not compare to the damage done to the hull during their encounter with Shinzon, but still, it was not a sight he could ever become accustomed to. The great crack overhead, the shimmering force field with stars just beyond, inspired an eerie sensation.

He felt relieved to have made his decision; he

was already impatient for action. He nodded briefly to Ensign Allen, who was back at his station, and at Lieutenant Nave, who had swiveled in her chair to face him, awaiting orders.

"Ensign," Worf said by way of greeting as he assumed the captain's chair. "Lieutenant. Welcome back."

"Thank you, sir," Nave said, and Allen echoed the sentiment. Nave hesitated, then colored faintly as she said, "I saw the course heading, sir. May I ask, are we running away?"

"No," he replied simply. "Just tending to repairs and getting out of the Borg sensor range. We'll be returning to the cube and I will be calling on your services as acting security chief shortly."

"Thank you, sir." Nave favored him with a somber smile before turning back to the helm.

As she did, the lift doors opened, and Geordi La Forge emerged. He came to stand beside Worf with a faintly worried expression.

"Report, Commander," Worf told him.

La Forge kept his voice low. "I've looked over your plan. I'm pretty sure it can be done in the time we have."

Worf scowled at him. "But?" Behind him, the lift doors opened, but he kept his attention on Geordi.

"Well, we're going to require a massive amount of energy. Energy we don't have right now, especially considering the damage to the saucer section."

"I have already taken that into consideration," Worf said. "We will need to separate the ship."

"Exactly what I was going to suggest," La Forge agreed. "In that case, I think we can do it. If you can manage to get those codes."

Worf nodded. "Considering the alternative, I do not think that will be a problem. How soon do you think you can be ready for us to return to the Borg cube?" As he asked the question, Counselor T'Lana arrived and soundlessly took her seat beside the Klingon. Worf watched her in the periphery of his vision. Being a Vulcan, she had doubtless heard his question even though they had spoken quietly.

"Within the hour," La Forge replied. "Depending on how extensive the process—"

Worf cut him off. "Prepare the ship."

"Yes, sir." La Forge nodded and left the bridge.

As soon as the turbolift doors closed, T'Lana addressed Worf suddenly, formally. "Sir. May I ask whether you intend to take the *Enterprise* back to the vicinity of the Borg vessel?"

Defiant, Worf looked down at her. "I do."

"Then I wish to make a formal objection, Commander."

Worf studied his expectant crew and considered the situation. "We will discuss this in the captain's ready room," he said, indicating for her to head in before him. She smoothly crossed the bridge while Worf moved to speak privately with Ensign Allen. He waited until the doors to the ready room closed behind the counselor before speaking so that he could not be overheard. He wanted to have his discussion with T'Lana before he revealed the nature of his plan.

T'Lana was still standing when Worf entered the ready room. The acting captain walked behind the captain's desk and gestured for T'Lana to sit first, but she remained on her feet. The situation was too serious for a relaxed discussion, and she expected the encounter to be brief. She felt no small amount of helplessness: the ship was heading for disaster, and she was unable to stop it. No one aboard the *Enterprise* had taken her advice, and she did not expect this time to be any different. But she felt compelled ethically to try again, to state her position—as forcefully as possible.

But before she could do so, Commander Worf faced her. His expression and posture were even more fearsome and challenging than usual as he asked, "Before our argument begins, I must have your answer: Why do you dislike Klingons?"

The question was entirely unexpected. "I neither like nor dislike Klingons," T'Lana said, "though I find your race to be more emotional and hot tempered than even humans. But your culture shares some values with that of Vulcans: personal honor, for example."

"Then is it *me* that you dislike?"

T'Lana stiffened. The question might have unnerved someone with less control; certainly, Worf's eyes were unsettling enough. Despite his defiant demeanor, T'Lana still saw the light of attraction in them.

And she did not, she told herself firmly, respond to it at all—although his fierce expression and stance reminded her of bold brush paintings she had seen of ancient Vulcan warriors.

"I see no point in pursuing such a useless topic," she said. "I urge you to reconsider returning to the Borg vessel. Captain Picard refused to listen to reason—and the away team was either killed or lost. Now he himself has been assimilated by the Borg and will be used to do the one thing he wished to avoid—destroy the *Enterprise* and harm Starfleet. How many more are you willing to sacrifice, Commander?"

Beneath his thick, knitted brows, his deep-set eyes were narrowed, his breathing had quickened. One of his hands had unconsciously clenched in a fist. T'Lana looked pointedly at it and said, "You see? If your return had anything to do with logic, you would not be angry at me, Commander. But it has nothing to do with reason and everything to do with emotion. *That* is why I do not approve of your being in charge of this vessel; you have demonstrated that you let emotion guide you in making the most critical of decisions." She realized that her pitch had risen slightly, almost as if it contained a trace of heat. *Impossible,* she told herself. She did not permit herself to indulge in anger. No doubt she was simply reflecting the Klingon's mannerisms back to him.

Had the desk not been between them, he would have stepped closer, a mere hand's breadth from her face. His eyes, his expression betrayed the fact that he knew precisely the incident to which she referred. Even so, he demanded, in a deadly low voice, "What are you speaking of, Counselor? When did I demonstrate such a thing?"

"When you rescued Jadzia Dax," she said, uncowed. "It was a rash, purely emotional act. The spy Lasaran was killed as a result . . . as were countless others, in a pointless war."

He recoiled at that. His expression went slack, and his broad, straight shoulders bowed slightly beneath the weight of an invisible, intolerable burden. T'Lana got the impression that he would have liked to sit down, but he was far too proud. He lifted his chin. "That is not common knowledge. The incident with Lasaran was classified. How is it that you learned of it?"

"I served as counselor," she said, "on the *Starship Indefatigable*. Karina Wozniak was my captain. We were on an errand of mercy on the outskirts of the Dominion War zone when we were attacked by the Jem'Hadar. Captain Wozniak and most of the bridge crew were killed in that attack." She paused. "Later I served as a diplomatic liaison to the Romulans. I worked for Starfleet Intelligence and, as a result, learned the details of Lasaran's murder."

"So this is why . . ." Worf began, then trailed off; he seemed to look past her, at a distant memory, then collected himself with singular dignity. "I agree, it was a poor decision, one that I have regretted each day since. I am sorry for the death of your captain and your crewmates. If it were possible, I would change the past. But I cannot. I want you to know that . . . I have refused a promotion to become the permanent first officer of the *Enterprise*— for the very reason you mention. I do not feel worthy of command. I asked Captain Picard to find a more appropriate replacement. In the meantime, I command this vessel, and I will decide the best course of action."

His words were uttered with perfect sincerity; humans would have said, *He has spoken from the heart.* This was not the hot-headed Klingon she had judged him to be. T'Lana looked on him and felt some of her resistance toward him melt away. "And you feel the best possible decision is to violate the order of your captain? I urge you: take the ship to safety and alert Starfleet. Await the arrival of Seven of Nine, who is now best qualified to find a solution."

Worf studied her a long moment, then said, "I have heard of the incredible loyalty of Vulcans to their commanding officers. Is this true?"

The image of Wozniak's charred features flashed in her mind as she answered, calmly, "It is."

"Your Captain Wozniak . . . were you with her during the attack?"

"We were both on the bridge."

Worf gave a slight, respectful nod, as if acknowledging the horrific memory. "Were you . . . able to help her?"

"She could not be helped," T'Lana answered, her voice tight, controlled. She had worked through the memory many times, she reminded herself; it no longer troubled her. The past was simply the past. Wozniak was gone and no longer suffered. "I could not tell whether she was alive or dead. Her injuries were too grievous. She certainly would not have survived being taken to sickbay."

"But you would have saved her life if you had been able."

"Of course."

"Does logic always override loyalty?"

T'Lana did not answer immediately, and the Klingon took advantage of her silence.

"You were loyal to your captain," Worf said. "That is something I respect. And I am loyal to mine—even though I am refusing to obey his last command to me. I will not leave and allow him to cause irreparable harm to Starfleet. He has suffered this dishonor once before. I will accomplish his goal: to stop the Borg." He paused. "In order to achieve what is best for the captain, and for the crew, I *must* disobey him. But emotion does not always have to be separate from logic. Ensign Allen is, right now, contacting Admiral Janeway so I may discuss the situation. If we fail, Starfleet needs to be prepared. At the same time, I need her permission for something as well. However, I should warn you that if she does not grant me that permission, we will be going back anyway. Because if we do not stop the Borg here and now, millions will die." A faint ripple of emotion— grief? T'Lana wondered—crossed his features. "Do you understand, Counselor? We have the opportunity to save millions. If this crew must die in order to do so, then we will do so willingly.

"I do this for the good of the many, not for the few or the one," Worf continued, with unaffected eloquence. "Is that not logical?"

T'Lana stared at him a long moment. She thought she had understood the Klingon; now she saw that her opinion of him had been one-sided and simplistic. She had failed to realize the depth of his intelligence or his wisdom. She opened her mouth to say, *Perhaps it is*. But a voice filtering through the ready room interrupted her.

"Crusher to Worf . . ."

Worf answered the signal. "One moment, Doctor." He glanced down at T'Lana. His defensiveness was entirely gone. His manner was solicitous, even gentle. "Did you have anything further to say, Counselor?"

She shook her head and answered just as gently, "No, sir."

"Dismissed."

Worf sat heavily at the captain's ready room desk. Confessing his feelings had been painful, but he felt that T'Lana had deserved the truth. He admired her for confronting him—he had expected no less of her—and for stating her opinion forcefully. She was very different from any other Vulcan he had met.

After he had explained his reasoning, he could not read her expression—it was too subtle for human, much less Klingon, eyes—but she seemed to have finally understood his decision.

At any rate, there was no time to argue with her any further on the subject.

He addressed the invisible Beverly Crusher. "Yes, Doctor?"

Her voice was filled with the exhilaration of discovery. *"Worf, remember you said that I should ask for whatever I needed to complete my research on the Borg?"*

"Yes . . ."

"Well," the doctor said exultantly, *"I need you."*

Worf frowned. "I don't understand."

"I mentioned the feminizing hormone that can transform a Borg drone into a queen . . . The human analogue would be estrogen. It's so simple, I should have seen it immediately—the antidote is an androgenic compound."

"A what compound?" The term sounded vaguely familiar, but he could not place it.

"Androgenic. Androgen is the human male hormone. Klingon males have a very similar one that produces masculine sexual characteristics; in fact, they have the most potent form around. If I could

have a blood sample from you, I know I could develop something fast acting that would neutralize the queen immediately."

Worf hesitated. In the interest of saving time, it was simplest to kill the Borg queen with conventional weapons. But he also realized the value of science. The more they could learn about the enemy, the better they would be able to defeat them.

"How soon do you need the sample?" he asked the doctor.

"*Now, if I'm to have any chance of developing something by the time we reach the Borg ship again.*"

"I will come to sickbay momentarily," he said as he cut the connection.

A moment later, Ensign Allen's voice broke in. "*Commander Worf, I have the admiral.*"

"Patch her through," Worf said as he sat behind the captain's desk.

He turned the screen to face him as the Starfleet insignia was replaced with the face of Admiral Janeway. Worf had never met the woman, but even on the small screen she appeared to be a formidable presence. She seemed particularly tense at the moment, in fact. Worf suspected that he knew why.

Not one for simple pleasantries, she got right down to business. "*I have recently received a communiqué from Seven of Nine, Commander Worf. She reports that her long-range scans do not show the* Enterprise *at the rendezvous coordinates. I assume you have an explanation for that as well as for why your captain is not the one speaking with me now?"*

"Yes, Admiral," he said stoically.

"And the reason?" she asked.

"We have engaged the Borg."

11

———◆———

SARA NAVE SAT IN SILENCE IN THE CONFERENCE
lounge along with T'Lana and Lieutenant Nelson
from engineering. It was an odd trio, to say the
least. Nave had known Nelson only in passing; the
few conversations they had were centered around
warp core specifications. She always found the information enlightening but not exactly interesting.
T'Lana, meanwhile, had already proved to be a
hard nut to crack, and Nave wasn't ready for another go-round. It was easier just to sit silently and
wait for Commander Worf than try to bother coming up with any topics for discussion. Regretfully,
that left her with her own dark thoughts.

Nave's heart was in a very strange place. After
she had heard Lio's dying screams, she had alter-
nated between excruciating grief and numbness.
Now she was in limbo, wanting to mourn, to cry,

but she couldn't. Because now she had hope of rescuing Lio, and now her mind was busy churning out a hundred different scenarios of how she would find Lio on the Borg ship, how she would feel when she saw him, how she would ultimately save him.

Intruding on all this was the single sinister thought: Was it possible that the Borg had simply killed him?

No. No. The Borg would have sent him back, like the others. Once they had finished using him for his comlink connection with the ship, they would have identified him as the leader of the away team and assimilated him for his tactical knowledge. What would be bad for the *Enterprise* meant hope for Nave.

So she was forced to hope that the Borg transformed him—the last thing he would have wanted. Since she had transferred to the *Enterprise,* she had occasionally overheard a senior officer making a comment about Captain Picard's time as Locutus, about how horrifying it had been for him and for the crew. About the sense of violation the captain must have felt.

Am I being selfish, wishing the same for Lio, just so that I can bring him back?

Anxiety clutched her midsection, made it difficult for her to draw in a deep breath.

Behind her, the conference room doors opened. She did not turn; she knew from the sound of his step that Commander Worf had returned from sickbay.

Immediately, she straightened in her chair and forced her dazed, grief-exhausted mind to still. *You need to remember only one thing: you're going to the Borg ship. No matter what happens to Lio, you'll have the chance to avenge him and your friends. And you'll have the satisfaction of helping to stop the Borg.*

She did not allow herself to consider for one second the possibility of failure.

She glanced up as Commander Worf took a seat at the head of the table: the captain's chair. Nave was surprised by how much she thought it suited him and worried that she was betraying Captain Picard in the process. Nave saw Worf and the counselor exchange quick looks. Apparently they had agreed to a truce: Worf's expression was determined; T'Lana's was of course more difficult to interpret, though it was definitely not unkind.

Despite her emotional turmoil, Nave was curious. After Commander Worf had ordered T'Lana to the ready room, the Vulcan had emerged first. Although she revealed no emotion, tension enveloped her like a cloud. But the counselor had remained on the bridge and sat quietly, as if nothing had happened. Worf had emerged a few minutes later and said he was going to sickbay, while T'Lana had remained maddeningly unreadable. Nave was not even sure she liked the woman.

But the larger question still hung in the air. *What had he discussed with Admiral Janeway?*

At that point, she banished all personal thoughts. Worf was ready to start the oddly attended briefing. She hoped she would find out the answers soon enough.

"As you all know, we will be heading back to the Borg cube," Worf said. "I have spoken with Admiral Janeway and, though she is displeased at how the situation has evolved, she agrees with my plan."

"Plan, sir?" Nave asked, realizing she was jumping the gun. She was just too afraid that whatever the commander was now planning would leave her out of the mix.

Worf had obviously guessed her concern. "You will have the chance to avenge the losses of your crewmates, Lieutenant," he assured her. "But we need to be cautious about this. We need to do it in a way that Captain Picard would never suspect."

"Surely the captain would never expect that you would disobey his orders in the first place," T'Lana said.

Worf paused for a moment. A rare smile played on his lips. "You are still new to this crew, Counselor. I assure you, the captain knows we're coming. We just need to make sure that he cannot see us returning."

Nave thought she knew what the commander was implying, but it was impossible. At the same time, it was a course of action the captain certainly would not anticipate. "Are you suggesting that we'll be . . . cloaked, sir?"

"Yes, Lieutenant."

Nave nearly laughed when she saw the questioning look on T'Lana's face. Surely the Vulcan wouldn't know how to process this information. It was clearly against the terms of the Treaty of Algeron for the Federation to possess a cloaking device, unless in a situation specially sanctioned by the Romulans. Honestly, Nave was a little confused herself. Where would they obtain a cloaking device in time?

Even taking Worf's communication with Admiral Janeway into account, there was no way she could have gotten through all the red tape to get permission from the Romulans already. In spite of the threat of another Borg incursion, bureaucrats simply did not move that quickly.

T'Lana was the first to speak. "The *Defiant* is the only Federation starship equipped with cloaking technology."

"That is not entirely correct," Worf said, evoking a look of shock from Nave and one of utter curiosity from T'Lana. Nelson alone looked as though he knew what the commander was talking about. Worf nodded to the lieutenant to explain.

"The Federation has been studying cloaking technology for over a century," he explained. "While the treaty forbids us to use the technology on our ships, it doesn't mean we can't possess it."

"That interpretation is a matter of semantics,"

T'Lana reasoned. "One that the Romulans would surely take issue with."

"True," Worf said. "But considering the recent coup in the Romulan Senate, combined with their unwarranted attack on the Federation—namely this ship—the Federation is taking a new look at their relationship with the Empire."

"Surely, the treaty has not been rescinded," T'Lana said.

"As far as Admiral Janeway is concerned," Worf said, "it is for the time being." He turned to Nelson. "Lieutenant."

"Cloaking technology has been encrypted in all starships' computers constructed within the past decade," Nelson explained. "The thought being that the technology should be available in cases of extreme need. The encryption does requires an admiral's access codes."

"Which we now possess," Worf added.

"So we're going to cloak the *Enterprise*?" Nave asked.

"Not exactly," the lieutenant replied. "To cloak the entire ship would require a massive amount of energy, which we don't exactly have at the moment. Since the saucer section is most damaged, we're going to have to separate from it and cloak only the stardrive section. Commander La Forge is working off the decrypted schematics and installing the cloaking device right now. He's the only one onboard with proper clearance for the procedure."

"Meanwhile, Doctor Crusher is working on a

neutralizer injection, a way to take out the Borg queen once and for all," Worf added. "In the meantime, we will need to evacuate all extraneous personnel to the saucer section. Counselor, I will leave you in command of that section. Your orders are simple: remain at this position, outside of the Borg sensor range, until we return. If you pick up *any* movement by the Borg, you will turn the ship around and head to the coordinates Admiral Janeway has ordered the fleet to mass. Do not attempt to slow the Borg ship. Your goal is to join the fight where you can be of the best advantage."

"Understood," T'Lana said with a nod. Nave didn't doubt for a second that T'Lana would do exactly as she was told.

Worf looked out at the three officers. "Lieutenant Nelson will be in command of the auxiliary bridge while we are on the cube. In the meantime, we must prepare for the separation."

"Aye, sir," the officers responded.

As T'Lana and Nelson left the conference room, Worf motioned for Nave to remain with him. "Once the cloak is active, we will be arriving in the vicinity of the Borg ship within the hour, Lieutenant," he said. "I need you to designate a security team. I will, of course, be leading the rescue efforts. But you will be responsible for coordinating them."

Thank you, Nave almost said. Worf had held the position of security chief several years earlier; he knew what was necessary in order to pull a team together on short notice. Perhaps Nave only imagined it, but it seemed he understood how important it was to her to organize the rescue efforts to find the captain. To find Lio.

Instead she answered, "Aye, sir. I've already thought about it. I'll want Chao, Leary, and Diasourakis." She'd worked out with Sandra Chao before; Chao was an ensign, only a year out of the academy, but she was tough and fast and smart. Margaret Leary was an experienced security veteran, and while Nave didn't know Gregory Diasourakis personally—he had transferred to the *Enterprise* only a month before—his Starfleet file was littered with commendations.

Worf grunted in approval. "Good choices. You will need to be sure your team is drilled in certain facts. First, phasers set on stun are useless against the Borg. Weapons must be set to kill. Second, when the Borg were last on the *Enterprise,* they learned to adapt to the frequency of our weapons. After we fired a few times, they became impervious, and so we had to constantly recalibrate our weapons. Your team should be prepared to do so as well."

The first fact worried Nave. She had assumed that all she had to do, if she encountered Lio on the Borg ship, was stun him and return him to the *Enterprise.* "I'll be sure to inform them." She paused. "Do we have any way of locating the captain, sir? Will we be aware of his position?"

Worf shook his head. "Our primary goal must be

to find the queen. Commander La Forge's team is currently trying to calibrate our scanners to determine whether we can single her out from among the drones. If we can destroy her, then the entire Borg colony will be disabled, and we can then try to locate the captain and Lieutenant Battaglia." He paused, then, with a look Nave could not interpret, said, "If we locate the queen, the captain will almost certainly be nearby."

"The neutralizer injection you mentioned Doctor Crusher was working on. Will that kill the queen?"

"Not exactly. The injection would transform the queen back into a drone—if it works. If it does not work quickly, or as planned, we will resort to conventional methods."

"Kill her, you mean."

The Klingon shot her a humorless look. "I believe that is what I said."

"Sir . . ." Nave began hesitantly. "You've fought the Borg before. I know that when the Borg overran the *Enterprise,* a lot of crew members were assimilated and . . . lost. What do you think our chances are of recovering Lio . . . Lieutenant Battaglia? Of actually bringing him home?"

"The same as our chances of bringing home the captain," Worf answered at once. But his tone held little hope, and he would not meet her eyes.

Worf sat in the command chair on the auxiliary bridge as the stardrive section disengaged from the saucer. He had never conducted a saucer separation before, though he had taken part in the procedure many times. The entire process was fully automated, but it still seemed unnatural to him to divide a ship and leave part of it behind. It was the equivalent of severing an arm or a leg to him. More to the point, it was almost unfathomable to leave behind most of the crew when heading into battle. True Klingon warriors would never consent to being left out of the fray. Then again, if the skeleton crew aboard the stardrive section with him failed, those aboard the saucer section would join in the battle soon enough.

"Separation complete," Nave reported from the conn of the auxiliary bridge.

"Very good, Lieutenant," Worf said as he tapped his combadge. "Worf to the main bridge."

T'Lana's voice replied. *"Aye, Commander."*

"Hold this position as instructed," he reiterated his previous orders. "Once we activate the cloak, we will have approximately two and a half hours to conduct our mission. If we do not contact you by the end of that time, or you read any movement from the Borg cube, you are to leave the area immediately."

"Understood," T'Lana said.

Worf briefly wondered if he was expecting too much to think she would wish him well in battle as she had wished the captain before his mission. He quickly put the idea out of his mind and severed the communication. This was not the time for such silliness. He pressed his combadge again and opened communications with La Forge.

"I've activated the cloaking device," La Forge reported from engineering. *"It's coming online now."*

If everything was going according to plan, the stardrive section would be in the process of disappearing from the main bridge's viewscreen. He could almost feel the anticipation from the crew seated around him. This was likely their first time on a cloaked ship. Not that they would be able to tell the difference from within the ship, but it was an odd sensation. Worf had experienced it many times onboard the *Defiant*. To be totally invisible to sensors gave one a feeling of power. Though some would say that sneaking up on an enemy was not an honorable way to conduct battle, it was a necessity in some cases. And he could think of none more important than this.

"The cloak is holding," La Forge reported. *"We're invisible."*

Worf set his eyes on the viewscreen in front of him. "Lieutenant Nave, set a course for the Borg cube. Maximum warp."

"Already set, sir," she replied. He heard the determination in her voice.

Worf then echoed the command his captain had used so many times before: "Engage."

Beverly Crusher moved rapidly down the corridor toward the transporter room. She had been working in one of the labs in the stardrive section up to the last possible moment and was positive that she had found success. Now, as she went to join the away team, her mind was utterly focused on her next challenge. A medkit was slung over her shoulder; a hypospray was securely fastened to her belt, a phaser beside it.

She was doing this, she told herself, for strictly professional reasons: for the sake of science, of research, for the sake of any sentient beings that might ever run the risk of being assimilated by the Borg. It had nothing to do with her inability to sit idly and wait for word of the away team's success or failure; it had nothing to do with her desire to go to the Borg ship and find Jean-Luc herself, to make sure—even if she had to do it herself—that the queen was destroyed and he was rescued and brought back to the *Enterprise* in one piece.

Be truthful. You're doing this because you want to go to him and not leave his side until you're sure he's safe and completely Jean-Luc again.

Yes. But I have another very good, very logical reason.

Fleeing the Borg when they had boarded the *Enterprise* was the second most frightening memory of her life—almost as frightening as the moment she had first set eyes on Locutus. But she felt no fear now, only horror, for Jean-Luc's sake. She was too busy trying to imagine where he was, what he was feeling . . . and what he had gone through.

In midstride, she realized that she was still

wearing her lab coat. Chagrined, she pulled it off without slowing her pace and flung it over her arm. She could not afford to be late: she needed time to make her case.

Two more steps, and she was in the transporter room. Worf stood in hawkish profile at the transporter console, next to Ensign Luptowski. The Klingon turned as she entered—and just behind her came Sara Nave, as tight-lipped and tense as Beverly had ever seen her. She was attended by three security crew members. Beverly recognized Chao, a muscular, dark-haired woman, and Leary, petite but formidable, but not the third, a thirtyish man with dark auburn hair and remarkably blue eyes who bore the relentlessly calm demeanor of a seasoned officer.

All of them, including Worf, were armed with ominous-looking phaser rifles.

As they all came to a stop and faced Worf, Nave shot Crusher a look and smiled in grim approval. Somehow, she had sized up the doctor; she understood what she was about to do, and she approved. Beverly shared a long look with her, then glanced back at Worf.

The Klingon turned to her. When Beverly had first met him, many years ago, his features had reminded her of an owl's: fiercely penetrating eyes beneath swooping brows that created a perpetual scowl. Worf briefly caught her gaze, then looked pointedly at the medkit slung over her shoulder.

"Thank you, Doctor. Is the injection in there?"

"No." She touched her belt. "It's here." She paused. "Actually . . . I'm going with you, Worf. When I was preparing the injection, my tests indicated that the feminizing hormone is in fact contained in a nutrient gel secreted by the drones' bodies, triggered by the loss of a queen. If I can get a sample of drone tissue—now that their body chemistry has altered to produce the hormone—I'm confident I can find a way to alter their DNA." It was Jean-Luc, actually, who had provided the clue, when he had spoken of the drones' protectiveness of the queen. *Not a directive,* he had said. *Something deeper.* Those words had haunted her until she at last realized what that "something deeper" was: DNA. "And if that's done . . ."

He lifted his chin, adamant. "I am afraid you must stay, Doctor. It is too dangerous for you to go."

"If you fail in your mission, it will be too dangerous to be on this *ship,* Commander. It hasn't been safe since we all agreed to accompany the captain on his search for the Borg queen." She pulled him aside and softened her tone. This was not a conversation for the junior officers to witness. "Hear me out, Worf. If I alter their DNA, it could spread to all the Borg in the Alpha Quadrant. They'll never be able to produce another queen. We could stop them *for good.*"

"I understand." Worf reached for the medkit. "But *I* can administer the injection. And I can take the sample."

"I have to do this," Beverly said sharply, stridently, as she pulled away from him with determination in her eyes. She knew that she was being unfair. She was counting on his Klingon sensibilities to kick in. Truthfully, anyone could make the injection. There was no need for a medical professional to administer it. Her request was personal. And she knew that Worf would see it that way, as more than a simple battle with the Borg. This was a fight to save the man she loved. In his eyes, it would be a deeply honorable action. "Please," she said softly. "I *have* to do this."

The tension in his features eased; the corner of his lip quirked in the small, exasperated gesture she knew so well.

"La Forge to Worf."

Worf pressed his combadge. "Go ahead, Commander."

Geordi's voice was uncharacteristically flat, defeated. *"We tried to pinpoint the queen on the Borg vessel, but there just wasn't enough time. If we had another hour, I could probably pull it off. She's a very small needle in a very big haystack. I'm sorry, Worf."*

"I know that you did your best, Commander," Worf said. He kept the channel open and turned to Luptowski at the transporter controls. "We will need to drop the cloak to beam to the cube. As soon as we are away, Commander La Forge can reinitialize the cloak. However, the Borg will be immediately alerted to our presence. If their behavior remains consistent, they will instantly perceive us as a threat and attack. Our only option, as I see it, is to beam into the same coordinates as the captain and the first away team had. Tactically, it will not be a strong position, but we won't have time to beam any farther away from the queen's chamber."

"Agreed," Nave said with a nod.

Worf addressed his security team. "We will provide cover for Doctor Crusher so that she can administer the injection to the queen. Once the Borg are disarmed, she will gather samples." He looked pointedly at Crusher and frowned. "You will need a phaser rifle."

The doctor shook her head. "I'll have to make do with the phaser. The rifle is too cumbersome with the medkit." Her hand fell on the hypospray. "Besides, *this* is all the weapon I need."

Worf spoke to the security team again. "Doctor Crusher will attempt to disable the queen—but the instant it seems that she is not successful, fire to kill." He paused, and his voice dropped even lower. "I realize that we want our captain and our crewmate to be recovered safely. But our first priority is to stop the Borg—at any cost. Am I understood?"

"Understood," Beverly said softly, along with the others. She caught Nave's eye at the instant it flickered with a ghost of pain. She was sure no one else saw it, no one but herself, because she felt the very same ache.

"Very well," Worf said. "According to Captain Picard, we have only two hours before the queen wakes and the Borg vessel is online. It is imperative that we accomplish our mission before either of those events occurs."

As they stepped onto the transporter pads, Beverly drew in a breath. The air was cool here and pleasant; she remembered how hot and dank it had been when the Borg had taken over the ship, and she steeled herself.

"Mister La Forge," Worf said into the air, "on my mark."

"Ready," La Forge's voice replied.

Worf nodded to Ensign Luptowski. "Energize."

Beverly watched as the normal world, the sane world, dissolved into nothingness around her.

12

NAVE MATERIALIZED WITH THE AWAY TEAM ON
one of the uppermost decks of the Borg cube.

She had been sitting at the helm of the *Enterprise* when the Borg ship had first loomed close on
the viewscreen. Hanging dark and ominous against
an incandescent moon, it had reminded Nave
oddly of images from old stories, of haunted Gothic
mansions peopled by white, soulless ghosts of the
ancient dead. The same feeling took hold of her
again, as she got her bearings on the catwalk sus-
pended high within the cavernous ship. This was
the exact spot where Lio had been taken, where De-
Vrie and Costas and Satchitanand had died. Their
ghosts whispered to her as she swayed a bit, staring
down at the spiraling decks below.

They now attack on sight . . .

The interior of the ship was as haphazard and

ungainly as the outside, dim and bland and shadowed—far dimmer, even, than the *Enterprise*'s night. What few colors existed were muted shades of dulled gray and bronze—the color of inanimate things.

Beneath Nave was a vast downward spiral, a maze of metal wrought like a spider's web but without the elegance. A conduit was stuck here, a railing there, another deck, a wall of circuitry fully exposed, as if someone had stripped away the bulkheads to reveal the internal workings of the ship, unable to be bothered by concerns of elegance or privacy.

Far below, so far they were no bigger than the first knuckle of Nave's little finger, Borg drones slept, mindless and dreamless, in tiny, dark alcoves. Nave's mind immediately went to Dante's *Inferno;* surely this was the innermost circle of hell, where souls were trapped in eternal suffering. And that brought her mind back to Lio.

But Dante had said that the innermost circle was bitterly cold; that was surely not the case on this ship, so humid that mists swirled about Nave's feet. Sweat already glazed her upper lip and forehead.

Nave forced her gaze upward, at the away team: Worf leading, then Leary, Crusher, and Diasourakis and Chao side by side. Clutching her phaser rifle close, its butt pressing into her collarbone, Nave brought up the rear, her body angled sideways in order to follow the movements of the team while still being alert to any threats approaching from her direction.

"There," Worf said softly. Nave craned her neck and looked beyond Chao's straight spill of dark hair, beyond Diasourakis and Leary and Crusher, to the Klingon, who pointed at a light—faint and pulsating and unmistakably green in the colorless landscape—emanating from an arched entryway in the near distance. "That would be the queen's chamber."

The team moved forward, each step punctuated by another pulse of the green light. In the silence, Nave heard the whisper of ghosts.

As the catwalk was intersected by a perpendicular walkway, Crusher hissed a warning. Nave turned, instantly on the alert. The phaser rifle was thicker than her two arms laid side by side, fastened to her body by a thick strap so there was no danger of her dropping it. Some officers complained that the weapon was unwieldy, but Nave swung it around as though it were an extension of herself.

A Borg drone was closing in on them from the side, moving faster than Nave had anticipated. By the time the away team slowed to react, Diasourakis was directly in the drone's path.

Nave saw no more than a blur of white and black and fired a split second before all the others; the rifle's blast was painfully dazzling. A small nova exploded at the level of the drone's chest. It staggered, bent neatly and impossibly backward at the waist, then steadied itself and straightened before restarting its inexorable move forward.

Nave fired again. This time, the beam from her rifle and Worf's converged and scalded the drone, brightening the shadowed corridors to daylight. It writhed briefly, then fell, scorched and lifeless, to the metal deck.

Her hands shook only slightly as she lowered her weapon.

Before she reacted, she had not even looked at the drone's face; she could not have said whether it had been Lio, whether it had been Picard. Along with the others, she stared down at the dead creature. Its features were indistinct, bland, unremarkable; Nave could do no more than identify the species as humanoid.

As she lifted her gaze, she caught the doctor's. Crusher had been gazing down at the drone's body; as she looked up, her eyes met Nave's. Neither woman spoke, neither gave any overt sign of acknowledgment, but Nave understood completely. She and Crusher had both come onto the Borg vessel for the same reason. She and Crusher had both been terrified by the possible identity of the murdered drone.

The away team moved on in silence.

It was no more than thirty meters to the source of the pulsing green light, the arching entrance to the lone walled-in structure on the ship. But the slow, stealthy march seemed interminable. Nave shifted her gaze constantly toward the rear, toward the sides, toward the front, where Worf led the way. It will happen, she told herself, and happen quickly. They would reach the queen's chamber. There would be a few more shots fired, then Crusher would inject the queen and all would be well. Picard and Lio would be discovered whole and be restored.

At least, she tried hard to believe it. She had thought, before she came aboard the Borg vessel, that she would have time to scan the chalky features of each drone before she fired, that she would have time to recognize Lio if he appeared and somehow magically stop the others from firing on him. Now she realized such a thing was impossible. She had hoped before to encounter Lio in his guise as Borg; now she wished for just the opposite.

Just as the away team neared the intersection of two catwalks, Nave saw them, approaching from the rear: six drones in pyramid formation, one in front, two in the second row, three in the last. They appeared out of the shadows as if materializing magically from the ether. They were all moving at speeds much faster than she had previously read in the reports. There was none of the lumbering that was typically associated with the hulking beings. They were fierce in their movements.

The lead drone wore a black optoscope that extended forward and rotated as it studied its prey; it caught Nave's gaze with its single humanoid eye, its expression frighteningly blank. At the sight of her, it lifted a cybernetic arm, which terminated in razor-sharp fingers that opened and closed, a deadly bloom. It reached for her, its blades champing together like the teeth of a hungry predator, ready to strike.

"Six approaching from the rear!" Nave shouted.

She fired on the drone, peripherally aware that Chao had closed in on her right flank, Diasourakis her left.

The Borg with the blooming blades moved in first. Nave's burst hit it squarely in the midsection. Like the first drone, this one buckled backward, then righted itself.

Nave fired a second time, a third, as Chao and Diasourakis followed suit; the dimness was lit by a rapid-fire series of dazzling blasts. She heard Worf's shouted orders to Leary, followed by phaser fire behind her, and realized that the Borg had attacked on two fronts.

Chao and Diasourakis were emptying their weapons on the second and third drones, trying to bring them down. But like Nave's, their targets stopped, rallied, then *kept coming.*

"Recalibrate weapons!" Nave yelled.

Somewhere behind her, Margaret Leary screamed.

Nave had no time to turn. The drone intended for her—its finger blades extended, clawing the air—was only two meters away.

But Leary's cry was too similar to Lio's; it filled her with murderous rage. She recalibrated with practiced swiftness, and the corner of her mouth tugged down as she fired. "I won't let you win this time," she said, her voice low, ragged.

The burst hit the drone in the gut, lifting it off its feet and propelling it backward. Nave stared through her scope and waited, but the creature did not rise; it lay on its back, the scorched black carapace smoldering.

Diasourakis had managed to take down his target, but Chao's had adapted again. As she struggled to recalibrate in time, a drone came within arm's reach, an instant away from striking. Nave and Diasourakis both fired on the drone, but it remained on its feet.

When it reached for Chao, Nave grabbed her arm.

"Retreat!" She pushed Chao to the left, onto the intersecting catwalk, giving them breathing room; Diasourakis followed.

Nave glanced over her shoulder. Behind Diasourakis, a cluster of drones—a black-and-white circle of flesh—had paused in the intersection of the two walkways, as if uncertain whom to pursue. Nave craned to look past them and caught a glimpse of Worf's russet hair and massive shoulders, of Crusher's and Leary's pale faces, of a flash of blood. They had veered right as Nave and her party had veered left; the drones who had attacked from front and rear had now converged, separating them.

Nave turned back to face the enemy, at the same time recalibrating her weapon; Diasourakis and Chao, shoulder to shoulder, did the same. As she moved, Nave took a quick head count: seven drones. Seven to six—almost even odds.

"Let's rejoin the others," she said. "Fire."

The darkness filled with dazzling light; a pair of bright bursts came from the opposite side as Worf and Leary attacked.

One drone dropped, then another; a third staggered, then slowly righted itself. Along with Diasourakis and Chao, Nave kept firing but slowly became aware that no further blasts were coming from Worf and Leary.

She thought of the flash of red she had seen—human blood—and quickly forced the image away, instead staying focused on her firing. The drones still stood in circular formation—backs together, fronts facing outward, but as Nave continued to fire, they moved slowly, deliberately, turning until every one of them faced Nave and her group.

They began to advance, moving out of the intersection and onto Nave's side of the catwalk.

"Keep firing!" Nave shouted. She could not see past them, to Worf and the others. Apparently, the Borg had decided that her group posed the greatest threat.

A series of rapid-fire phaser blasts flared, limning the dark bodies of the drones, dazzling Nave's eyes and clouding her vision with afterimages. Even so, she could see that none of the Borg hesitated when struck. They were moving steadily forward, forcing Nave and her officers to move steadily back.

"Recalibrate!" she called, as she did so to her own weapon. Chao and Diasourakis obeyed, but the slight hesitation allowed the drones to draw uncomfortably closer.

Nave gripped the trigger and squeezed it repeatedly, faster than she ever had in practice, faster than she ever had in her life. Her officers were firing madly beside her; white-hot bursts turned the dimness to daylight. One Borg fell, only one.

The others kept advancing. They were adapting to the phaser blasts more quickly now, she realized, and moving in faster. She could no longer see Commander Worf and his group and did not know whether they had escaped. She did not want to abandon them or separate the away team, but she had a responsibility to her own group. When the drones were no more than two steps away, she called out to Chao and Diasourakis.

"Retreat! Retreat!"

Nave turned and caught the crook of Chao's elbow with her free hand and pulled her along; Diasourakis followed.

She ran madly, blinking as sweat stung her eyes, gasping at the hot, stifling air. The phaser rifle, strapped snugly to her, jammed against her ribs so that she found it hard to draw a breath. She could hear her own boot heels hammering against the metal deck, followed, too quickly, by the inexorable tromp of the Borg's.

After the brightness of the phaser blasts, the corridor seemed darker than ever. Nave dashed recklessly through the faint mists, trying to ignore the fact that she might very well run directly into a waiting group of hostiles.

Abruptly, the deck forked in three directions.

"This way!" She veered hard to the right. The momentum flung her briefly against the railing. She grasped it tightly and caught a vertiginous glance of the hundred or more levels beneath her.

Chao almost collided with her. They caught each other for balance, then separated again. Nave straightened and led the flight.

She ran at top speed, throat and lungs burning, for a full minute, by which time her eyes had re-adjusted to the dimness. Another stride, two, then she pulled up short, panting.

A few meters in front of her, the deck terminated in a solid bulkhead. Swiftly, Nave glanced behind her. The Borg were following and closing the distance. It was impossible to go back, to try a different route.

Bringing up the rear, Diasourakis had noticed as well. "We're trapped, Lieutenant!"

Nave scanned the area, squinting at the shadows. She tried her combadge. Nothing. There seemed to be no way out, short of crawling over the railing and jumping to one's death—an option she refused to accept. She stared hard at the bulkhead, at the deck and the railings, until she spotted something to her left: a metal hatch covering a broad, enclosed cylindrical shaft. She hurried to it, Chao sticking close to her side, and pulled on the hatch until it yielded.

Inside, illuminated with faint, eerie gray twilight, was a shaft leading down several levels, equipped with metal rungs for climbing. Nave decided it existed because she had simply willed it. She looked up at the approaching drones, then motioned quickly to Chao.

Without a word, Chao tightened the body strap on her rifle, then crawled into the shaft and started climbing down.

Nave turned to Diasourakis. "Go."

He shook his head. "I'll bring up the rear, sir."

Nave did not care to waste time arguing. She lowered herself and started climbing down. The act seemed exceptionally precarious, given that her hands were slick with sweat, the nose of her rifle kept catching on the smooth metal rungs, and the shaft was uncomfortably wide, making her feel exposed. It didn't help matters that the drop below her was dizzyingly infinite.

Don't think about it. Just move.

Below her, Chao's dark head bobbed. To make moving easier, she had pushed her strap so that her rifle now hung on her back. Nave refused to follow suit; she wanted her weapon as close to her hands as possible.

Overhead, Diasourakis closed the hatch with a dull, final sound. Nave didn't look up. She was too busy concentrating on gripping each new rung firmly, taking care that neither her hands nor her heels slipped, matching her pace to Chao's. They made fair time; less than a minute had passed when Chao suddenly slowed her pace.

Nave glanced down, concerned.

"There's a landing here, sir." Chao's voice echoed endlessly.

Nave saw it. It was more like a small ledge, with just enough room for a body to step onto and then reach out to the side to catch hold of a rung. The Borg were apparently none too concerned about personal safety.

"Keep going," she called down. "Let's put a couple more levels between us and them." At the same time, she was aware they could not go *too* far; the away team now had less than two hours to accomplish its goal.

"Aye, sir."

They kept descending. The atmosphere in the shaft was a steam bath; Nave remained vigilant about gripping the rungs as tightly as possible with her sweating hands. At times, she paused to carefully wipe a hand on her uniform, then to glance overhead to see whether the drones were still in pursuit.

Blessedly, she saw nothing above her but Diasourakis's legs. Ahead of her was the little landing, just below a hatch; she glanced at it as she made her way past it. After five minutes, she decided she would direct Chao to take the next landing. And then it would be a matter of surviving long enough to find another shaft that would take them back up to Worf and the others. Once they had some breathing room, she would try to contact Worf and ascertain the other away team members' status . . .

Her thoughts were interrupted by a hoarse cry. She jerked her head back and stared up at Greg Diasourakis's right leg, which had slipped off the rung and kicked out suddenly to the side.

No, she realized, it hadn't been kicked out. It had been *pulled,* by a long, dark arm that had snaked out from the landing. By a drone, whose upper torso emerged from the hatch; its shoulders rested on the landing as its white hand gripped Diasourakis's ankle. It and Diasourakis's foot were an arm's length from the top of Nave's head.

His cry was wordless, but Nave understood it nonetheless. With her left hand, she gripped the metal rung. Her body swung precariously to the left, but she ignored it, along with Chao's shouts, and focused instead on catching hold of her phaser rifle. Using her shoulder and right hand, she managed to get the nose up and her fingers on the trigger.

Diasourakis was thrashing wildly now. The drone had wriggled farther out so that its waist and hip rested on the landing. Its humanoid hand still clung to the security officer; its prosthetic saw arm was raised, and the blade was rotating, ready. Slowly, it was pulling him down. Down, and in, to the landing.

Nave leaned back as far as she dared and pushed the nose of her weapon high, higher, then called up.

"Greg! Hold still! *Hold still!*"

Diasourakis flailed a few more times; Nave couldn't get a bead on the drone without killing them both. And then his leg relaxed—for an instant, only an instant, but it was enough time for Nave to fire.

Given its proximity, the blast blinded her; she felt heat on her face. Instinctively, she dropped the phaser rifle and clung to the rail with both hands, pressing her face against them, squeezing shut her eyes.

In the same instant, she cried out as a deluge of tangled limbs, flesh and bone and hard metal, pummeled her, struck her head and shoulders and back; something razor sharp nicked the back of her thigh. It should have washed her away, taken her down with it, but impossibly, she held on.

She held on and raised her face at the scream, at first high-pitched and in her ear, then rapidly growing lower, fainter, until it faded into nothingness.

She blinked, trying to force her vision to clear, and shouted down at Chao. "What happened? *What happened?*"

Moments earlier, as the away team neared the intersection of two catwalks—only steps away from the chamber filled with pulsating green light—

Beverly Crusher saw the drones approaching from the front.

They had come from what Beverly instinctively knew was the queen's chamber. There were six of them, and she craned her neck anxiously to see past Leary and over Worf's shoulder; she wanted to know if Jean-Luc was among them. He was not, and she did not know whether to be relieved or disappointed.

Either way, she fought to suppress a wave of fear. The Borg were advancing with their prosthetic weapons wielded.

Worf had led the way, with Leary a close second. Leary at once moved into position beside the Klingon; the two formed a barrier in front of Crusher.

"Open fire!" Worf shouted, and Leary obeyed. One Borg, caught in the brilliant beam from Worf's rifle, spasmed briefly as the energy surge enveloped its body; it dropped quickly as the blast faded.

Crusher held back, thinking to let the other security team members move past her to join the fight— but she glanced over her shoulder to see Nave and the two others standing shoulder to shoulder, firing on a second group of drones who were attacking from the rear.

"There are other Borg behind us," she shouted, pulling her phaser from its holster. Worf was far too engaged in the battle to acknowledge if he heard. She considered her options as a second Borg fell, then a third reeled from a blow but recovered to continue its approach. Worf and Leary kept firing, but the drones reacted not at all to the blasts, not even pausing when directly hit.

"Recalibrate!" Worf ordered. At the same time, Beverly fired her own phaser, dropping the Borg.

Worf adjusted his weapon smoothly, swiftly, and resumed firing at the next oncoming Borg, but Leary's malfunctioned. She frowned at it as she repeatedly pressed a control.

The lead drone—its prosthetic arm terminating in a slowly rotating claw hook—sensed her weakness and lunged forward. Leary glanced up, startled, and fired her unrecalibrated weapon. It had no effect, and before she could step back out of the way, the drone sunk its claw into her shoulder.

Leary cried out sharply. Miraculously, she stayed on her feet, the hook still in her flesh, and jammed the hilt of her rifle into the drone's jaw. It staggered backward, just long enough for Worf and Beverly to dispatch it, firing in unison.

Crusher holstered her phaser and, with hand on her medkit, darted to Leary's side. The claw had bitten into the young woman's right deltoid, then ripped a ragged seam all the way into her biceps. Blood rapidly soaked the shoulder and sleeve of her uniform, and began to drip onto the deck. Amazingly, Leary was still standing. She had shifted her weapon over to her left side, nestling it against her rib cage as she adjusted it one-handed. She discharged a blast as Crusher did a quick scan of the damage.

"You have to let me help you," Beverly half shouted in her ear. "That's a deep laceration. If I don't fix it, you'll wind up fainting from blood loss."

"No time," Leary mouthed, but her eyes were dazed, her skin pale; a dark curl had fallen forward and clung to her sweat-dampened forehead. Even so, she kept firing.

Resolutely ignoring the approaching Borg, Beverly focused on her patient's wound. She couldn't reverse the blood loss Leary had already experienced, but she could at least slow it. She pulled her stimulator from her kit and applied it to Leary's wound. At the same time, she fumbled in the kit with her free hand, searching for her emergency hypospray.

Leary fired twice more, then swayed on her feet; her hand dropped from the trigger, leaving the rifle to dangle from her body by a strap. Crusher caught her before she fell.

"Worf!"

He did not slow his pattern of firing and recalibrating, but his gaze flickered to the side and took in Crusher and Leary—able to stay on her feet only because the doctor wound a supporting arm beneath her shoulders. The Klingon moved immediately in front of them and gestured for Beverly to go to the right, onto the intersecting catwalk.

Desperation encouraged Crusher to move herself and her burden fast, even though Leary's boots dragged against the deck. Worf followed, still firing at the Borg, his back to Crusher. Pulling Leary with her, Beverly staggered along a good twenty meters until she realized that Worf was no longer firing.

She looked back over her shoulder, awkwardly, trying not to discomfit Leary.

Worf was still behind her, though she could not see Nave and the others. But the Borg had gathered in the intersection of the two walkways. Inexplicably, they turned away from Crusher and Leary, away from Worf, and as a whole began to move toward the source of the firing.

Worf hesitated, then took a step in the direction of the drones, clearly thinking to join his stranded colleagues. At that same instant, Leary fainted, and Crusher sank beneath her weight.

"Worf! Help!"

The Klingon hurried to her side and scooped Leary up into his arms. They moved quickly out of the Borg's line of sight. At last, Worf stopped and gently lowered Leary to the floor.

Crusher knelt beside her patient and did a quick scan. "It's blood loss," she said, and Worf hovered above her. She ferreted the hypo from her medkit. "I can give her some tri-ox to keep her going for a while, but ultimately we're going to need to get her back to the ship for a transfusion."

"How much time does she have, Doctor?"

"A few hours."

Worf gave her a pointed look. "If we do not make it back to the ship in less than two hours, it will not make any difference for her."

Beverly fell silent. She had been thinking only of her patient, but if the away team was still here after the queen and all the drones awoke, no amount of tri-ox would save Leary.

She emptied the hypo into Leary's good shoulder, then sat back on her heels and counted the seconds. On five, Leary's eyes fluttered open.

"Ooh," she said. "Dizzy."

"It'll pass," Crusher soothed.

Leary blinked a few times, then tried to push herself up. Crusher helped her sit. "You're right," Leary said. "That *is* better."

"Good. Now, how about you hold still for me this time? I'm going to apply some more stimulation to speed up the healing."

"Sure." Leary sighed. She leaned back against the bulkhead.

As Beverly applied the stimulator, she glanced up at Worf, who was repeatedly pressing his combadge and frowning. "What's wrong?"

"I was attempting to contact the other members of the away team. My communicator is inoperative."

Instinctively, Beverly pressed hers; it, too, was dead. Without thinking, she said at once, "Jean-Luc." Locutus was of course expecting them—and would do everything possible to make their mission more difficult. Trying to find the missing crew members would cost precious time. And they were separated not only from Nave and the others but from the *Enterprise* as well.

Worf gave a grim nod. "I would suspect a damping field."

Beverly looked around her. They had wandered into a more sheltered area, where the open railings were replaced by bulkheads on either side. A bit farther down was an ominous sight: dark, empty alcoves, the alcoves where the drones slept. Would they be returning, she wondered, or were these reserved for the soon-to-be assimilated?

Worf paced warily beside her, his hand resting on his rifle. "I suspect the drones that attacked us had been guarding the queen. And I expect there are many more in her chamber . . . If we cannot locate the other members of the away team, we will need to come up with a new strategy."

"I've come up with a hypothesis," Beverly said. "I think that the same mechanism that prompts the Borg to secrete the queen's nutrient gel is the same one that triggers their hypervigilance in guarding her."

"Interesting," Worf said.

Beverly checked Leary's wound; the dermis was starting to knit together nicely, enough to check any further bleeding. "You're good for now," she told her patient.

Leary got at once to her feet and turned to Worf. "I'm ready for action, sir. I know we don't have much time . . ."

"Good," the Klingon said. "We will head back toward the queen's chamber. There are only three of us and there are no doubt several drones guarding the queen. We will have to create a distraction so that Doctor Crusher can administer the hypospray that will deactivate the queen."

"What if I'm the distraction?" Beverly asked.

Worf turned sharply to look at her, but his expression was faintly pleased; he had, she realized, been thinking of suggesting it. "It could work," he said.

Leary wasn't following. Slightly aghast, she looked from Worf to Crusher. "But the doctor . . ."

Beverly gave a tight little smile. "The Borg may be moving faster, but they still don't run," she said. "But I sure can."

13

"HE FELL."

Sandra Chao's voice, soft yet ragged, filtered up to Nave and echoed in the wide, empty shaft. Nave closed her eyes and pressed her forehead hard against her knuckles as she clung to the metal rung. At least Diasourakis's scream had stopped reverberating.

"He—" Chao broke off and took a few seconds to gather herself before continuing. "It was hard for me to see. When you fired . . . the Borg fell, I think, and knocked Greg off the ladder."

Nave kept her eyes closed a long moment. When she was able, she opened them and raised her face. Overhead, there was no sign that anyone else had followed. "Let's keep going," she told Chao. "Two more landings, then we'll see where we are."

They continued down in miserable silence. They

passed another landing; then, as Chao neared the second, she reached out carefully, caught hold of a guardrail, and pulled herself onto the landing. Her boots clattered against the metal. "I think it'd be best if you waited, sir," she called to Nave, then cautiously opened the hatch and peered beyond it.

She looked back at Nave. "It's all right. The corridor's empty."

The landing was large enough only for one. Chao stepped through the open hatch, then turned and waited.

Nave reached for the guardrail above the landing and made the mistake of glancing down at the fathomless drop; she jerked her gaze up sharply and instead focused on Chao, who stood on the other side of the hatch, offering her hand.

Using the guardrail, Nave swung herself over and came down hard, on both feet, on the landing. Chao helped her climb through the hatch; both women paused to study their surroundings. The deck was similar to the one above, except that there were no drones within sight.

Nave hit her combadge. "Nave to Worf . . ." She let go a sound of disgust. "It's dead."

Chao tried hers, with the same result. "They must all know we're here."

Nave raised her face to study the outer bulkheads, trying to figure out the ship's skeleton in hopes of finding another shaft that would take them back up to the queen's chamber and, with luck, the rest of the away team.

"It's not your fault," Chao said suddenly, softly.
Nave scowled down at her.

"About Greg. You were trying to save him. It
wasn't your fault, the way it happened."

Nave averted her gaze and shrugged. Chao was
wrong; it *was* her fault. The shot from her rifle had
hit the Borg—who struck Diasourakis when it fell.
And Greg had fallen such a horribly long way that
his body had to have been completely shattered—
too damaged for human medicine or even Borg
technology to repair. He was utterly, irrevocably
gone. But there was no point in arguing about her
innocence or guilt with Chao.

"There's nothing either of us can do about it,"
she said shortly, then let go a breath and looked
back at Chao. "We can only get back up, to the
queen's chamber, and do what we're here to do."

"Aye, sir."

Nave stared up at the distant bulkheads again
and finally saw what she was looking for. "And to
get there"—she pointed—"we need to go *that* way."

As the two made their way forward, they encountered a series of steps leading down to a semi-
enclosed area. Nave didn't like it; it was harder to
see if anyone was coming in either direction. And,
like Chao, she found the surroundings distracting.
Built into the bulkheads were blinking consoles—
ungainly, cluttered things with masses of exposed
circuitry so that Nave found it impossible to distin-

guish the working parts from the controls. On the opposite side stood a massive workstation, large enough to accommodate six standing workers; its main screen displayed a rotating, glowing red legend, but all other controls were dark, as if the main systems had been shut down.

Nave frowned at it. "It's a schematic of this ship."

Beside her, Chao spoke. "This could be the helm."

Nave grunted. "And the weapons station." She lingered an instant. It was tempting to discharge her weapon into the heart of the station, destroying it—but the risk of alerting the Borg was too great. Her primary responsibility was to locate Commander Worf and assist him in destroying the queen.

"Makes you wonder where everybody is," Chao said softly.

"Waiting," Nave answered and started moving again.

They wandered past more stations and equipment, a jumble of consoles and controls, panels and dark monitors. To Nave it looked as though every department of a starship—engineering, life support, communications, weapons, navigation—had been crammed together in a one-hundred-meter space.

Another handful of steps led them up to a narrower, curving corridor, one even darker than the rest of the Borg vessel. Nave found it claustrophobic: the curve and darkness both restricted her line of sight. And it did not help matters that the corridor was lined on both sides with rows of empty Borg alcoves.

"These are their alcoves," she whispered to Chao. When Chao shot her a quizzical glance, she added, "Where they sleep."

"Do you think they're all awake now?" Chao whispered back.

Nave shook her head—if they were, she doubted the ship's stations would be unmanned—but her reply was unnecessary. In the next instant, Chao's question was answered.

Nave froze as she spotted a dark form in the alcove that had just come into view on her left. She raised her rifle, aware that Chao, beside her, had done the same.

If it had moved, she would have instantly killed it.

But it stayed motionless in its narrow cubicle, bathed in faintly pulsating gray light. Chao raised her weapon to fire; Nave reached out to the side and pressed her hand against the nose of her companion's weapon, lowering it. The Borg was not moving and posed no immediate threat. It was best to save the power cell. The more they fired, the more the Borg would adapt. This one still seemed to be in hibernation.

Not daring to breathe, Nave neared cautiously; as she did, she passed through the elbow of the curve. Beyond stretched a hundred more alcoves, each one inhabited by a solitary dark silhouette. It was like stumbling onto a graveyard of unburied dead—worse, because these dead might well spring back to life in the blink of an eye.

For an instant, she considered forging ahead into the forest of sleeping Borg and hoping they did not wake—it would be faster than turning around. But the prospect of what would happen if they *did* made her stop and turn to Chao. Better to face the few drones they had left behind than to be caught in the middle of a swarm.

"Double back." Nave spoke so softly she could scarcely hear herself, but Chao—wide-eyed, solemn with fear—nodded in reply.

They turned and headed the way they had come. Rifle gripped tightly, Nave took the rear and kept glancing over her shoulder, expecting at any moment to see movement in the shadowy alcoves, to see eyes open, bodies stir, limbs move . . .

They attack on sight . . .

But the dreamers remained silent and still. Even so, it was not until Nave had made it back past the area of the ship's jumbled, artless control consoles that she finally released a long breath and realized she had been holding it the entire while.

Chao flashed a shaky smile over her shoulder. *"That* was more than a little nerve-racking."

"Yeah," Nave said. The corridor changed into an open catwalk with railings again; she lifted her face and scanned the overhead maze of pipes, circuitry, and interconnecting walkways. She was looking for another shaft, a lift, anything that would take them up. She sighed and looked back down at Chao.

"We're going to have to go back to the shaft where . . ." She barely managed to catch herself in time. Sara had almost said *where Diasourakis fell*. "We need to get back to the away team. And if we can't find them, we'll need to figure out a way to destroy the queen ourselves."

Chao's expression darkened at the unspoken words. "Aye, sir."

They moved on in silence, Nave yielding constantly to the impulse to look behind her, to make sure none of the sleeping Borg had awakened and followed. She suspected that most of the conscious Borg were on the uppermost level along with the queen. And if she and Chao were unable to find Worf and the others, there was very little chance that two security officers could get very close to the queen.

But Nave would certainly try.

Her vision, always sharp, had adjusted completely to the feeble light. She had been scanning for the small hatch leading to the shaft; it finally came into view, some fifty meters distant. Nave broke into a loping run. There was little time left, she realized, to complete the mission—less than ninety minutes.

Chao followed close on her heels.

So intent was Nave on her destination that she failed to notice two figures approaching from a walkway to her left. By the time she saw them and drew herself up short, they stood directly in front of her, blocking access to the hatch.

Immediately, she raised her rifle—but a second quick look at the pair made her hesitate to fire.

They were Borg. The first was hairless, sporting the black carapace, the optoscopic eye, the prosthetic arm that doubled as a weapon. Its features were bland, unremarkable, as if worn away by years of service to the Collective.

The second was newly assimilated, apparently being escorted back from recent surgery. Its hair was covered by black metal molded to its cranium; tubes emerged from the crown of its head and connected to apparently random spots on its neck, cheek, chest. Like other Borg, its movements were stiff, its expression wooden, but the face was not altogether pale. It wore a slight flush, and the areas on its skin where the tubes had been inserted were still red from the insult.

It still had two hands—human hands—and two human eyes. Despite the distance, despite the dimness, Nave knew that they were still clear and green.

"Lio," she breathed. "Oh, Lio."

Beverly listened to the sound of her heels ringing against the metal deck—a lonely, solitary sound—as she slowly approached the Borg queen's chamber.

She could not see inside, of course—a quartet of drones, standing shoulder to shoulder, guarded the entry. Their silhouettes were black against the ghastly greenish glow beyond. Their faces were hidden, but Beverly knew instinctively that Jean-Luc was not among them, just as she knew instinctively that he was inside the chamber, somewhere very close to the queen.

"Excuse me," Beverly said to them lightly, just as they lifted their heads to indicate they had spotted her. She saw an odd humor in the situation, even though she was trembling in her Starfleet-issue boots. "There's something I'd like to show you. If you would just follow me . . ." To sweeten the offer, she fired her phaser at one, just to get it riled up. The setting had been on stun. She wasn't about to waste a usable setting on a distraction.

One took a single forward step, and Beverly did not wait. She turned and ran at full tilt in the opposite direction, glancing only once over her shoulder to be sure they followed. She dashed back over the metal catwalk, then careened to the left at the first intersecting walkway.

She ran until the rails turned into bulkheads, until the bulkheads turned into empty regeneration chambers. At last she passed two occupied cells, their inhabitants shrouded in shadows. A few more strides and she slowed and turned.

Her four pursuers were twenty meters behind, walking more rapidly than she had ever seen the Borg move before. But there was only so much speed their cumbersome bodies could muster. They clomped through the walkways in unison, two abreast, their arms raised like swords, ready to strike.

Beverly spread her own arms. "Here I am. Come and get me!"

The drones neared. For all her apparent bravado, she found the sight terrifying; not all the sweat that dripped from her brow was inspired by the heat. As their steps clattered against the deck, she felt them vibrate in the soles of her feet, felt her own heart beat in rhythm. She counted each step in her head: *one, two, three, four* . . .

Ten meters away. Eight. Seven. Six . . .

"Now," a low voice commanded, and she dropped to the deck.

She knew better than to stare into the phaser fire and be blinded by the glow. Instead, she kept her gaze tightly focused on the drones' extremities—on their legs—as she readjusted her phaser and fired. She watched as they stumbled, then dropped on their arms, as they thrashed, then grew still.

She counted, too, as they fell. One. Two. Three . . .

But the fourth staggered, then straightened. Worf and Leary tried to stop the creature with a volley of blasts, but it remained upright and began again to walk.

Toward Crusher.

She adjusted her phaser, but the new setting was useless.

Crusher scrambled to her feet and began again to run, turning to look behind her. The Borg had passed Worf and Leary in their alcoves; it was still following her.

"Recalibrate!"

And the phaser fire was following it. An errant blast struck the bulkhead near her, dazzling her, throwing off sparks.

"Doctor, *get down!*"

Agonized by indecision, she glanced back. The drone was closer now, barely four meters away.

"Get down! *That's an order!*"

Beverly censored the thought of what would happen if the next shot failed to stop the drone. She dove for the deck and landed facedown, hands instinctively shielding the back of her head.

She heard the phaser fire as it struck, then heard the soft, mechanical grunt of the drone and Leary's triumphant cry.

"Got him!"

But she was unprepared for the impact as the drone's body—propelled forward by the blast—collided with hers. She cried out as heavy limbs struck her head, her back; the skin covering her ribs stung suddenly and smartly.

"Doctor!" Worf's and Leary's voices formed a chorus.

She pushed herself free of the drone's upper torso, which covered her shoulders and back, then got unsteadily to her knees. Worf and Leary hurried to either side of her; gratefully, she took their proffered hands and got to her feet.

"You're bleeding!" Leary said.

Beverly reached a hand around to touch her back; it came away bloodied. She shook her head.

"It doesn't feel that bad." She was far more concerned about the hypospray for the queen; she touched her belt to reassure herself it was still there.

Worf bent down to examine the wound. "It appears to be shallow."

"It is." Beverly let go a long, shaky breath, then forced a grim smile. "Well, then. Shall we do it all again?"

No other drones had followed Beverly, and she encountered no one on the way back to the queen's chamber. Now only two drones stood shoulder to shoulder barring entry. Beverly drew close enough only to be seen. She could not see much beyond them, into the chamber, but she caught blurs of one or two other dark bodies.

This time, when she called out to the drones, her tone was not as light; this time, when Worf told her to drop, she did so immediately and did not let herself look up.

When it was over and two more drones lay motionless on the deck, she sat back on her haunches and gazed up at Worf, who had stepped out of the darkened alcove, his rifle gripped by both hands. Leary moved out of the alcove directly across from his.

"There are a few others in the chamber," Beverly said. "Maybe only one or two. I couldn't tell exactly."

"There cannot be too many," the Klingon responded, "if they cut the number guarding the chamber by half."

"Or if there *are* more, they're all needed to tend the queen."

Worf considered this, nodding faintly. His intense gaze strayed beyond her, in the direction of the great chamber.

"Are we going, sir?" Leary asked. In the gray light, her skin was sallow, her eyes shadowed. Beverly began to worry that the effects of the tri-ox were starting to wear off—Leary needed to get back to the *Enterprise* in less than an hour. But it was a moot point, she realized. If Leary *didn't* get back to the ship by then, no transfusion in the world would save her life.

"We are," Worf replied. "Doctor Crusher, you will remain between Ensign Leary and me until we are in the chamber. We will clear a path for you to the queen and cover you while you administer the hypospray. But if you are unsuccessful—or if circumstances require it—I will not hesitate to destroy her with our weapons. I appreciate the importance of scientific research, but we cannot fail in our mission."

"Of course," she said. "I wouldn't expect it to be otherwise. But . . . Worf," she began, then paused, hesitant. "If we encounter the captain—"

"I will do whatever I can to avoid harming the captain," Worf countered swiftly, his tone uncharacteristically soft. "But that might not be possible."

"I know. I just wanted to say that . . . whatever happens . . . I know that you have to do what's necessary. I . . . I trust you to do what's right, however hard that might be. And I know that he trusts you, too."

Worf glanced down—humbly, she thought—and let go a long breath. As he did, the natural sternness of his features eased to something fleetingly but remarkably gentle. *This,* she thought, *is what his wife must have seen in him.* And then just as quickly, his fierce pride returned, though his voice was very quiet and not quite so deep.

"A Klingon would do everything possible to save the life of his commander. But he also would not permit that commander to live if living brought dishonor upon him. I will try," he said, "to be Klingon for him."

14

A SINGLE DRONE STOOD GUARD AT THE ENTRY TO
the queen's chamber, its face obscured by shadow,
its body backlit by pulsating greenish light.

Beverly's phaser had already proved useless
once. She knew that she couldn't rely on it in the
queen's chamber. Besides, she had a more important weapon to focus on once they were inside.
With Worf's permission, she set the phaser to over-
load and sent it skidding along the ground toward
the lone Borg. It stopped a meter in front of the
drone.

She held her breath as the drone took a step forward to examine the mystery object. That was all
they needed as the phaser exploded beneath the
drone. For one millisecond, its body froze, the dark
mass at the center of a dazzling nova. Then the
blast faded, and the drone crumpled and dropped.

Leary and Worf stood motionless in place, weapons trained on the open entry to the chamber. Like them, Beverly did not move but held perfectly still, listening for the sound of approaching footfalls.

She could hear only her own rapid breath. The corridor and chamber were eerily silent—*as though,* she thought, *someone is waiting.*

Several seconds passed before Worf at last gave a nod and began to move; Leary and Beverly followed. As they stepped over the drone's body and over the threshold of the queen's chamber, Beverly felt an unpleasant thrill in the pit of her stomach.

There were black-and-white forms in the near distance. Someone was indeed waiting.

The chamber was a huge, high-ceilinged vault, so open and hushed it reminded Beverly oddly of a cathedral. She had never before set eyes on the queen, but she recognized her at once.

The queen was standing upright—or rather, her flesh-and-metal head and shoulders were supported by an entirely prosthetic body. Her arms, legs, and torso all were constructed of the same brittle black carapace worn by the drones but vastly different at the same time. It was a young body, strong, distinctly feminine.

As was the face, pale and still as sculpted stone beneath a shimmering, transparent layer of gel. It was a strangely beautiful face, naked of hair, including brows and lashes; the skin was so translucent that the veins showed through, giving it a mottled appearance. The queen's expression was serene, beatific; her lips curved upward in a languid smile. Her eyes were closed, as if she were dead or sleeping.

To her right was a bier, from which she had recently been resurrected. Mounds of the gelatinous substance—glinting opalescent mother-of-pearl in the light—still lay faintly quivering on the bed; some had spilled onto the deck, and a shining trail could be traced directly to the feet of the queen.

High above her, draped in shadow, was a vast cybernetic structure vaguely like the core of a ship's engine. Faintly phosphorescent, it was the source of the pulsating green light. From it dangled dozens of long, slender black tubes that drifted, oddly sentient, like the stinging tendrils of a jellyfish at sea.

Indifferent to the intruders, a pair of drones fawned over her like courtiers. One knelt beside her as he slowly unhooked her from overhead tendrils; the other used a scanner to check the connections of the body's self-sustaining tubing, which ran from the crown of her bare skull to her neck, back, and shoulders.

And Jean-Luc stood beside them. He was watching not the queen but the away team. He had seen them kill the drone guard and followed their every move.

Not Jean-Luc, Beverly corrected herself at once. She looked into his eyes—blank, emotionless, soulless—and knew they were the eyes of Locutus, the enemy. Jean-Luc had been eclipsed. She reined in the emotions that hit her at the sight and rested her hand on the hypospray attached to her belt—a reminder of why she had come.

"Captain Picard," Worf murmured but fell silent at once.

Locutus looked away, at the courtier drones. Merely looked, but the drones immediately stopped what they were doing, as if they had heard a command, and left the queen's side. They moved toward Locutus, who in turn stepped closer to the away team.

Worf raised his weapon and took aim at the queen. Beverly said nothing; it was his prerogative as commander to end this swiftly, if he deemed it best.

Yet in the instant before he fired, before Leary had managed to train her rifle on the others, Locutus reached to one side and grazed a control on the bulkhead.

A pale, glittering force field leaped in place around the queen—and the queen alone—leaving Locutus and the other drones to do battle with the intruders. It happened so swiftly that Worf could not stop himself: the beam from his rifle flared brilliantly, blindingly against the field, which absorbed the energy with a crackle.

Picard had known they were coming, Beverly realized. And Locutus had used that knowledge to prepare for them: the field looked to be Federation technology.

Locutus moved again, before Worf could retrain

his weapon, catching an overhead tangle of snake-like tubing and propelling it forward. Still attached to the ceiling, it glided with serpentine speed at the away team. Beverly cried out, shielding her face as dozens of whips lashed against her, knocking her to the deck.

Somehow, Locutus's harsh monotone penetrated the chaos.

"You will not escape. We have commanded all the others to wake to assist us in disarming you. And the queen will wake momentarily. You will be assimilated, and the *Enterprise* and those aboard her will be destroyed."

Cut and bruised, Beverly fought back to her feet and thrashed her way free of the tangles. Worf, too, had risen and was lifting his weapon from the deck when they both glanced up at the sound of deliberate but rapid footsteps.

A half dozen drones appeared in the entryway. Worf reeled about and fired into their midst; as Beverly oriented herself, Leary appeared from the tangles, rifle blasting.

Locutus, in the meantime, had activated his prosthesis so that the saw blade was whirring; he and the two courtier-drones advanced on the Starfleet officers' unprotected backs.

"Look out!" Beverly shouted beside them. And as Worf wheeled about, firing, Beverly saw her opportunity: Locutus had deserted his post where the force field controls were located. He and the courtiers were ignoring her, since they considered her unarmed, and were converging instead on the embattled Worf and Leary.

She drew in a long, deep breath and ran, crossing from behind her fellow officers to head past Locutus and his companions. She made a beeline for the control on the bulkhead, and when she reached it, she slapped it hard, gasping.

The field dissolved. "Worf!" she shouted. "Worf, she's open! The queen's open! Leary!"

But neither Leary nor the Klingon could spare the time to look at her, to listen; they were firing rapidly, then stopping to recalibrate every few seconds. They were in danger of being overtaken.

Beverly dashed toward the motionless queen.

She was barely two meters away when, from the periphery of her vision, she saw Locutus stop, turn, gaze at her. He abandoned the fight at once and moved toward Beverly.

For a minute she thought he was pursuing her—and then he stopped at the bulkhead control and stared at her again. She stopped at once; she dropped her arms to her sides, intentionally covering the hypospray on her belt.

He blinked, once . . . then pressed the control.

Beverly sighed in silent relief as the force field snapped back into place—leaving her inside it, with the queen. She held still for a painfully long moment, until Locutus, satisfied she was no real threat, turned his attention back to Worf and Leary.

She sidled cautiously up to the sleeping queen,

then quickly reached for her hypo and settled it against the queen's slender white neck.

The queen's hand snaked across her body and caught Beverly's so rapidly that the doctor let go a startled sound. She tried to pull away; the queen's fingers, steel talons, held her fast.

The queen turned her face toward Beverly's. Her eyes were dark, quicksilver, malevolent. She increased the pressure on Beverly's wrist until the doctor cried out at the pain; the hypo fell from her grasp and clattered to the deck.

"Pathetic little creature." The queen's voice was distinctly un–Borg-like, distinctly unmechanical. It was animated, thoroughly laced with emotion: amusement, haughtiness, gloating, scorn. "Did you really think I would let you take him away from me again?"

Beverly looked on her with profound hate. "Did you think I would let *you?*"

The queen's delicately wrought lips twisted. Her grip grew fiercer, until Beverly felt her own feet rise slightly off the deck. There came a soft, grisly sound, as the bones of her wrist snapped.

Agony, bright blue and electric, more dazzling than the phaser beams, flashed in front of her eyes. The queen casually released her grip; Beverly fell at once to her knees.

Worf watched as the captain—Locutus, he reminded himself sternly—erected the force field around the queen, leaving Doctor Crusher closed inside. He trusted the doctor to do her job; his greatest worry at the moment was how to render Locutus harmless without killing him. *Fast acting,* she had called the hypospray. He only hoped that it would act quickly enough.

Of the six drones that had swarmed inside the entryway, two were already downed. Leary had moved to crouch beside Worf. She fought valiantly, but she had grown noticeably pale and haggard; she would not be able to stay on her feet much longer. She kept firing at the drones near the entryway. The Klingon faced the opposite direction, addressing himself to Locutus and the two drones who had attended the queen.

Worf took down the latter two quickly, but Locutus gave him pause; he kept his rifle's sights trained on the recently assimilated Picard but waited to fire. The drone kept steadily, fearlessly advancing, lifting its arm and causing the saw blade at its tip to whir ominously. Clearly it shared the captain's knowledge that his second-in-command would do everything possible to avoid killing him.

Behind Locutus, within the safe confines of the force field, Doctor Crusher hurried to the side of the queen.

"*Got* him," Leary murmured beside the Klingon. Worf recalibrated his weapon, and without another instant's hesitation, fired.

The blast struck exactly as he intended: at the far

outermost edge of the force field. It was too shallow to be absorbed; instead, it banked off the edge and detonated a few meters away—dangerously close to where Locutus stood. The burst knocked the captain-drone to the deck.

Worf turned, recalibrating as he did so, and tried to help Leary, but it was too late. In her weakened state, Leary had been overwhelmed by the drones. It had happened so quickly that she could not even let out a sound. Worf had not been aware. With a howl of rage, Worf fired and brought down her killer, then wheeled about again to look behind him.

Locutus was back on his feet, a mere five meters away. Worf recalibrated and banked another shot. This time, his aim was off, and the field absorbed the blast. And as the field brightened from the impact, Worf recalibrated, stealing another glance at the queen as he did so.

Doctor Crusher had fallen, and the queen—now conscious—stood glaring down at her.

He would, the Klingon realized, have to shoot to kill. There was no longer any time to spare; he would have to find a way to the queen himself and destroy her.

He lifted his rifle again, prepared to take aim— and frowned. Locutus had, in the wink of an eye, disappeared.

A millisecond later, the nutrient bed on which the queen had lain slammed against Worf's legs and hips, knocking him to the deck. He fell hard onto his tailbone but managed, through supreme effort, to keep his grip on his weapon. He slapped one palm against the deck, thinking to push himself immediately to his feet . . .

. . . But before he could, he looked up to see Locutus, standing over him, the saw arm lifted.

The saw arm came down, biting into the rifle with sparks and a harsh grinding sound. Locutus lifted the arm; the weapon came with it, and with a sharp jerk, he sent it flying through the air. It struck the field and clattered to the deck, sliding to a stop on the opposite side of the chamber.

Before the saw arm came down again, Worf rolled to his side. Locutus followed, relentless.

It was not in the Klingon's nature to flee. Determined, he threw himself on the drone. With one hand, he caught hold of Locutus's forearm and forced it away; with the other, he seized hold of the drone's neck.

He intended to overpower the captain-drone, then get to the queen in order to kill her—but Locutus was far too strong; the whining saw drew inexorably closer to the Klingon's chest. Worf realized he would not even be able to hold his ground, and he let go a roar of fury and frustration.

There was only one thing left to do: die, killing Locutus. It would save the captain from further dishonor . . . and it would give Worf an honorable death.

An honorable death, he told Jadzia silently, *for both of us.*

As the saw blade neared his heart, Worf increased the pressure on Locutus's neck until it was strong enough to kill a human.

Without an instant's reflection, Nave fired her phaser rifle at the guard-drone, felling it. The blast was so near Lio that he staggered—Nave could not bring herself to think of him as a drone, an "it"—and bounced off the railing before regaining his footing.

She had a choice, she realized as she and Chao quickly recalibrated their weapons. They could leave him here, turn and head back to the forest of the sleeping Borg—but other than the obvious risk, it would waste even more priceless time. Or they could attempt to get past him—a possibility, since he was unarmed and with only two human hands to fight them.

The question was resolved in a heartbeat: in the distance behind her, lights flashed on.

"The console area," Chao said quickly. Nave heard the faint sound of footsteps. "They're waking up."

Nave fired at the deck in front of Lio's feet. The reflected blast stopped him, made him raise an arm to shield his face—a distinctly human gesture, she decided, she *hoped*. Once it faded, he began to move steadily forward again.

"Don't fire!" she told Chao as she recalibrated. "Get ready to run past him. I'll aim at the center, in front of his feet, so steer clear when you go. If you get yourself hit, I won't be able to help you."

Chao gave a swift nod. Nave fired again at the deck, squinting at the brilliance as Chao, compact and muscular, dashed past Lio's tall, lanky form. She swung out as she did, brushing against the railing—and Lio, as he lifted his arms in response to the blast.

But she made it to the other side, a bit shaken from the proximity of the burst, then turned to Nave.

"Over here, Lio!" she called to the drone. "Over here!" And as she lifted her rifle, she directed a nod and a pointed glance at Nave.

Nave lowered her own weapon and readied herself to run.

"Now," Chao said.

Nave sprinted, careful to veer to the side. The burst from the rifle was blinding. She kept her head down, her gaze averted as she brushed against the railing, and did not think about the precipitous drop just past it.

When the blow came, she was entirely surprised. It caught her across the brow, snapping her head sharply back. She reeled, then dropped to her knees, dizzied, nauseated by the pain. For one disoriented instant, she thought she had somehow collided with a low-hanging conduit.

And then hands grasped the uniform fabric atop her collarbone and yanked her onto her unreliable feet.

"Stop!" Chao shouted. "Lieutenant, get away from him! Run! I have to shoot!"

"No," Nave said, vainly trying to make her eyes focus. She could see nothing but Lio's Borg face, unsmiling and pale—or, rather, one and a half faces. She reached for her rifle, thinking not to fire it—shooting a body so close to hers would prove fatal for them both—but to wield it like a club. Her fingers had barely touched it when it was tugged from her. She felt the strap over her shoulder break and give way, heard the weapon strike the deck with a loud ring in the distance. "No, just *go!* We don't have time. Find the queen . . ."

Phaser fire rushed past her. Chao was taking aim at the approaching Borg, giving Nave the time to break free of Lio.

She tottered on her feet in a pathetic effort to move away. Running was impossible; her body had become uncoordinated, uncooperative. Something dark loomed toward her—Lio's arm, she realized, as it slammed against the side of her head. There came a breathtaking stab of pain in her neck. Her ribs collided with the railing, which she instinctively clutched as her head and shoulders lurched over the side.

She opened her eyes. Her gaze was fixed on the infinite downward spiral of deck after deck after deck, dissolving into vertiginous darkness: the abyss. The decks swam and shifted, doubling in number, then shifted back, accompanied by a fierce throbbing in her skull; Nave thought she would be sick. Behind her, Chao was still firing, her screams shrill against the dull, steady thrum of Borg footsteps.

"Go!" Nave screamed, but her voice came out faint, weak. *"Find the queen . . . That's an order!"*

As she cried out, a roar filled her ears; her own voice, and Chao's, faded to silence. She turned and looked up.

Lio was reaching for her shoulders; he pushed sideways against her, trying to use the weight of her body to loosen her grip, to send her tumbling over the side. Nave held on as she stared up into his eyes.

They were green and clear, lifeless and mindless, Lio's eyes absent Lio's soul. They were the most horrifying thing she had ever seen, and she realized, quite clearly, that she was an instant from death—and that those terrible eyes were the last things she would ever see.

She looked back down at the dizzying darkness. *Let go,* she told herself. *Why force him to kill you? Just let go and die . . .* It was a better way, to fall into oblivion and decay, rather than survive in eternal purgatory as a drone.

Just hold on, someone said suddenly, calmly, clearly, as if lips had been pressed to her ear. It might have been Chao; it might have been her father.

There was no hope, none at all. The drones were waking up, which meant that the queen had wakened, and there was no more hope of stopping her.

The Borg would win, and Lio and Captain Picard would spend eternity as drones. Chao would find herself alone and overwhelmed, and be torn to pieces.

And she, Sara, was already dead, gone as surely as her mother and father had one day disappeared from the living to become memories.

No hope, Nave repeated to herself, as Lio pressed against her, killing her. She tried one last time to find the warmth in his eyes, but there was none, no recognition at all. In that moment, she gave up all hope of saving Lio, all hope of saving herself. She would do as she had promised him before he had left the *Enterprise.* She would do what he said he had not been able to do for his friend Joel.

With herculean strength borne out of her love and sorrow, Nave pulled Lio with her as she allowed herself to fall over the railing. She could hear Chao's scream follow her as they dropped down the seemingly endless pit until she was too far to hear anything.

Sara had been right earlier.

The last thing she saw were Lio's cold eyes.

Behind the force field, Beverly sat back on her haunches. The sound of Locutus's saw drilling into Worf's rifle brought her back to full consciousness; the pain had caused her nearly to faint. She stared clinically down at her injury and assessed it. The wrist of her dominant right hand was shattered, useless; she could not bear the attempt to articulate her fingers.

But Worf had fallen, and Locutus was moving in for the kill. There was no time to think about something as unimportant as pain. She had one good hand. Gritting her teeth, she propped herself on it, the injured arm tucked close to her body. The missing hypospray had rolled only a few meters away; she crawled to it on her knees.

Nearby, the fully born queen had grown impatient with her restricted mobility. Rather than wait for her courtiers, she reached clumsily, with unaccustomed hands, for the cables that attached her neck, shoulders, and crown to her overhead energy source.

Beverly clutched the errant hypo. Unseen, she rose awkwardly to her feet and, crouching, approached her enemy from the back.

The queen's hands were behind her neck as she unfastened a piece of sinuous black tubing the way a woman might a necklace. Beverly reached out with the hypo, aiming for one of the queen's upraised arms.

The instant before she could rest it against the queen's flesh, the black body, the mottled white head, whipped about and faced her.

The liquid bronze eyes were narrowed with fury. *"Insect,"* the queen hissed. She reached out with a bone-pale hand and wrapped it about Beverly's throat; her touch was cool, unctuous, metal hard.

Beverly felt a flare of pain as her trachea, her larynx, were slowly crushed—but she felt no fear, only disgust and determination. She did not waste time considering the fact that she would now certainly die. She had no more than a split second to act, and in that second, she concentrated all of her energy, all of her will, on her unsteady left hand and the hypospray it held.

The queen bore down. Beverly grew lightheaded; her vision began to dim. But her left hand continued to move. She felt rather than saw the hypo meet the flesh of the queen's shoulder; she pressed her thumb down and heard it whisper. Only then did she permit her eyes to close and yield to darkness.

15

———•———

A KLINGON'S STRENGTH DID NOT QUITE MATCH
that of a Borg. Worf's hand began to tremble with
the effort of holding Locutus's saw arm back. The
blade grew closer, closer, until at last it sliced
through the fabric of his uniform just beneath his
chest.

And then it stung his skin. Worf felt the
warmth of blood as it ran down his midsection;
the realization made him roar and squeeze his fingers even more deeply into Locutus's throat. The
drone's eyes bulged slightly; its lips parted as it
gasped for air.

The saw blade stuttered as it hit the edges of the
Klingon's ribs. Worf did not flinch at the pain; instead, he came to a decision. He would let go of the
saw arm, let it take him—so that he could seize Locutus's neck with both of his hands and kill him.

We will die together, he promised the captain. It would be a good way to die.

Yet, in the fleeting second that Worf let go of the thick prosthetic arm, it went suddenly limp and fell to hang at the drone's side. Astonished, the Klingon let go of his grip, thinking that he had somehow managed to kill first.

He pushed himself free and rose to find that Locutus was still standing. He was not dead, merely immobile. Hopeful, Worf glanced quickly in the direction of the force field. Behind it, the queen was motionless, her head bowed.

Beside her, Doctor Crusher lay, just as lifeless and unmoving on the deck.

Worf called out to her. "Doctor Crusher! Can you hear me?"

There was no response.

Worf went immediately to the force field control; a hum, and the field disappeared. He then moved, unsteadily, to Crusher's side. She was breathing. It was shallow but steady. Worf found the medkit, stripped it from Crusher's leg, and opened it to find a scanner. He ran it over the doctor, then looked at the readout in dismay. Her throat had been crushed.

Finally, there was merciful silence. The pain was still there, but the noise had ceased. She wanted to sleep. But in the back of her mind, Beverly knew that she could not do that. To sleep meant to die.

Although, at the moment, either would be preferable to the pain.

She barely felt the press of metal against her neck as the world returned around her in a sudden rush. Beverly came to with a cough, then immediately put a hand to her aching throat. For an instant, she was disoriented, half thinking she was in bed, in the captain's quarters—in *their* quarters— and then she started, remembering the queen, and opened her eyes.

Worf was standing over her with a medical stimulator in her hand. He was wan and weak looking, but alive. "How are you feeling, Doctor?"

Beverly pushed herself to sitting, grimacing at the stab of pain in her right wrist, then squeezed her eyes shut at the wave of dizziness. She was having trouble speaking.

Worf put a steadying hand on her shoulder. "It is going to take you a while to mend completely. Your wrist is not yet thoroughly knitted. I had to spend most of the time on your throat."

Beverly gave another cough, then said, "The queen . . ."

"Dead," Worf said, nodding at a point beyond Beverly's left shoulder. "It was quite impressive."

Beverly turned her head—gingerly, carefully— and followed Worf's gaze.

Standing motionless atop her black prosthetic body, the queen slumped, face toward the deck, her eyes lifeless and empty. Beverly gasped at the profile: every distinctive, identifying feature—the full lips, the feminine curve of the jaw and neck, the sharp nose, the upward slanting eyes—had been washed away, blunted so that it was now completely androgynous. Beverly gave a faint victorious smile.

She turned back to Worf and said suddenly, "Jean-Luc . . ."

"There." Worf pointed to where the captain stood, silent and still as the queen.

"Is he—?"

"Alive," Worf said. "But in hibernation. I believe all of the Borg have gone into their sleeping state."

Beverly tried to stand up but failed. "I need samples of the drones' DNA so that we can prevent the mechanism that allows them to create a new queen . . ."

"You need to rest," Worf said.

She frowned. "I don't think so. Hand me my medkit."

Worf considered the request for a moment, then complied. "I need to locate the control for the damping field so that we can use our communicators to locate the rest of the away team and contact the *Enterprise*." He helped her to her feet before moving to the console.

Beverly nodded that she understood, then rifled through her medkit where she found the hypo and collected a sample from the nearest drone.

"I think I've brought down the damping field,"

Worf said as he pressed his combadge. "Worf to security team."

"This is Chao," a relieved voice replied, though Beverly could hear a strain in it as well. *"The rest of the team is . . . gone."*

"Understood," Worf said, simply. "Stand by to beam out."

Worf then contacted the *Enterprise,* where Nelson reported from the auxiliary bridge that they were ready to drop the cloak and transfer the surviving members of the away team back.

Beverly confirmed that she had collected enough DNA samples and joined Worf as he took a position beside the captain.

Jean-Luc stood passive and unresponsive. His eyes were distant, blank, but Beverly knew from experience that somewhere, deep within, Jean-Luc was there, watching, listening. She took his limp hand and whispered, "We're going home now." And as the beam caught hold of them, causing the queen's chamber to dissolve like an ill-remembered nightmare, she smiled.

Picard drew in a breath. The air against his skin, in his lungs, was no longer forbiddingly cold and dry; it was comfortable, fresh, invigorating. He opened his eyes. Beverly stood over him, smiling. "Welcome home."

She was no longer painted in the blacks and whites and grays of monochrome; her hair was pale copper, glinting and glorious against the vivid blue of her lab coat. The world was once again alive with color.

"Beverly." His voice seemed hoarse, unused. "You have no idea how good it feels to be back." He stretched his arms out in front of him and flexed his hands and fingers—warm, living flesh and blood—with pleasure. "The queen . . . ?"

"No longer a threat," she said. "Remember I mentioned I had a hunch? The queen's nutrient gel, which the drones were feeding her, contained an estrogenic-type compound. It can be neutralized by its male analogue, an androgenic compound."

"And the cube?"

"Dormant," she reported. "The drones are little more than empty shells. All consciousness left them when we destroyed the queen. With no connection to the hive and no way to activate a new queen, they effectively shut themselves down. Possibly waiting for a new directive that, we hope, will never come. Admiral Janeway is sending a contingent of science vessels to examine the craft."

"Worf has been in touch with the admiral?" he asked.

"Don't worry," she said. "He left you to give her the full report."

"I will have to remember to thank him later," Picard said with a smile.

"Now, as for you," Beverly said, "it wasn't so easy transforming you back again. The Borg had developed a new generation of nanoprobes. It took a few hours, but I figured it out . . . and now the Starfleet research files on the Borg are updated. Oh, and we have fresh samples of Borg DNA, too. We're working on a way to chemically short-circuit the mechanisms that propel the drones to create a new queen so that it can never happen again."

Picard had to say the words himself to make sure he understood them. "Never again?"

"Never again," Beverly repeated. "I'm confident we'll be able to find a way."

Her words provided infinite relief, but it was short-lived. A question troubled him deeply, and he dreaded the answer. "Were there casualties in my rescue?"

"Three lost," she said with sadness. "Sara Nave was among them."

Picard took in her words with regret.

"And we were unable to save Lieutenant Battaglia," she added.

He looked away and down. He should have been grateful, he told himself, that this time it had been only a few and not thousands. And yet the guilt, the sorrow, was no less acute. "Did I . . . ?"

"You didn't harm anyone," she said. "Not permanently. But you did give Worf a run for his money."

"I'm surprised *I* survived an encounter with a Klingon. Is he all right?"

"He mended pretty quickly. I released him a couple of hours ago."

Picard looked up at her more keenly and saw the

fading greenish bruises, like dark pearls, encircling her neck. "Those are *fingerprints* . . . What happened?" He reached a hand toward them.

She touched them absently; her smile was dark but self-satisfied. "A memento."

"A drone attacked you?"

"The queen."

"The queen . . . ?" He blinked at her, impressed. "You did it, didn't you? *You* saved me."

"We all saved you," she said modestly. "Worf, Leary, Nave—all of us. None of us could have done it alone." The dark little smile returned. "Let's just say I had a score to settle."

"With such a formidable opponent, then, the queen never had a chance." He returned her smile. "Am I fit for duty, Doctor?"

"As fit as you'll ever be."

Picard reached for his combadge, then frowned as he realized it was no longer there. Beverly saw and—reading his mind—pressed her own.

"Crusher to bridge."

"Worf here, Doctor."

"Worf." Her tone turned faintly playful. "There's someone here who'd like to speak to you."

Picard slid off the edge of the diagnostic bed and stood next to Beverly. "Commander," he said. "Report."

The Klingon kept his tone formal but could not entirely hide the warmth and pleasure he felt. *"Aye, Captain. We are currently still in the vicinity of the Borg ship. We have disabled her engines.*

During an earlier attack, the Enterprise*'s hull sustained major damage in the area of the bridge. Now that we have reintegrated the saucer section, Commander La Forge is overseeing temporary repairs. He says that a structural overhaul should be done in drydock."* Picard shot a questioning look at the doctor upon hearing Worf mention reintegrating the saucer section, but she just nodded in a way that he inferred meant that she would explain later.

"Understood," Picard said. A sense of heaviness crept over him; he had no doubt that the Borg had once again used his knowledge to inflict the damage.

"We have also received a signal from an approaching Federation shuttle," Worf continued. *"Seven of Nine will be arriving shortly."*

The news gave him pause. "Very good. Let me know when she arrives. I'll be in my quarters. Picard out." He looked up at Beverly and sighed. "Time to pay the piper. Let's hope this goes more easily than it did with the queen."

Kathryn Janeway was not smiling.

In the captain's quarters, Picard stared down at her image on the monitor. Janeway sat leaning forward, elbows on her desk, hands tightly folded. She did not scowl, but her eyes were bright and cold. She knew what was coming.

"Admiral," he said. "Seven of Nine is due to

arrive aboard the *Enterprise* momentarily. I understand that you are already aware that her presence is no longer needed. At this time, I would like to take full responsibility for my actions. I decided to have the *Enterprise* intercept the Borg cube. My crew was only functioning under my orders."

Janeway's lips thinned. For the space of several seconds, she remained silent, staring hard at the captain. Picard held her gaze without faltering.

At last she spoke, her tone one of carefully contained fury. *"You violated a direct order, Captain."*

"I did, Admiral. I offer no defense; I expect no leniency."

"And you'll get none from me." Her chin tilted upward; her eyes flashed once, twice. *"You're very lucky things worked out to Starfleet's advantage—and yours. But I've never believed that luck should excuse insubordination."* She leaned farther forward. *"Let's imagine that things had gone differently. That the* Enterprise *was destroyed and your kidnapping had been a success. We'd have another Wolf 359 on our hands then—or worse—wouldn't we? I was very clear and emphatic about my reasoning, Picard. And you chose to ignore it completely. I suppose you expect me to say, 'All's well that ends well,' and leave it at that? Perhaps slap your wrist with a reprimand in your file?"*

"I expect nothing," Picard answered honestly.

"Nor should you. I'll be informing others at

*Command about this. In fact, I may very well initi-
ate court-martial proceedings. Am I understood?"*

"You are, Admiral."

*"Good. Have Seven of Nine contact me when she
arrives. Janeway out."*

The screen darkened; Picard bowed his head
and released a low sigh. At a different time, the
prospect of court-martial—of losing Starfleet, the
only life he had ever known—would have seemed
devastating. As it was, a career seemed a small
price to pay to prevent the loss of billions of lives.
Janeway had been wrong: it hadn't all been luck.
They had beaten back the Borg out of sheer determination, sheer will.

Beverly's dark little smile, her voice, glimmered
in his imagination. *Let's just say I had a score to
settle.*

"And I still had one, too," Picard whispered. "I
had one, too."

"To Commander Worf," Picard intoned, "now the
official first officer of the *Enterprise.*" He paused as
Doctor Crusher whispered something in his ear,
then corrected himself. "Make that the official *permanent* first officer."

"Here, here," La Forge called with the others and
joined in the enthusiastic applause.

The tables in the Happy Bottom Riding Club had
been cleared away. Picard and Crusher stood in the
center, with a clearly uncomfortable Worf nearby.

The gathering wasn't remotely as small as the Klingon had requested. Actually, one might say that it was quite large, in fact. But Picard had realized that it was the first public gathering since the memorial service for their fallen comrades and the crew needed something to celebrate.

A few days had passed since the *Enterprise* had left the directiveless Borg behind, in the care of Seven of Nine; the crew was headed now for dry-dock and shore leave.

Picard made his way past the well-wishers as they encircled Worf. There was a playful gleam in the captain's eye as he knew how uncomfortable his new first officer was under the spotlight.

"You're enjoying this, aren't you?" Beverly quietly asked with a straight face.

"It's not a dip in the ocean," he remarked, remembering Worf's last promotion under his command, "but it will do." Picard regarded her for a moment. "But you don't seem to be having much fun."

Beverly let out a sigh. "For a while," she said, holding her champagne flute at chin level, "I thought we'd never be able to transform you back into yourself. The nanites had evolved radically . . ." She shook her head. "I figured it out because I had to. But it was the hardest thing I've ever done."

"The hardest thing?" Picard asked softly. His tone was mildly teasing. She had been terribly serious and preoccupied the past few days. The experience with the Borg had been hard enough on her, but then she ferreted out the fact that Janeway had seriously threatened him with court-martial. He had hoped that the little celebration for Worf would help raise everyone's spirits—including hers.

Beverly caught his little half smile, but her tone did not lighten. "Actually, the *second* hardest thing. The hardest was seeing you as Locutus again." She looked down and shook her head, her hair swinging against her shoulders. "I took a great deal of pleasure in destroying the queen. I only wish I could have hurt her as badly as she hurt you."

"It doesn't matter," Picard said gently. "The queen doesn't exist anymore. All that's left is a pathetic creature that has to be taught to think for itself. Besides . . ." He fought the impulse to reach out and smooth her hair, an act he would never permit himself to do in front of the crew. "Hurting her wouldn't make me feel any better. But being here with you again *does.*"

His words had the desired effect; she smiled, and took another sip of champagne.

Picard let his gaze sweep over the crowd. It lit on the bar, where Worf had managed to escape to and was having a discussion with the Vulcan counselor. "I was very glad Mister Worf came to his senses about his assignment," he said. "I just don't understand what made him change his mind."

Beverly looked down slyly into her glass as her lips quirked upward.

"Wait a minute," Picard said. "Out with it."

She gazed up at him with mock innocence. "Out with *what?*"

"You know something. That cat-that-caught-the-canary smirk. Why did Worf change his mind?"

"I really don't know," she replied. "All *I* did was tell him to be Klingon."

He frowned, puzzled. "Be Klingon?" He turned toward Worf, who seemed to be hard at work trying to make another convert.

"It is prune juice," Worf explained. "A suitable drink for a warrior."

He poured the thick purplish-brown liquid from a flagon into the short, narrow glass in front of the Vulcan counselor and studied her as she stared noncommittally at it. He had not spoken to her privately since he had returned from the Borg vessel; he did not know whether she still resented him. He wanted to foster cordial relations between them, especially now that he was the official second-in-command.

"Vulcans do not believe in war," she said.

"One does not need to shed blood in order to be a warrior," Worf countered. "Victory comes in many guises."

T'Lana seemed to consider this a moment, then lifted the glass and downed it in one swallow. She looked over at him, her expression utterly serious. "It is more agreeable than its appearance indicates."

Worf immediately poured her a second glass. "So you must now admit that the captain was correct in pursuing the Borg." As he spoke, Captain Picard wandered up and stood beside the Vulcan.

"Counselor," he said, by way of greeting.

She nodded graciously. "Captain."

Picard favored the Klingon with a smile. "So, Number One, are you enjoying the festivities?"

Worf winced inwardly at the term of address. It seemed wrong for the captain to use it to refer to anyone other than Will Riker. "Not really, sir."

The captain seemed to find the honest answer amusing. "Don't worry. They'll end soon enough." He paused and glanced at T'Lana. "I'm sorry. I interrupted your conversation. Please continue."

Worf shot the Vulcan a warning glance, which she ignored. "No, Commander," she said in reply to Worf's previous question. "I do not believe that the captain was justified in disobeying orders. The captain was indeed correct about his mental connection to the Borg collective. And I am pleased that you were successful in neutralizing the queen. However, it does not logically follow that the captain's good fortune means that he was correct."

"I'm afraid Admiral Janeway agrees with you," Picard said dryly. He took a sip from his glass. "And I suppose that if you always agreed with me, you wouldn't be much of a counselor."

T'Lana gave another courteous nod. "If you will excuse me, gentlemen. I have matters to attend to."

Worf noted that when she left the lounge, she took her drink with her.

"Mister Worf," Picard said, his voice low, his tone suddenly serious. "Doctor Crusher says that you were prepared to kill me—to kill Locutus—if necessary. Is that true?"

"Yes, sir."

He gave a grim smile. "Good. You're already thinking like a captain." He drew in a deep breath, then said, very softly, "The hardest thing about having a command is realizing that one is . . . fallible. That one *isn't* always right. I failed, Worf. I was no hero this time; I endangered my own people. Had you not rescued me, I would have been responsible for the deaths of billions of people." He paused to scrutinize the Klingon's expression. "Do you understand?"

Worf's look did not waver. "Yes, Captain."

Picard's gaze was searching; at last, he seemed to find the answer he sought. He nodded slowly. "I believe you do, Mister Worf. I believe you do." His expression softened. "Congratulations. You've more than earned this."

"Thank you, sir," Worf said as the captain moved on. The Klingon turned back to the bar and his glass of fragrant juice. He imagined his dead wife smiling before him and remembered her words.

None of us knows for certain how our actions will affect others. We can only do what we judge to be right at the time. You acted from your heart. You couldn't have done anything else and remained true to yourself.

He had followed his heart and inadvertently caused the death of innocents; he had followed his heart and saved the lives of many more.

Worf lifted his glass. "To Jadzia," he said softly. *"tlhIngah jIH."*

I am Klingon.

STAR TREK

THE NEXT GENERATION®

BEFORE DISHONOR

Peter David

Available November 2007

1

———

The *Einstein*

KATHRYN JANEWAY NEEDED TO SEE IT FOR HERSELF.

She had read the detailed reports provided her by Seven of Nine. She had spoken at length with Captain Jean-Luc Picard, about whom she was still seething. In short, she had all the information she really required. Going to the Borg cube wasn't going to accomplish a damned thing.

Yet here she was, on her way, just the same.

Although she was entitled, by her rank of vice-admiral, to commandeer an entire starship for the purpose of essaying the trip, she had opted not to do so. She considered it a waste of resources. Instead she had been content to catch a ride on the *Einstein,* a standard science-exploration vessel. The commander of the *Einstein,* Howard Rappaport, had been enthused to welcome Janeway aboard. Short, stocky, but with eyes that displayed a piercing intellect, Rappaport had peppered her with questions about all the races that she had encountered during the *Voyager*'s odyssey from the Delta quadrant. It hadn't been something that she'd been overly interested in discussing, but turning down Rappaport's incessant interrogation would have felt like kicking an eager puppy, and so she had accommodated him during their trip as often as she had felt reasonable.

At least she knew he was paying attention, because not only did he hang on every word she spoke, but he kept asking intelligent follow-up questions. Still, at one point he said eagerly, "I wish I'd been there."

Upon hearing that, Janeway had promptly shut him down with a curt "No. You really don't." When she said that, he looked as if he wanted to ask more about her attitude in that regard, but wisely opted to back off when he saw the slightly haunted look in Janeway's eyes.

There were three other Starfleet officers traveling on the *Einstein* with Janeway, all of them purported experts on the Borg. The officers—Commanders Andy Brevoort and Tom Schmidt, and Lieutenant Commander Mark Wacker—were experienced xenobiologists who had been given a simple mandate by Starfleet: Find a way to develop an absolute protection against the Borg should they launch another attack. The general feeling of the United Federation of Planets Council and Starfleet in particular was that, even though they had managed to dodge destruction at the hands of the Borg each and every time, they owed a measure of that success to sheer luck.

The plan was to try to remove luck from the equation and replace it with a practical, proven solution.

The *Einstein* was long on durability but short on amenities. It was designed to cater to scientists, not to top brass or ambassadors or any of that ilk. Janeway's quarters were consequently the most luxurious the ship had to offer yet still quite spare. The admiral didn't care. She didn't tend to stand on ceremony in such matters. Give her breathable atmosphere, functioning gravity, and a steady source of coffee, and Janeway was content.

The admiral was worried she was becoming an addict. The last time she'd been on a starship, she'd studied the warp core too long and decided that it looked like a gigantic antique coffee maker. She'd sworn—at that point—to give up the hideously addictive brew. Yet here she was now, nursing a cup of black coffee while she read over yet again the reports from all the various sources about the monstrous Borg cube that the *Enterprise* had managed to take down pretty much single-handedly. There was a transcript of all of Picard's log entries on the subject, as well as the entries from other crew members, including, most notably, the Vulcan counselor, T'Lana. Janeway shook her head as she read it all, still bristling at the very thought of all that had transpired contrary to her orders.

"How could you, Picard?" she asked rhetorically of the empty room. "How could you put me in that kind of position, just on a hunch?"

"It's what I would have done."

The voice caught her by surprise, because she

had naturally thought she was alone. She turned and, uncharacteristically but understandably, let out a startled yelp.

James T. Kirk was standing in her quarters.

"*What the hell*—?!" Janeway was on her feet, gaping.

Kirk was wearing a very old-style Starfleet uniform, a simple yellow shirt with black collar. He smoothed it down and gave her a wry smile. "Hello, Admiral. Or Kathryn, perhaps? Would it be too forward if I addressed you as Kathryn? Feel free to call me Jim."

Fortunately for Janeway, she had been in enough bizarre situations, had enough experiences that would have made lesser men and women question their sanity, that she was thrown only for a few moments. She recovered quickly from her initial shock, and then said briskly, "I'm quite certain I'm not dreaming."

"How would you know?" asked Kirk. He walked casually around the small quarters, looking disapproving.

"I know because I dream in black and white."

"Perhaps you're only dreaming that you're dreaming in color," he countered. He gestured around himself. "Space may be infinite, but obviously not in here. They couldn't provide you with larger accommodations?"

"I wasn't expecting to share them. Who are you?" she demanded. She felt no need to summon help at that point; she didn't feel as if she were in any immediate danger. Besides, it was a science vessel, not a starship, so it wasn't as if a crack security team was going to come running.

"I'm James T. Kirk." He tilted his head slightly, quizzically. "Are you having short-term memory difficulties? You may want to see somebody about that."

"I know you're supposed to be James T. Kirk. That's who you're presenting yourself as. But obviously you're not."

"Why are you fighting it, Kathryn?" he asked with what he doubtless thought was suavity. He smiled wryly. "You once said you wish you could have teamed up with me. So what's wrong with getting your wish once in a while?"

Her eyes narrowed, her mind racing toward an inevitable conclusion. There was no trace of amusement in her voice. "All right. Drop it."

"Come on, Kathryn," Kirk said wheedlingly. "I was famous for flaunting Starfleet regulations. You know that. Everybody knows that. Picard's mistake wasn't disobeying your direct order to wait for Seven of Nine and then, and only then, seek out the Borg cube that his 'link' to their hive mind had detected. His mistake was consulting you at all. He should have done just what I always did: Send off a brisk message telling you what he was up to, gone off and done it, and then waited for you to tell me that you trusted him to make the right call. Or is that the problem?" He regarded her thoughtfully. "Are you having trust issues, Kathryn? That's it, isn't it. You dislike having to reach into yourself and trust others."

"I," said Janeway through clenched teeth, "am

not about to discuss any of my personality traits, real or imagined, with you . . ." And then she paused and added with a firm flourish, "Q."

Kirk blinked in overblown surprise. "Is that a failed attempt to utter a profanity? I hardly think it's warranted."

"What is it this time, Q? Another civil war under way in your Q Continuum? More problems with your son? Or were you just sitting around in whatever plane it is that you reside and you suddenly thought, 'You know what? It's been ages since I tried to annoy Kathryn Janeway, so I think I'll have a go of it. But maybe, just maybe, if I show up looking like someone else, she'll be stupid enough to fall for it. Nice try, and it might have worked were I monumentally stupid. So drop the façade. It's not as if you even knew James T. Kirk."

"Don't be so sure of everything you think you know, Kathryn. You see"—Kirk smiled—"even I, who truly *do* know everything, know enough to know what I don't know."

Kirk's form suddenly shifted, and Janeway was fully expecting to see the smug face of the cosmic entity known as Q standing before her. Who else, after all, would it be? Who else would show up out of nowhere, looking like someone who was long dead, and acting in an overly familiar and generally insufferable manner?

So she was understandably startled when she saw something other than what she was expecting.